Off Script
The Backlot Series - Book 5

Kimberly Page

Off Script

Published by: PageMedia, LLC

Copyright © 2026 by Kimberly Page

Cover Design by: Quirky Bird

All rights reserved. No part of this book may be reproduced, distributed, or transmitted in any form or by any means, including photocopying, recording, or other electronic or mechanical methods, without the prior written permission of the author, except in the case of brief quotations embodied in critical reviews and certain other noncommercial uses permitted by copyright law.

This is a work of fiction. Names, characters, places, and incidents either are the product of the author's imagination or are used fictitiously and not to be construed as real. Any resemblance to actual persons, living or dead, events, or locales is entirely coincidental.

All brand names and product names used in this book are trademarks, registered trademarks, or trade names of their respective holders. The publisher and author are not associated with any real likeness, product, or vendor mentioned in this book. Any likeness referenced within the book has not endorsed the book.

ISBN: 979-8-9918472-9-2

Editing: Emerald Edits and First Editing

*For everyone who's ever been blindsided by life—
may you stay open to hope,
even when the script changes mid-scene.*

author's note

Dear Reader,

Welcome to *Off Script* and the final book in *The Backlot Series*. I can't believe I get to say that.

Before we begin, I want to acknowledge that pregnancy can be a deeply emotional topic. Everyone's experience with it is different, and some journeys are complicated, painful, or layered in ways that don't always get talked about. I approached Natalie's story with a lot of care, and I hope her experience feels thoughtful, honest, and respectful, even when it's messy.

At its heart, this book is about hope and how differently we all relate to it. Natalie carries some real demons, and she doesn't always make things easy on herself or on the very best man alive who is trying, repeatedly, to show up for her. She may frustrate you at times. I hope you'll give her grace. Growth isn't always pretty, and sometimes the bravest thing a woman can do is let herself want more than she planned for.

Writing this final book also gave me space to look back at

the women who started this journey with me. Five stories. Five women finding their voices, claiming their ambition, learning how to love themselves fully and vulnerably, and deciding they get to take up space. I don't know that I set out to write such badass women, but I'm so damn proud that I did. They represent the friends I have, the women who inspire me, and the ones I hope to keep collecting along the way. Each of them carries something I admire and something I'm still learning to embody myself.

Thank you for coming along for the ride. It's meant more to me than I can put into words.

And one last thing, just so expectations are set...This is still an open-door romance. The language is strong, the chemistry is very real, and the bedroom scenes are absolutely not fade-to-black 😉.

Happy reading,
Kimberly

Devil In A Dress - Rhea Raj
Bed Chem - Sabrina Carpenter
Let's Fall in Love for the Night - FINNEAS
Out of My League - Fitz and The Tantrums
Hey Daddy (Daddy's Home) - USHER
Never Be the Same - Camila Cabello
Mystical Magical - Benson Boone
bad idea right? - Olivia Rodrigo
Wonder - Shawn Mendes
All That Really Matters - ILLENIUM, Teddy Swims
Best Part (feat. H.E.R.)- Daniel Caesar, H.E.R.
Sunday Morning - Maroon 5
I Was Made For Lovin' You - YUNGBLUD
I Won't Give Up - Jason Mraz
Love Me Like You Do - Ellie Goulding
I Like Me Better - Lauv
Right Now - One Direction
Opalite - Taylor Swift
Nobody Gets Me - SZA
Ordinary - Alex Warren
Man I Need - Olivia Dean

prologue

. . .

Jake - The Fourth of July

"YOU'RE STARING."

Natalie Cruz doesn't even look at me when she says it. She's leaning against the railing of my deck, watching the fireworks explode over the Hollywood Hills like she has all the time in the world. The display paints her skin in shifting shades of red, blue, and gold.

"I'm appreciating the view," I counter, moving to stand beside her.

She turns her head toward me, her dark eyes sharp and assessing, a smile playing at the corner of her mouth. "Is that what you're going with?"

"I could lie and pretend I haven't been watching you all night."

"I prefer the honesty." She takes a sip of her champagne, her gaze steady on mine. "It's refreshing."

Below us, my backyard is packed with people. Music thumps from the speakers as laughter carries on the warm night air. I'm supposed to be hosting, mingling, and making sure everyone has what they need, but instead, I've spent the last two hours tracking Natalie's movements.

We've crossed paths before at industry events and mutual friends' parties. Each time, there's been this pull between us. This awareness. But she always slips away before I can do anything about it. Until now.

Tonight, she came to my party.

"You want to get out of here?" The words come out before I can second-guess them.

She arches an eyebrow. "That's very direct, Mr. Reyes."

"Jake. And I thought you appreciated honesty."

"I do." She sets her champagne glass on the railing, then turns to face me fully. "Lead the way."

My heart kicks hard against my ribs as I guide her through the house, past clusters of people, and up the stairs to my bedroom. I close the door behind us, muffling the party noise below, and then back her against it. The scent of her hits me. Jasmine and something darker, woodsy. Sandalwood, maybe. It's been driving me insane all night, every time she laughed at something I said, every time she leaned in close.

I trace my thumb along her jawline, watching her eyes flutter closed. "I've been thinking about this. About you. What you'd taste like. The sounds you'd make. How you'd feel."

"Jake?" My name comes out breathy, needy, and something primal sparks in my chest.

"Yeah?"

"Less talking. More action."

I kiss her hard and deep and claiming. She melts against me and slides her hands up my chest, scraping her nails across my shirt. She tastes like champagne and apple pie. Sweet and sharp and addictive.

My hands find the zipper at the back of her dress. I drag it down slowly, feeling the fabric loosen under my fingers. She gasps against my mouth, and I smile.

"Patience," I murmur against her lips.

"I don't have any."

"I can see that."

The dress pools at her feet, and I pull back to look at her.

Jesus Christ.

No bra. Just black lace panties and expanses of smooth skin. She's lean but curvy in all the right places. Small, perfect breasts with pink nipples already hard. And there's a delicate tattoo of a crescent moon with wildflowers twining through it on her ribs. Witchy and feminine and absolutely her.

"See something you like?" she asks, but there's no self-consciousness in her voice. Just heat.

"You're stunning." I reach for my shirt, pulling it over my head. "Fucking perfect."

Her hands immediately go to my chest, fingers tracing the lines of muscle I've earned from early mornings boxing at the gym. Her touch sends ripples of electricity down my spine, making my dick grow hard.

"Your body is insane," she breathes, her palms flattening against my pecs, sliding down my abs, and I press against her, letting her know I feel the same about her body.

I grab her by the hips, lift her, and walk her over to my bed. She gasps, legs automatically wrapping around my waist. The bed dips under our combined weight, and I brace myself above her.

"You sure about this?" I ask, even though it's killing me to give her an out.

She rolls her eyes. "Jake, I swear to God, if you get noble on me right now, I will leave."

"I'm not getting noble. I just want to make sure we're on the same page."

"I'm a big girl. I know what I want." She hooks her leg around my hip, pulling me closer. The friction makes us both groan. "I want one unforgettable night. I want you. So stop overthinking and fuck me already."

The crude words in that smoky voice nearly undo me.

I kiss her again, cutting off whatever smartass comment she's about to make next, and pour everything I'm feeling into it. She melts against me, her nails sliding over my back and digging in hard enough to sting.

When I finally pull back, we're both breathing hard.

"Okay?" I ask against her lips.

"More than okay. Now take your pants off before I do it for you."

I stand up long enough to shed my jeans and boxer briefs, and her eyes go wide when she sees me. I'm already hard as steel, and the way she's looking at me makes it worse.

"Holy shit," she mutters.

"Is that a compliment?"

"Definitely." Then the softest whisper to herself, or maybe to me, "Please know how to use that thing."

A soft chuckle escapes as I crawl back over her, settling

between her thighs. "Oh, I do. But first, I'm going to make you come with my mouth."

"Fuck," she breathes.

I trail kisses down her throat, feeling her pulse jump under my tongue. She arches into me as I move lower. The hollow of her collarbone. The swell of her breasts. I circle one nipple with my tongue, and she gasps, fingers tightening on my shoulders.

I move to the other breast, giving it the same attention, and she writhes beneath me. Her skin tastes faintly of salt and summer and something sweet.

"Jake, please."

"Please what?"

"Touch me. Taste me. Stop teasing and just—" Her words cut off in a moan as I slide my hand down her stomach and hook my fingers in those black lace panties.

She lifts her hips, and I drag them down slowly, watching her face the whole time. The flush spreading across her chest. The way her teeth catch her bottom lip.

"You're so fucking beautiful," I tell her, meaning every word.

I toss the panties aside and settle between her legs, pushing her thighs wider. The scent of her arousal hits me, and my mouth waters.

"Don't tease," she warns, but her voice is unsteady now.

"I'm not." I press a kiss to the inside of her thigh. "I'm savoring."

Then I put my mouth on her, and she cries out.

I take my time. Learning what makes her gasp. What makes her hips buck. What makes her knees squeeze my head hard enough to hurt. She's responsive as hell, and I'm memorizing every reaction. When I slide two fingers inside her, curling them just right, her whole body arches off the bed.

"Oh God, yes, right there." Her words tumble out, desperate and raw. "Don't stop, that feels so fucking good."

I don't let up. I pump my fingers faster, seal my lips around her clit and suck, and she shatters above me.

"Jake, fuck, I'm coming, oh God—"

Her thighs tremble against my shoulders as she rides it out, gasping my name. I've never seen anything sexier in my entire life.

Before she can catch her breath, I'm reaching for my nightstand, grabbing a condom from the drawer. My hands are unsteady as I tear it open and roll it on.

She props herself up on her elbows, watching me with dazed eyes. "That was..."

"Just the warm-up." I crawl back over her, and she reaches up to pull me down into a kiss. She can probably taste herself on my tongue, and that makes everything hotter.

I reach between us, lining myself up. "Look at me."

Her eyes meet mine as I push inside slowly, letting her feel every inch of me as I watch her face the entire time. Her eyes flutter closed. Her mouth falls open. And the feel of her, tight and wet and perfect around me, I know I'm completely ruined for anyone else.

"Eyes on me," I say, my voice rough.

She opens them, and for a moment, everything else falls away. It's just us. Just this.

"Move," she breathes. "Please, Jake, I need you to move."

I pull almost all the way out, then drive back in. Hard. Deep. She gasps, nails digging into my shoulders.

"Like that?" I ask.

"Yes. Fuck, yes. Harder."

I obey, setting a rhythm that has us both panting. She matches me thrust for thrust, her hips rolling to take me deeper. I can feel the sweat building between us, hear the slap of skin on skin, the headboard hitting the wall with each thrust.

"God, you feel so good," she moans. "So fucking deep."

I slide one hand under her ass, angling her hips higher, and she cries out.

"There, right there, don't stop, please don't fucking stop."

Outside, fireworks explode in cascades of color, lighting up the room and framing her perfect gorgeous face. I can't look away from her. The way her eyes go unfocused or the way her lips part. She looks at me like I'm giving her everything she needs.

I feel her tighten around me, her breath shallow and desperate. I can barely hold back.

"Touch yourself," I tell her. "I want to feel you come around me."

She slides her hand between us without hesitation, her fingers finding her clit. The moment she touches herself, she moans, and I nearly lose it.

"That's it," I encourage, my voice rough. "Make yourself come. Let me feel it."

"Jake, I'm so close, I'm so—oh fuck—"

She comes hard, clenching around me, her whole body going taut as she cries out. The sight of her, the feel of her pulsing around me, pushes me over the edge. I bury myself deep and let go, pleasure flooding through me so powerfully I see stars.

For a long moment, neither of us moves. Both of us breathing heavy, hearts pounding against each other.

Finally, I pull out and deal with the condom, then collapse beside her on the bed.

"That was..." She trails off.

"Yeah." I turn my head to look at her. "It was."

She sits up, swinging her legs over the side of the bed. I watch as she gathers her clothes, and something tightens in my chest.

"You're leaving?"

"That's usually how these things work." She pulls on her panties, then reaches for her dress.

"It doesn't have to be." I sit up, keeping my voice casual even though my pulse is racing. "You could stay. We could order food. Talk. Go for round two."

She pauses, dress in hand, and looks at me. For a second, I think she might say yes.

"Fuck, the zipper broke." And just like that she's shifted back into a guest at my party. Like nothing even happened in this room tonight. I watch as she looks down at my shirt on the floor and bends to scoop it up. "I'm stealing this."

"Keep it." The words come out rougher than I intend.

"This was fun, Jake." She finishes dressing, folding the dress so it's a skirt, tucking the T-shirt to make the outfit look like it was intentionally designed to be worn that way, then looks around for her shoes.

I stand, pulling on my boxers. "For the record, I'd like to see you again."

"Jake...this was a one-time thing. I don't do complicated."

"Who said it would be complicated?" She doesn't respond and I scramble to walk her to the door, opening it for her. "If you change your mind..."

She rises on her toes and presses a quick kiss to my cheek. "I won't. But thank you. For tonight."

Then she's gone, disappearing down the hallway toward the stairs.

I close the door and lean against it, running my hand over my head and down my face. Fuck.

My sheets smell like her, my skin still tingles where she touched me, and I already know that one night isn't going to be enough.

I don't care what she said. I'm going to see Natalie Cruz again.

one
. . .

Natalie - Three months later

THE ANXIETY MAKES ME NAUSEOUS.

I roll onto my side and shove my face into the pillow, breathing in laundry detergent. Light slices through the gap in my blackout curtains, striping my floor in the harsh Los Angeles light. Deep breath in. Slow breath out. My pulse still skips like it's late to its own meeting.

Big day. Career-changing day. Let's not puke on it.

My phone buzzes on the nightstand. Then again. Then again. Whoever's messaging is certainly committed, so I grope for it and squint at the screen.

The writers' group chat is going off.

> **JONAH**
> Still can't believe you actually did it!
>
> **WREN**
> FlixPix!! Do you know how huge this is??

> **ERIC**
> When's the contract signing? We need to celebrate properly 🥂
>
> **IRIS**
> You are my idol.
>
> **BRODY**
> Does this mean you're going to forget about us little people?

A slow, stupid smile creeps in despite the nerves jangling in my stomach. They've been hyped since I told them last week, but seeing the words this morning makes it feel less like a dream and more like my actual life.

Seven years of writing. Five pilots that went nowhere. An inbox full of polite "no" emails that said the same thing in slightly different fonts.

And then *Spellbound* happened.

My phone buzzes again, pulling me away from the group chat. Stella. My best friend since she took my yoga class three years ago and declared we were soulmates over post-class smoothies.

> **STELLA**
> Don't forget we're getting drinks tonight to celebrate. And by drinks I mean YOU'RE buying because you're about to be RICH and FAMOUS 😎
>
> **ME**
> I'm not rich yet. And definitely not famous.
>
> **STELLA**
> Details. See you at 7!

I finally peel myself out of bed. My feet hit the cool hardwood and I shiver as I shuffle to the kitchen. The electric kettle is already full, because last night Me set it up for this morning Me. Thoughtful bitch.

I flip it on and open my laptop while I wait. Nineteen new emails since I crashed at two in the morning.

Most are trash. One isn't.

From: Victoria Wexler
Subject: This morning – see you at 9:45!

My stomach flips so hard it feels like whiplash.

Natalie,
Confirming we're all set for 10 a.m. at Hays & Cole. I'll meet you in the lobby at 9:45. The contract looks great – looks like everything we negotiated is in there. Congrats!

See you soon,
Victoria

I read it twice, fingers tightening around the counter. This is real. In less than three hours, I'll walk into the most prestigious entertainment law firm in Los Angeles and sign something that changes everything.

The kettle clicks off. I grab my mug and move on autopilot, whisking matcha and hot water until smooth before topping it off with oat milk and a little honey. The ritual steadies me. If I can make matcha, I can sign a contract.

At my desk, I curl into my chair with the mug and flip

open my notebook. Pages and pages of messy notes stare back at me. Episode ideas. Character arcs. Monster-of-the-week options. I haven't even met the room yet, and I'm already trying to break the season.

Of course I am. My brain doesn't know how to chill; it only knows how to plan.

My phone rattles across the desk again.

> **MOM**
>
> Big day for my favorite daughter! Call me after. I want to hear everything. Love you so much.

My chest tightens, in a good way. My mom doesn't gush, exactly, but she never misses when it matters.

She was twenty-two when she got pregnant with me after a one-night stand with a guy on his way to law school on the East Coast. She could have called him. She didn't. She pressed pause on her own law school plans instead, raised me, and then went back when I started elementary school.

She graduated at the top of her class and then built her own family law firm. And she never once made me feel like I was the thing that derailed her life.

> **ME**
>
> Love you. I'll call later.

A second text pops up as I hit send.

> **DAD**
>
> See you this morning. So proud of you, kiddo.

I smile before I can stop myself.

Because that extremely prestigious entertainment law firm I'm heading to?

It's my dad's.

When my mom found out he'd moved back to LA, she eventually told him about me. I'd just started fifth grade and he had a wife and a baby on the way. Complicated doesn't even begin to cover it.

But I'll give him this, he stepped in without hesitation and hasn't missed a moment of my life since.

Most people don't know he's my father. Partly because I kept my mom's last name. Mostly because I didn't want anyone assuming the only reason I made it in Hollywood was because *Ryan Cole* happens to be the guy who helped raise me. Don't get me wrong—I had advantages. A solid education. Connections I could tap if I was desperate enough. A safety net most aspiring writers would kill for. But I also worked my ass off. Every pitch, every draft, every rejection—that was mine. The privilege opened a few doors. My work is what kept me in the room.

When I told him about the FlixPix offer last month, he practically vibrated through the phone. Then he got quiet and said he wanted *his* firm to handle my contract.

Contracts? Legal landmines? That's where I'm perfectly happy to ride the nepotism bus, right up in the front row.

I take another sip of matcha and push away from the desk. Time to face the other big question: What the hell do you wear to sign your first TV deal?

My closet is a collection of thrifted band tees, yoga gear, vintage jackets, and black. A lot of black. I push hangers aside until my fingers hit the black blazer I bought for pitch meetings. I tug it out and pair it with dark jeans and boots. Professional, but still me, and maybe some writer chic vibes.

Reaching back in for an old band tee I know I have somewhere in my closet, my hand brushes soft cotton. I pull it free without looking.

A faded gray T-shirt.

My heart stutters.

Jake's shirt sags between my hands, smelling faintly like fireworks and the ghost of a cologne that isn't really there anymore, but which my brain insists is.

Heat creeps up my neck as the memory crashes in.

His hands on my hips. His mouth at my throat. The easy way he made me laugh. How his eyes, almost translucent in the low light, tracked every move I made, like he'd been waiting for me. How it felt when I pulled this shirt over my head after, skin still humming, and he just watched, looking like he wanted more.

I'd told him it was one night. No complications.

He'd actually listened.

We haven't crossed paths once since. Not at premieres, not at mutual friends' parties, not even on social media. It's like the ground swallowed him up.

Probably better that way. Cleaner.

And yet, sometimes I catch myself scanning crowds at industry events. Wondering if he's thinking about me too. Not that I've been missing him or keeping an eye out. Of course not. I don't do that.

I clutch the cotton for a second too long, then shake my head and shove it back into the closet.

Today is not about a one-night stand with a ridiculously hot guy. Today is about *Spellbound*. About the fact that some junior executive at FlixPix read my pilot and didn't send a form rejection. About the years of working two jobs and writing on my breaks and watching everyone else move on with their lives while I chased this thing that might never work.

I take a quick shower, and get ready, keeping my makeup light but polished. Concealer, liner, mascara, a swipe of berry on my lips. I make a few attempts to twist my dark hair up and clip it, then pull loose a few lavender streaks around my face. In the mirror, I look like a woman who signs TV contracts on weekday mornings.

Perfect.

I grab my bag, double-check I have my notebook and a pen, then head downstairs to meet the Uber idling at the curb.

As we pull away from my place, I press my forehead lightly to the window and watch my city slide by. My stomach roils, a queasy flutter. Just nerves, I tell myself. Excitement mixed with terror mixed with the reality that today actually matters.

I was born here, raised here, and even attended UCLA. LA isn't a dream to me; it's just home. Messy and loud and overcrowded and mine.

We pass the coffee shop where I wrote the first draft of *Spellbound* in between yoga classes. The studio where I still teach three times a week to keep my body and bank account from collapsing. The bar where the writers' group meets once a month to celebrate any win, no matter how small.

All these tiny, ordinary places that got me to this very unordinary morning.

By the time downtown rises up ahead of us, glass and steel catching the sun, my palms are damp again.

The Uber stops in front of a high-rise that looks like it was designed to intimidate people. It's filled with law firms. Hays & Cole takes up the top floors, because of course it does.

I stare up at it, heart thumping. I head inside to the lobby where everything is marble and glass and very intentional art. My boots squeak faintly on the polished floor.

Victoria stands near the elevator bank with her phone to her ear and gesturing like she's closing another big deal for the day. She's in a sleek red blazer, black trousers, and heels that could be used as weapons. Her face breaks into a grin when she spots me. My agent has been with me for the last eighteen months, and believed in *Spellbound* even when it was still rough around the edges. She was also one of the only agents who agreed to respect my need to make it on my own terms.

She ends the call, slips her phone into her bag, and waves me over.

Here we go.

two
. . .
Jake

THE BAG SWINGS back hard and I catch it with both hands, my palms slamming into the vinyl as I steady it before driving my right fist forward again. The impact reverberates all the way up my arm, a sharp jolt that I'm hoping knocks a memory of one perfect night out of my brain.

It doesn't.

Left hook. Right cross. Another combination, faster this time, my shoulders burning, breath coming rough and shallow.

Three months.

It's been three months and I still can't stop thinking about her.

I shift my stance, roll my shoulders, and go again. Jab, jab, cross. I try to punch the memory out of my head, like maybe if I hit hard enough I can knock July out of my skull and send it skidding across the slick gym floor.

No luck.

"You trying to murder that bag or just maim it?"

I glance over my shoulder. Wyatt is leaning against the wall like he has all the time in the world, one ankle crossed over the other, gym bag slung over his shoulder, eyebrows raised in that knowing way that makes me want to hide from him, knowing the questions that are coming my way.

He's been my best friend since our first day on campus at UCLA. We were roommates all through undergrad and law school. After years pretending to enjoy working for his dad's company, he finally bailed and joined me at Hays & Cole. I've been at the firm for seven years, working my way up from junior associate to someone people actually trust with the big deals. With luck, I'll make partner in the next few years.

The gym is halfway between our houses and the office downtown, so we try to meet up here early a few days a week to get a workout in before the day swallows us whole.

"I'm working out," I say, turning back to the bag and letting another punch fly.

He pushes off the wall and walks closer, adjusting his bag. "It's quite the workout."

"I'm fine."

"Liar."

I huff out a breath and stop, palms flattening against the bag to hold it still. My chest heaves as I drag in air that smells like rubber mats, old sweat, and the faint citrus cleaner the staff uses right before the place opens.

"You've been off for weeks," Wyatt says, not bothering to soften it. "And before you deny it, Blair noticed too. She asked me last night if you were okay."

Blair notices everything. She is wired that way. She and Wyatt have this whole high-school-sweethearts-who-found-their-way-back love story. They now also have a baby girl, who arrived about six months ago and ruined their sleep schedule in the cutest way possible. Watching them together is like watching hope pull up a chair, pour a drink, and settle in.

"I'm fine," I say again, because if I say it enough maybe it will be true. I peel off my gloves, fingers stiff and sweat-slick. "Just got a lot on my mind."

Wyatt watches me for a beat. "It's not Lauren, is it?"

I catch the concern in his face and shut that door fast. "No. Nothing like that."

For a long time, every bad mood was linked to Lauren. She was a dark period in my life for sure. I fell hard and fast and I really believed I was doing the whole forever thing. Then her true colors started to show and the demands for introductions started. Or she would make passive-aggressive comments when I wouldn't leverage a client to get her an audition. Then the stories about my clients that somehow made it to the tabloids with details only I was supposed to know about.

By the time I understood what she was doing with my life and my reputation, the marriage was already hollowed out from the inside. Getting out was the only sane choice I had left.

Some days that history sits heavy, like a weight on my chest. Most days, though, I'm just grateful it ended when it did and I was able to salvage my reputation.

But now I fear that I may be in worse shape. I can't stop thinking about a woman who looked me in the eye and told me she doesn't do relationships.

Fuck.

Wyatt doesn't look completely convinced, but he lets it go. That's one of the things I love about the guy. He knows when to push, and when to back all the way off and act like he never asked.

"Blair wants you to come over for dinner this weekend," he says, switching lanes like only a seasoned litigator can. "Fair warning, she is absolutely going to try to set you up with one of her friends again."

I groan, scrubbing my towel over my face. "Tell her I'm not interested."

Unless she wants to set me up with Natalie. Then I would be very, very interested.

"I did tell her," he says, smirking. "She ignored me. Apparently you've been single too long and it's making her nervous."

"The divorce was finalized in January."

"You know Blair. She just wants you happy."

"I know," I sigh.

"Just come to dinner. Eat something that isn't takeout. Hold the baby. You don't have to agree to any dates."

I blow out a breath and weigh my options. It's dinner with people I love and a small squishy human; or another lonely night in my kitchen pretending frozen pizza is a food group.

"Fine," I say. "But if she ambushes me with someone, I'm leaving."

"Deal." His grin widens. "I'll at least try to give you a heads-up before the ambush."

We head to the locker room together, the two of us falling

into the familiar rhythm of post-workout chatter. He talks about Blair's latest signing, some up-and-coming actor she's excited about. The baby, who apparently thinks sleep is for cowards. The nightmare that is preschool waitlists in Los Angeles. I half-listen, throwing in a comment or a laugh when it feels right, but beneath the surface my brain is already drifting toward the day ahead.

"You good to grab coffee on the way in?" Wyatt asks as we step out into the parking lot, the sun way too bright for this early in the day.

"Raincheck? I don't have to be in until ten this morning, so I was going to run home for a bit."

He nods, shifting his gym bag higher on his shoulder as he walks toward his car. It's a practical sedan with the baby seat strapped in the back. I can only imagine the abundance of soft toys scattered across the floorboards. "Sounds good. See you at the office," he says.

I unlock my BMW and slide into the driver's seat, the interior already warm from the sun. I crank the AC, rest my head against the headrest for a second, and then pull out, letting muscle memory do the work as I wind my way through streets I know by heart.

My house sits in the hills, glass and mid-century lines and the kind of view my younger self thought existed only on TV. I pull into the driveway, kill the engine, and sit there for a moment in the quiet.

The house waits empty, like always. No shoes kicked off by the door. No jacket thrown across the back of a chair. No voice calling my name from down the hall.

Most days, I'm okay with the silence and the lack of

drama. The knowledge that everything inside these walls is mine and no one is rifling through it for things to sell. Some days, though, the quiet gets loud.

I climb out of the car and head inside, dropping my keys in the bowl by the door. I jog upstairs to my bedroom, stripping my sweaty clothes off on the way to the bathroom and leaving a trail I'll pick up later.

The shower comes on with a hiss. I step under the hot spray and let it pound into my shoulders, steam fogging up the glass. It takes all of thirty seconds for my brain to betray me.

It's three months ago and Natalie's soft skin is under me, her head tipped back, that little gasp she made when I slowed down instead of rushing like she wanted. Her dark hair spread over my pillow.

I've stopped pretending I feel bad when I grip my cock. I have replayed that night more times than I should probably admit. Like some kind of masochist torturing myself with things I can't have.

The first time I saw her was at Sophia and Grant's wedding. Sophia is Wyatt's sister and an Oscar-winning actress who married Grant Hall, the head of Wonderland Studios. Their wedding was this glamorous circus of producers and actors and family that somehow came together for one of the most memorable evenings. Especially when I spotted Natalie.

She walked past me on the terrace, laughing at something her friend said, and the sound went straight through me like an electrical shock. Dark hair, sharp eyes, and a black dress that looked like it had been designed precisely for her. I tried to come up with something clever to say. She smiled. And then she was gone, swallowed by the crowd.

I scrub my hands over my face and force my brain back into the present. I finish rinsing off, turn off the water, and step out into the fogged-up bathroom. I wrap a towel low around my hips, and wipe a circle in the mirror. My reflection show faint shadows under my eyes and a look of longing. Or maybe desperation.

"Get it together, man," I mutter.

I dress on autopilot. Light blue shirt, the one that somehow makes me look more awake than I am. Charcoal jacket with matching slacks that pulls the whole thing into lawyer territory without feeling suffocating. I slip on my watch and the whole routine settles my nerves, the way it always does.

In the kitchen, I grab my travel mug, pour in some coffee, and the smell fills the space instantly. My phone lights up on the counter and I slip into work mode at the sight of my boss's name.

RYAN

Can you join me for a new client meeting at 10am. Our offices.

I relax. Just routine work.

JAKE

No problem. Need me to prepare anything?

The bubble with his reply pops up almost immediately.

> **RYAN**
> She's a first-time writer-producer. Just sold a show to FlixPix. Contracts done, just want fresh eyes and ears at the signing.

> **JAKE**
> I'll be there.

The drive to Hays & Cole isn't bad today. Traffic is actually moving which is a rarity for LA. By the time I pull into the garage under the downtown high-rise, the city is fully awake.

I step on to the elevator the ride smooth all the way up. The doors open onto the fifteenth floor, and that familiar burst of cool air and quiet power rolls over me.

The firm's offices are sleek in a way that feels intentional. Floor-to-ceiling windows, dark wood against brushed metal, soft lighting that makes everyone look more put together than they probably feel, and the faint smell of coffee, paper, and money.

I swing by my office to drop my laptop off and grab a legal pad and pen. I step back out into the hallway, and head to the meeting with a stranger whose life is about to change.

I have no idea mine is about to shift too.

three
...
Natalie

THE ELEVATOR GLIDES UPWARD SO SMOOTHLY it feels like we're not even moving.

Victoria is beside me, scrolling through her phone with the kind of casual focus I envy, her thumb moving in clean, efficient flicks. Nothing rattles her. Not studio notes, not last-minute schedule changes, not even the fact that I am about to sign the biggest contract of my life and my heart is currently trying to punch through my ribs.

"You ready for this?" Victoria asks, glancing up long enough to take me in.

"I've been ready for seven years," I say.

She smiles, pride showing on her face. "You earned this, Natalie. I hope you take a moment and really soak it in."

"I'm trying to."

The elevator dings and the doors slide open onto the fifteenth floor of Hays & Cole. The reception area hits me with that uncanny jolt of recognition mixed with foreignness.

I've been here a few times, but today feels different. I'm not here as Ryan Cole's kid. Today I'm here as a client.

The receptionist looks up as we approach. Her face brightens the second she recognizes me. "Natalie!" she says, already half out of her chair. "We are so excited for you. Your dad has been talking about your show nonstop."

"Sorry," I say, leaning in to return her hug.

"Oh, trust me, we love it," she says. "It sounds amazing."

A flutter starts somewhere under my ribs. People who don't share DNA with me think *Spellbound* sounds amazing.

"Let me take you back. Can I get you anything? Water? Tea?"

"Water," I start, then pause. "Actually...orange juice?"

She blinks, surprised, but recovers quickly. "Absolutely. I'll bring it in."

Orange juice? I don't even like orange juice that much. Too acidic. Too morning-y. But right now the idea of cold citrus pulsing into my bloodstream sounds perfect.

We walk down the hallway past glass-walled conference rooms, each one alive with early-morning negotiations. The machinery of Hollywood is grinding away around me and today I'm part of it.

"Here we are," the receptionist says, opening the door. "Your father will be right with you."

She steps aside and Victoria and I enter the conference room. The table stretches the length of the room, dark wood gleaming under recessed lights. The floor-to-ceiling windows frame downtown LA like a city-sized movie still. Sunlight glints off skyscrapers. Cars crawl along streets far below. The whole thing feels big and alive and somehow not quite real.

But there, in the center of the table, is my contract. Seven years of work, distilled into paper and ink and clauses. I walk toward it without thinking, fingers brushing the edge of the folder.

This is real.

Behind me, the door opens.

"There she is."

I turn, already smiling, because I know that voice. Dad is crossing the room with his arms already opening, and for a second I am twelve years old again and he is arriving at the school play in a suit and tie with a bouquet of flowers he swears he got "for the whole cast."

"Hi, Dad," I say.

"Hi, kiddo." He pulls me into a hug that is all warm cologne and familiar. The kind of hug that says everything without words. "Big day."

"Huge day," I agree, my voice muffled against his shoulder.

He pulls back, but keeps his hands on my shoulders like he needs the physical proof that I am here and this is happening. His eyes shine in a way that makes my throat tighten.

"You did it," he says, like he still cannot quite believe it, even though he has seen every stage of this journey. "You really did it."

"I did," I reply, and even saying it out loud feels surreal.

"I am so damn proud of you, Natalie." His voice goes rough around the edges. "You know that, right?"

"I know." I smile up at him. I do know. He's not exactly been subtle about it.

He grins, the emotion easing back into his usual

composed, charming, lawyer face. He gestures toward the table, toward the folder. "Ready to make it official?"

"More than ready."

And that's when I see him. My stomach drops straight to my shoes, then bounces back up and lodges somewhere in my throat.

He's standing near the windows, one hand resting lightly on the back of a chair, the other holding a legal pad and pen. Charcoal suit. Light blue shirt. No tie. The sleeves of his jacket pull just enough to hint at the muscles I already know are underneath, because I've had my hands on them.

Jake.

I take a moment to admire him in the daylight. He's tall, easily over six feet, with an athletic build that comes from actual training, not just genetics. His hair is cut close and neat, the kind of precise fade that requires maintenance and looks effortlessly sharp. Those eyes, pale green with hints of blue, are striking and intense. They looked at me like I was the only person in the world that night. A faint scar cuts through his left eyebrow. I remember tracing it with my thumb as he hovered over me.

He carries himself with the easy confidence of someone who knows exactly what he's good at and doesn't need to prove it. For a second, my brain just blanks and I can't speak.

This is karma. What else could it be? The man to whom I very specifically said "this is just one night" is standing here in my father's conference room, looking like an ad for a competent, trustworthy attorney who will absolutely rail you against a headboard and then kiss your forehead.

What the hell is he doing here?

As if he hears the question, he looks up.

Our eyes meet across the table and the recognition hits like a physical force, like someone snapped a rubber band between us. For half a heartbeat, his expression shifts into a surprised flare, and maybe excitement, but then I watch him pull it back.

His features smooth. His mouth settles into a polite line. His whole face rearranges itself into professional neutrality like someone flipped a switch labeled "courtroom demeanor."

He's so fucking hot.

"Jake, this is my daughter, Natalie," my dad says, completely oblivious to the emotional car crash currently occurring inside my chest. "Nat, this is Jake Reyes. He is one of our top attorneys. I asked him to sit in today, make sure everything is airtight."

There is a hot little spark of humiliation blooming under my skin now, tangling up with the nausea and adrenaline that were already there. Have they worked together for years? Has Dad ever said his name in front of me and I just didn't connect the dots? Did I really sleep with someone who shares an office with my father and not think to ask?

Jake takes a step forward. "Ms. Cruz," he says, extending his hand like we haven't already had our hands all over each other. His voice is that same low, steady baritone that sent chills down my spine in his bedroom, except now it is dressed up in polite vowels and professional distance. "Pleasure to meet you."

The formality scrapes across my nerves. For a second I just look at his hand, then at his face, searching for any crack in the mask. Any sign of the man who gave me one of my most memorable nights ever, who told me I was beautiful, who looked at me like he wanted more and then actually respected me when I said I did not.

Nothing. He is a wall. It's what I should want. I'm the one who said one night. No relationships, no complications, no messy aftermath. And it's not like he could do anything here. This is him honoring what I asked for. So why is there a tiny, petty voice in the back of my brain going, "Seriously, that's it? Not even a flicker?"

I make my fingers move, step forward, and slide my hand into his. His hand closes around mine, warm and solid and too familiar. For half a second, my body forgets where we are and my brain flashes back to his weight above me, his grip on my hips, the way he held my gaze when he moved inside me and it felt like my whole life shifted half an inch.

I shove the memory away so hard I almost stumble.

"Mr. Reyes," I say, my voice surprisingly steady. "Nice to meet you."

His eyes hold mine for a fraction longer than necessary, and that is the only evidence I get that he remembers too. Then he releases my hand, stepping back like this is just another day in Conference Room 3.

Thank God he's being professional. Thank God he's not making jokes or letting his expression slip or doing anything that would make my dad tilt his head and go, "Wait a second."

The last thing I need is Ryan Cole realizing that his golden girl and one of his star attorneys have already met. Intimately.

"Heard great things about your script," Jake says, still in full attorney mode. "Congratulations."

"Thank you," I reply, not trusting myself to say anything more.

We step apart, and I take the opportunity to put a respectable amount of table between us.

Dad gestures toward the chairs. "Why don't we all sit?" he says. "Natalie, come here next to me. Victoria, Jake, wherever you like."

I sink into the seat beside my dad, my legs suddenly made of gelatin. The room feels both too big and too small now. Too much glass. Too many reflective surfaces where I might accidentally catch Jake looking at me or he might catch me looking at him.

Jake takes the chair directly across from me, which feels personal even though I know it's not. It gives him a perfect view of my face and me a perfect view of his.

This is fine. Everything is fine. I am a grown woman who can handle sitting across from the man she slept with while her father explains the fine print.

"So," Dad says, flipping open the folder. "Let's walk through this. Natalie, the contract is straightforward. Victoria and I have gone through it, but I wanted another set of eyes today."

"Sounds good," I say, even though my heart is pounding so loudly I am pretty sure everyone on the fifteenth floor can hear it.

Jake leans forward slightly, pen poised over his pad, the picture of attentiveness. "Everything looks solid from what I have seen," he says to my dad, then glances at me. "Terms are fair, language is clear."

Dad nods and starts talking, his voice slipping into that rhythm I know so well, the one that has soothed nervous actors and terrified studio execs alike. He goes clause by clause. Credit. Fees. Writers' room guarantees. He walked me through all this on the phone, but hearing it out loud, with this view and this table and this pen in front of me, makes it feel like the universe has slid into some new position.

Victoria jumps in every so often to clarify a point in plain English or to remind me where this matches our wish list from the first round. Jake makes small notes in the margins, his handwriting neat and each stroke deliberate.

I try to stay anchored in the conversation and focus on the pages in front of me. This is my show. My name is on the title page, these are my weird witches with supernatural powers, and my chance to prove I am not just a girl in a yoga studio promising people that stretching their hamstrings can change their lives.

But there is an annoying, insistent part of my brain that will not stop narrating.

Jake is three feet away from you. Jake has seen you naked. Jake has heard the sounds you make when you are falling apart and now he is saying "morals clause" with a straight face like none of that happened.

I drag my focus back to the page as Dad reaches one of the big sections we fought hardest for.

"As we discussed, the created by credit is locked," he says, tapping the paragraph. "Your name appears on screen with that language and cannot be removed. You are guaranteed a producer role for season one with an option to continue, and they are committed to a writers' room where you are present and participating, not just handing in drafts from the outside."

I rest my fingers on the edge of the contract. This is it. The thing I have wanted since I sat on my mom's couch as a kid and watched TV like it was religion.

I take a slow breath and let it out. I'm not going to let anything distract me from that.

Not even him.

four

• • •

Jake

"MY DAUGHTER." Ryan's words land like a punch to the sternum.

Natalie.

In our conference room. Sitting right there. Looking at me with the same perfect, unmistakable shock I'm definitely failing to hide. I school my face into professional neutrality—or at least the closest approximation I can manage when my nervous system is busy staging a coup.

I slept with Ryan's daughter. *Fuck me.*

The air in the room shifts. It's thinner, tighter, like someone dialed the oxygen down without warning. I try to breathe normally, but every inhale scratches against the memory of her. The soft, warm slide of her body under my hands.

Shaking her hand just now. Jesus. Touching her again felt like plugging myself back into a current I never wanted to walk away from. She's still soft. Still warm. Still very much the woman my brain keeps replaying in dark, inconvenient hours. And now she's three feet away pretending none of that ever happened. Because what else can we do?

"If everything looks good," her father says, "we just need your signature here, here, and here."

Natalie picks up the pen, her hand steady. Her signature is deliberate, neat, and confident. Everything about her is confident, except for that half-second when our eyes met and she went still, like she couldn't decide whether to bolt or throw the table at me.

"Congratulations," Ryan says, pulling her up into a hug that makes something in my chest twist. Pride looks good on him.

"Thank you, Dad."

I stand with everyone else, keeping my breathing even. I turn to Victoria first, fearing my expression might betray me if I face Natalie too quickly.

"Congratulations," I say to Victoria, shaking her hand. "Great deal."

"Thanks for the assist," she says before stepping away to answer a buzzing phone.

And then there's only one hand left to shake.

Her hand is small in mine. I force myself to shut everything down. Every instinct. Every memory. Every piece of me that remembers the way she whispered my name against my mouth that night.

"Congratulations, Ms. Cruz," I say as smooth and controlled as I can. Like we haven't already been tangled together. "I'm sure your show is going to be great."

"Thank you," she says quietly.

We're still standing too close when Ryan's phone rings. He checks the screen, his face shifting back into his high-powered-lawyer look.

"I have to take this," he says. "Victoria, can I steal you for a second? You may want to listen in."

"Of course," she says, already stepping out with him.

The door closes behind them and suddenly it's just the two of us. Natalie quickly crosses her arms like she's bracing herself for impact.

"Small world," she says, her voice a little higher, a little tighter.

"Indeed."

Her head lowers as she exhales. "Of all the law firms in Los Angeles."

"I didn't know," I say immediately. Too quickly, probably, but I need it out there. "I swear, I had no idea Ryan had a daughter named Natalie. You go by Cruz—"

"I know." She holds up a hand, cutting me off. "There's no way you would've known. Nobody knows."

"Why?"

Before the question can land, her knees buckle. Not a sway. Not a slight wobble. Her legs give out completely.

I move on pure instinct. My arm shoots out and catches her around the waist before she can hit the floor, pulling her against my chest. She's light in my arms, too light, and her skin is cool and clammy under my palm.

"Whoa. Hey." I keep my voice low, steady, even though my heart is slamming against my ribs. "I've got you."

Her hand grips my forearm, fingers digging in like she's trying to anchor herself. Her breathing is shallow and fast.

"I'm fine," she says, her voice—thin, shaky—contradicting her.

"You're not." I guide her carefully back into the chair, keeping one hand on her elbow, feeling the slight tremor running through her body. "Just sit. Breathe."

She nods, eyes squeezed shut, and I crouch beside her, my hand still steadying her arm. My thumb brushes against the inside of her wrist without thinking, finding her pulse. It's fast but steady.

"When's the last time you ate?" I ask.

"I don't know. This morning." She winces. "Toast."

"Toast," I repeat. "That's it?"

"I was too nervous to eat."

Before I can push further, Ryan reappears in the doorway, phone still in hand. "Everything okay?"

"I stood up too fast," Natalie says. "I just need a minute."

Ryan's beside her in an instant. "Are you sure? You look a little pale."

"I'm fine, Dad. I swear. Just dizzy."

Ryan's jaw tightens. "I'm calling 911."

"No." She sits straighter, eyes wide. "Don't. I'm okay. I just need to sit for a second."

"Natalie—"

"Dad, I promise. I probably just need to eat something."

He doesn't look convinced. Neither am I.

"There's a minute clinic across the street," I say. "She could get a quick check, in and out."

Ryan hesitates. I can see the tug-of-war happening behind his eyes.

"I have a client in fifteen minutes," he mutters.

"I'll take her," I say immediately.

Natalie opens her mouth, either to argue or tell me to mind my own business, but Ryan cuts her off.

"Clinic or 911. Your choice."

She sighs, defeated. "Clinic."

Ryan helps her up. I stay close, just in case she wobbles again. She steadies, but she's still pale.

Victoria reappears in the doorway, phone pressed to her ear. She covers the mic. "Emergency with another client. I have to run. You good?"

"I'm good," Natalie says.

"Text me later," Victoria says, before continuing her call.

Ryan cups Natalie's face with both hands, full dad mode. "If they tell you to go to the hospital, you go. No arguments."

"No arguments," she echoes softly.

He kisses her forehead and steps back.

I offer her my arm and she hesitates for half a heartbeat but then she takes it. Her fingers curl around my elbow, soft and warm and familiar in a way that makes my stomach clench. We walk out of the conference room together and I keep my expression professional and not like I'm escorting the woman I slept with out of her father's law firm.

The elevator ride is quiet. She leans back against the wall, eyes closed, breathing slow. I don't touch her. Don't talk. I just stay close in case she needs me.

Outside, the sunlight is too bright. She lifts a hand to shield her eyes, and I guide her across the street to the clinic.

"Hi," I say to the receptionist. "She's not feeling well. Light-headed. Almost fainted."

"Have her fill these out," the woman says, handing over a clipboard.

I take it and hand it to Natalie as she sinks into the nearest seat. I sit beside her so I'm close enough to help, far enough not to crowd her. She fills out her name, birthday and insurance info.

"You don't have to stay," she murmurs. "I can handle it from here."

"I'll stay."

Thankfully, she doesn't argue.

When she's completed the forms, I return them and we wait. Five minutes, ten. A cooking show plays on the TV mounted in the corner and a chef aggressively whisks something in a copper bowl. The waiting room hums with low conversation, a kid coughing in the corner, and the receptionist typing.

I glance at Natalie from the corner of my eye. She's still pale, her breathing a little too careful, like she's concentrating on each inhale. Her hands are folded in her lap, fingers laced tight.

My dad died of a heart attack at fifty-eight years old. He collapsed in his office on a Tuesday afternoon. I was in my second year at the firm, and at work reviewing a contract when my mom called to let me know. By the time I made it to Connecticut, he was gone.

I shake the thought away, but it clings. Natalie's young and healthy. This is probably nothing. But what if it's not nothing?

I want to reach over, take her hand, but before I can, a nurse steps into the doorway. "Natalie?"

We both stand. Natalie steadies herself, and I follow her down the hall into a small exam room. She sits on the paper-covered table, and I hover near the doorway.

"I can wait outside," I say. "If you want privacy."

She looks at me for a long moment, something unreadable flickering across her face. Then she shakes her head. "Stay," she says quietly. "Please."

The invitation settles me somehow. She's letting me in, just a crack, and I'm not about to waste it. "Okay," I say, stepping inside and closing the door behind me. I lean against the wall, close enough to be there if she needs me, far enough to give her space.

The nurse checks her vitals and lets her know the doctor will be right in. The silence stretches, that awkward kind that's too loud for such a small room. Finally, there's a knock and a woman in a white coat walks in.

"Hi, Natalie. I'm Dr. Patel. I hear you had a dizzy spell?"

"Yeah," Natalie says. "I'm sure it's nothing."

"Let's just make sure." Dr. Patel reviews her notes. "Start from the beginning."

Natalie explains waking up nauseous, her nerves, the meeting, and standing up and feeling like the room shifted.

Dr. Patel nods, listening carefully. "Any other symptoms? Fatigue? Headaches?"

"I've been tired," Natalie says. "But I've also been stressed. Big week."

"Understandable." Another note. "Okay, I want to run a

few tests. Standard bloodwork, urine sample. Just to rule things out."

Natalie nods. "Okay."

The nurse returns with supplies, and I step into the hallway, giving her privacy. When they let me back in, Natalie's perched on the table again, a bandage on her arm.

"They said about fifteen minutes," she says softly.

I nod, then return to my vigil against the wall.

five
. . .
Natalie

THE EXAM ROOM feels smaller with every passing minute, like the walls are quietly inching closer while we pretend not to notice.

I sit on the thin paper that keeps crackling under my thighs, hands clasped in my lap so I don't fidget with them. The fluorescent light above me hums in a way that makes my already-frayed nerves feel like exposed wires.

This is ridiculous. I'm fine. I stood up too fast. I probably need a sandwich and a nap, not a full medical workup. My dad and Jake are being dramatic, which would be sweet if it wasn't also mildly suffocating.

Across from me, Jake is leaning against the wall, one ankle crossed over the other, scrolling through his phone. He looks casual and relaxed. Or at least putting on a very convincing performance. His still looks annoyingly perfect, even after the walk over here. His top button is undone and every time he tips his head back to stretch his neck, I can see the long, clean line of his throat.

I remember exactly how that neck feels under my lips. How he sounded when I kissed him there. How his pulse jumped against my mouth.

Stop it.

But there's something about having him here that makes the room feel less clinical. Less scary. Like as long as he's standing there, solid and steady and present, nothing too terrible can happen. It's infuriating how much I don't hate it.

I drag my gaze away from him and fix it on the poster beside the door. A rainbow gradient background and big, blocky letters: YOUR HEALTH IS YOUR WEALTH. There's a smiling cartoon heart in the corner, like it personally endorses preventive care.

Across from me, temptation in a suit clears his throat.

"You okay?" Jake asks.

I tear my eyes away from the poster and back to him. His phone is still in his hand, but he's not looking at it. He's looking at me. Really looking at me. Eyes soft, forehead slightly creased, like he's trying to gauge if I'm about to keel over.

"Yeah," I say. "Just ready to get out of here."

"I know." He glances at his screen again. "Won't be much longer."

He scrolls, thumb moving in lazy strokes, then pauses. "Says here dizziness can be caused by low blood sugar, dehydration, stress..." His gaze lifts to mine. "Have you been drinking enough water?"

I make a face. "I don't know. Probably not."

"That might be it. Combined with not eating enough and the stress of the contract signing."

The fact that he's googling my symptoms is annoyingly sweet. "You don't have to stay, you know," I tell him. "I'm fine to wait by myself."

"I know I don't have to." He slips his phone into his pocket and gives me his full attention. "I want to."

Something in my chest does a small, traitorous flip. My brain immediately hyper-focuses on every detail. The watch on his wrist—expensive but understated, the kind chosen by a man who knows how much it costs and doesn't need anyone else to. The way his fingers tap absently against his thigh when he's thinking. Those hands. Strong, capable, steady. I remember those hands on my skin, in my hair, on my hips, holding me down and holding me together and—

The door opens, mercifully cutting off that mental highlight reel.

Dr. Patel steps in with her tablet, smiling. "Okay, good news," she says. "Blood work looks normal. Your blood sugar's a little on the lower end, which explains the dizziness. You'll want to eat more regularly, but that should happen naturally."

"Naturally?" I repeat.

"Well, yes." She glances at the tablet again. "Since you're pregnant, I'm surprised your appetite hasn't increased already. Most women start eating more as they head into the second trimester."

The world stops. Everything inside me goes still. Like someone took my entire reality and just hit pause.

"I'm...what?" The words scrape out of my throat, barely there.

Dr. Patel's smile falters just a fraction. "Pregnant," she repeats gently.

"Pregnant?" I echo automatically—except the voice that says it isn't mine. It's Jake's. He sounds like he's been shoved off a cliff and is still waiting to hit the ground. The voice in my head, however, is screaming *What the actual fuck* on a loop.

Dr. Patel looks between us, then back at her tablet. "Based on your HCG levels, I'd say you're around twelve weeks," she continues. "You're headed into your second trimester."

Twelve weeks.

My brain is spinning, cataloging, trying to make sense of this. Pregnant. Twelve weeks. How did I not know?

My weight hasn't changed. My stomach is still flat. There's no bump. No obvious sign. I teach yoga three times a week. I would have noticed.

Morning sickness? I've been nauseous, sure, but I chalked that up to stress and nerves about the deal. And my period. Oh God, my period. When was the last time I had one? I try to remember, scrolling back through my mental calendar. There was that light bleeding in August. I thought it was my period. It was short, barely there, but I didn't question it because my cycle has never been reliable.

I've been so busy. Pitching. Rewriting. Meeting with Victoria. Celebrating the FlixPix deal. I didn't even notice I'd missed it. Didn't think twice about it. How did I not see this?

"That's not possible," I say. It comes out flat. Distant. Like someone else is speaking from somewhere very far away.

"I know it can be a shock," Dr. Patel says. "But the test is very accurate." She taps something on her screen. "Twelve weeks would put conception around...early July?"

The words land like a freight train. Fireworks. Jake's bed. My dress on his floor. His shirt on my body. The condom wrapper in his hand. I turn to look at him.

Jake is staring at me like he's watching his entire life get rewritten in real time. Shock, yes. But underneath that, there's something else cracking through his expression. Something fierce and bright and completely unguarded that looks a hell of a lot like hope. And fear. And maybe a little wonder.

I don't have room for any of that. My emotional capacity is currently maxed out.

"I'll give you two some privacy," Dr. Patel says softly. "Take all the time you need. The front desk can give you a referral to an OB-GYN if you need one." She sets a pamphlet on the counter—*Your First Trimester: What to Expect*—complete with a cartoon stork that looks way too cheerful for the moment. Then she slips out of the room.

The silence that follows is deafening. Like being locked in a soundproof booth with only your own heartbeat and every bad decision you've ever made.

I stare at the pamphlet. At the pastel colors and the friendly font and the little list of bullet points I refuse to read. This cannot be my life.

"Natalie," Jake says quietly.

I can't look at him. I can't. If I look at him, this becomes real in a way I'm not ready for. I fix my eyes on the wall instead. That stupid heart poster with that sage advice. Whoever wrote that has clearly never had their entire future ambushed in an exam room on a random morning.

"It's mine," Jake says.

It's not a question. It lands in the air between us with heavy certainty. I force myself to turn my head. To meet his eyes. He's closer now, only a few feet away. He slides his hands in his pockets like he's physically restraining himself from reaching out. His jaw is tight. His eyes are steady.

"I don't want to assume anything," he says, voice careful, measured. "But—"

"It's yours." I cut him off, because if I don't say it now, it's going to choke me. "There hasn't been anyone else. Not since you." I swallow hard. "Not for a while before that, either."

Something in his face loosens. Just a fraction. His shoulders drop half an inch. That flicker of relief is so obvious I almost want to punch him and hug him at the same time.

"Okay," he says.

"Okay?" I repeat, half hysterical laugh, half challenge. "That's it? Just...okay?"

I stare at him, waiting for the rest. Waiting for anger or panic or some sort of *Why didn't you call me?* or anything that matches the chaos ricocheting inside my skull.

But he just stands there, looking at me like I'm something precious he's afraid to touch too quickly. Like if he moves wrong, I might bolt. Which is a great idea.

"I need to get out of here," I say suddenly. The room tilts when I stand, a slow, unpleasant roll. Jake is beside me in a heartbeat, his hand firm on my elbow.

"Easy," he says. "Just breathe."

"I'm fine."

"I know. But let's take it slow anyway."

He keeps his hand on my arm, steadying but not controlling, guiding me out of the exam room and down the hall. The fluorescent lights, the harsh disinfectant smell, the shuffle of nurses—it all blurs at the edges, like someone smeared my life with their thumb.

We pass the front desk, where the receptionist is already pulling some printout off the printer for me. Something about referrals. I nod like I'm absorbing information when really my brain is just repeating *pregnant* like a skipping record.

Outside, the air hits my face—warm, bright, too clear. The sky is aggressively blue. People are walking dogs, juggling coffee cups, living their lives like the ground hasn't just shifted three feet to the left.

"I can't be pregnant," I say, tipping my head back to stare at the sky, talking to the clouds or the universe or whoever decided now was a good time for chaos. "I just sold my show. This is everything I've worked for. I'm supposed to start in the writers' room in December. I'm supposed to be on set in the spring. And now—"

My voice cracks. I swallow hard, but it doesn't fix the wobble.

"And now it's all going to blow up," I finish, quieter.

"Now we figure it out," Jake says.

"You don't understand." I shake my head, frustration and fear burning hot behind my eyes. "You know what happens to women in this industry when they get pregnant? They get replaced. Pushed out. Everyone says they're supportive, but the second you become 'unreliable' or 'unavailable' or 'tired' or 'needing accommodations,' there's someone else waiting to take your spot. Someone without a uterus."

"Natalie—"

"I finally made it," I say, and my voice breaks completely this time. "I finally got everything I wanted, and now it's all going to fall apart."

He's quiet for a second. Long enough for me to feel stupid for saying it out loud.

"What do you want to do?" he asks.

The question stops me cold.

What do I want to do?

"I don't know," I whisper.

Jake reaches out, slowly, like he's approaching a skittish animal. His hand lands on top of mine where it's pressed against my stomach. Warm. Solid. Steady. The contact sends a jolt through me.

"Whatever you decide," he says, his voice low and certain, "I'm here. I'm not going anywhere. We'll figure this out together."

That certainty in his voice hits something deep and unsteady in me. Part of me wants to lean into it. To believe him. To let myself be held up for a second when everything feels like it's tipping sideways.

Another part of me is absolutely terrified of what "together" might mean. Because together sounds like feelings and responsibility and future, and I am barely keeping my own future in a straight line.

"Where do you live?" he asks, pulling his hand back before I can decide if I miss it. "I'll take you home."

I hesitate, but the thought of summoning a stranger to make small talk with while my life is unraveling is laughable, so I give him my address.

We find his car, and he unlocks it with a chirp. He opens

the door and helps me as I slide into the passenger seat. The city moves past the window—shops, billboards, palm trees, the same streets that felt hopeful and bright this morning and now feel like they belong to someone else.

We don't talk. The silence isn't exactly comfortable, but it isn't hostile either. It's fragile. Like if either of us says the wrong thing, it'll snap whatever thin thread is holding me together.

My brain keeps circling back to that night. We used a condom. I know we did. I remember him tearing open the wrapper and rolling it on. I'm on birth control. Have been for years. Sure, I miss a pill here and there, but that's why there was backup. That is literally the point of backup.

Jake pulls up in front of my house and puts the car in park. The engine idles. For a moment, neither of us moves.

"Thank you," I say finally. "For taking me to the clinic. For staying. For driving me home." My voice wobbles. "For... all of this."

"Of course," he says simply.

I reach for the door handle, but he says my name.

"Natalie."

I turn back.

"I meant what I said," he tells me. His eyes are steady, clear. "I'm here. Whatever you need, whenever you need it. Okay?"

I nod, because my vocal cords are apparently on strike.

He pulls his phone out. "Can I get your number?" he asks. "So we can...talk. When you're ready."

I give it to him. A second later, my phone buzzes in my

pocket. *Unknown number.* I save the contact and tuck my phone away like that somehow makes this all manageable.

"I need time to think," I say.

"I know." His voice softens. "Stay there."

Before I can ask what he means, he's out of the car, circling around to my side and opening my door. He offers his hand, and I take it, letting him help me up. He walks me to my front door, slow and patient.

"Thanks again," I say when we reach the top step. "For everything."

He reaches out, gently tucks a piece of hair behind my ear. His fingers linger for half a second longer than strictly necessary. My breath catches.

"If you need anything..." he says quietly. It isn't a line. It's a promise.

"I will," I say. "I'll call soon." It's the best I can give him.

I slip inside before I can change my mind, closing the door softly behind me. For a second, I just stand there with my back against the wood, taking in my living room like I've stepped into a set of my own life. Everything is exactly where I left it this morning. Notebook open on the desk next to my laptop. The throw blanket I kicked off the couch last night when I fell asleep revising a scene.

Same room. Same stuff. Completely different life.

I drop my bag on the couch and sink down beside it, elbows on my knees, head in my hands. I'm pregnant with Jake Reyes's baby.

My hand drifts to my stomach again, almost on instinct. Twelve weeks. There is a baby in there. A tiny, impossible cluster of cells that somehow already has the power to blow up my entire carefully constructed plan.

The thought terrifies me. The career implications. The financial questions. The logistics. The conversations I'm going to have to have.

But under all of that—buried way down deep under the panic and the anger and the fear—there's something else. Something warm. Something that feels suspiciously like... awe. And maybe the tiniest flicker of excitement I'm not ready to admit to anyone, including myself.

I pull my hand away like I've been burned. I reach for my phone instead, scrolling through my contacts until I land on the one person who might understand how your entire life can tilt on its axis because of one night.

The phone rings once, twice.

"Hey! How'd the signing go?"

Her voice is so normal, so her, that something inside me cracks wide open.

"Mom," I say, my voice breaking. "I need you."

six

...

Jake

I DRIVE ON AUTOPILOT, my hands on the wheel and mind stuck on a loop. I went back to the office, but after an hour I canceled the rest of my day and left. I had to get out of there and think.

I might be a dad.

The city moves around me like it always does. Same clogged on-ramps, same half-faded billboards, same guy in a black SUV who thinks a turn signal is an optional suggestion rather than a necessary element of the highway code. By the time I turn onto my street, my brain has repeated the sentence so many times it has lost all meaning.

I might be a dad.

A baby.

The word is ridiculous and enormous at the same time. It sends a jolt through my chest, some wild mix of terror, awe, and something close to joy.

I have always wanted this. Kids. A family. The whole thing. Not in a white picket fence way, more in a Sunday mornings in pajamas with cartoons and cereal on the couch way. After the divorce, I kept telling myself it would still happen eventually, that I had time. But there was this small, quiet worry in the back of my mind.

But I definitely did not see this happening from a one-night stand, and certainly not with my boss's daughter.

I pull into my driveway and put the car in park, but I don't get out right away. My phone sits in the center console, silent. I grab it and see three missed calls from the office. Two texts from my assistant telling me to look at my email. One from the client I was supposed to meet confirming he's fine to reschedule.

I fire off quick responses. Then I stare at Ryan's name in my contacts. What am I supposed to say?

Hey, your daughter's fine, just a little dizzy from low blood sugar. Oh, and by the way, she's pregnant with my baby from a one-night stand we had three months ago.

Tomorrow. I'll figure out what to say to Ryan tomorrow. Right now, I need to talk to someone who won't fire me.

I dial Wyatt and wait for him to answer.

"Hey man, what's up?"

"Um, just letting you know I left early today."

"Oh, ok. How was the contract signing?"

"It was fine," I say. My voice sounds rougher than usual.

There's a pause. I can picture him on the other end, eyebrows up, reading between every line.

"Everything okay?" he asks.

"Yeah. Just a long day."

"I'm about to head out. Blair's making lasagna." His tone is casual, but there is a thread of concern under it he doesn't even try to hide. "Why don't you come over and eat with us? We have plenty, and you can fill me in on your day."

I look at the front door of my house and consider the quiet waiting for me inside. There is a part of me that wants to go in, shut the door, and sit on the floor until all of this sorts itself out in my head. But I know that's not how my brain works.

"Yeah," I say. "Okay. I'll head over."

"Great. See you soon."

An hour later, I am standing on Wyatt and Blair's front porch. The house is lit up from the inside, warm and bright. Before I can knock, the door swings open and Blair stands there with Ruby hitched on her hip like it is the easiest thing in the world.

"Jake." She smiles and steps back to let me in. "Perfect timing. Dinner is almost ready, come on in."

Their place has always felt like a home, but tonight it hits different. The air is warm and smells like tomatoes and garlic. There is baby gear in every direction, but none of it feels like clutter. My eyes catch on the swing, then shift to the row of bottles lined up to dry next to the sink, and over to the little suction bowl stuck to the highchair tray.

This might be my life soon. Some version of it, at least.

Wyatt greets me with a dish towel over his shoulder and a wooden spoon in his hand, like he has fully leaned into the domestic life. "Hey man," he says. "Lasagna is almost perfect. Hope you're hungry."

"Starving." I realize I haven't eaten since this morning and my stomach chooses that moment to agree loudly.

They herd me toward the dining room, and I can't help

notice how they've made space for Ruby's highchair at the table. When the food is ready, Blair brings it out and we all dig in. It's delicious.

"So," Wyatt says finally, wiping his mouth with his napkin and giving me his full attention. "What made it such a long day."

I set my fork down, take a breath as my heart rate kicks up. "Ryan asked me to sit in on a new contract client today," I say. "It was Natalie."

Blair's fork stops halfway to her mouth. "Natalie?" she repeats. "Our Natalie?"

"Yeah."

"Natalie from yoga?" Wyatt says, brows up.

"Yep."

"Wait," Blair says. She puts her fork down completely. "What was she doing at a contract signing?"

"Turns out she's a screenwriter," I say. "Just sold a show to FlixPix."

Wyatt blinks. "Natalie is a screenwriter?"

"Apparently a damn good one," I say.

"I remember she mentioned something about being a writer, but she's never talked about it," Blair mutters, almost to herself.

I push the food around my plate, thinking about how little any of us actually know about Natalie. Blair's been friends with her ever since she rented her house to her when she moved in with Wyatt—and she had no idea she was a screenwriter.

She's kept herself hidden from everyone. Not in a dishonest way, more like she's protecting something. Like she's built walls so carefully that even the people who care about her can only see what she wants them to see.

Most people would find that frustrating, but it makes me want to know her better. I want to understand why she keeps herself so guarded, and I want to be someone she trusts enough to let in.

"That is a surprise, but what made it such a long day?" Wyatt asks, as he continues eating.

I push a piece of lasagna around my plate with my fork.

"Well," I say slowly, "after the signing, she stood up and almost fainted."

Blair's head snaps up. "What? Is she okay?"

"I walked her across the street to the minute clinic," I say. "Ryan had another meeting and I offered to go with her."

"That was nice of you," Blair says softly.

"Yeah." I stare at my plate, mind half on the food, half on the storm I'm about to unleash. "They ran some tests."

Wyatt stops chewing. "And?"

I swallow. My fork trembles just slightly in my hand. My chest tightens. How do I even say this? There's no preparation for moments like this. No script. No way to soften it.

I set my fork down and look up at them. At my best friends sitting across from me, completely unaware that the next bit of info is going to shock them.

"It turns out she's pregnant."

Ruby bangs her hand on the highchair tray, the only sound in the room, completely oblivious to the bomb that just dropped.

"Did she know?" Blair asks, her voice careful.

"No. She had no idea."

"Oh my god." Blair presses her hand to her mouth. "She must be freaking out."

"I bet she is," Wyatt adds quietly. "She just signed the biggest deal of her life."

"Yeah," I say. My stomach twists. "She's terrified about what this means for the show."

"Did she tell you who the father is?" Blair asks.

Here we go. I take a breath, and my hands grip the edge of the table. "It's me," I say. "I'm the father."

Complete silence.

The weight of it settles on all of us. Blair's eyes go wide. Wyatt's face goes through about fifteen different expressions in three seconds. Ruby throws a Cheerio. It bounces off the table and lands on the floor. No one moves to pick it up.

"I'm sorry," Blair says after a long beat, her voice calm and direct. "Did you just say you're the father?"

"When did you sleep with Natalie?" Wyatt blurts.

"Wyatt," Blair hisses, swatting at his arm. "What he meant to say is we didn't realize you and Natalie were dating."

"We're not," I say. "We, uh... We hooked up at my Fourth of July party."

Blair's mouth forms a small oh. Wyatt drags a hand through his hair, processing.

"And it gets worse," I add, because apparently my mouth wants all of this out at once. "Ryan is her father."

Blair's fork slips out of her hand and clatters onto her plate. The noise is loud enough to make Ruby jump. Under it, I still hear her very clear, very quiet, "Holy fuck."

Wyatt just leans back in his chair like someone hit him

with a wave. "Wow," he says finally. "Okay. So you slept with Ryan's daughter, who you did not know was Ryan's daughter, and then had to sit through a contract signing with both of them, pretending you don't know her biblically. And she's pregnant."

"That's the summary, yes," I say.

Ruby chooses that moment to rediscover her spoon and smacks it against the tray, babbling happily. Blair automatically hands her another Cheerio, eyes never leaving my face.

"How are you feeling?" she asks. Her voice is soft. There's no humor, just concern.

"Honestly," I say, "I am all over the place. Nervous. Excited. Worried." I blow out a breath. "But also kind of... okay. Which sounds insane."

"It doesn't sound insane," Blair says, quick and firm.

"The situation is a mess," I say. "She barely knows me. I work for her dad. There are about eight million ways this can go wrong."

Wyatt nods.

"That night still plays on repeat in my head," I admit. "I wanted more than one night, but she was very clear that she doesn't do relationships, doesn't do complicated, this was a one-time thing."

"Maybe," Blair says, "you get another chance. Different circumstances, yeah. Messier ones. But a chance."

"If she lets me," I say. "She's scared. She's panicking about the show and what this means, and she has every right to. I told her I'm not going anywhere. That we'll figure it out together. I meant it."

Blair reaches across the table and squeezes my hand.

"Jake, once she realizes who you are she's going to realize she hit the jackpot. You're one of the good ones."

"I hope so," I say.

Ruby decides that is the perfect moment to launch a Cheerio at me. It bounces off my shoulder and lands in my lap. She screeches with glee like she has invented a new sport. Despite everything, I laugh.

"That's my cue to go wrestle her into pajamas," Blair says, scooping her up. "Stay as long as you want, Jake. There's more wine."

After Wyatt and I catch up on a few work things and schedule our next round of golf, I stand to leave. "I should get out of your hair," I say. "Thank you for feeding me."

"Any time," Wyatt says, walking me to the door. "And hey, we're here if you need anything. You're not alone in this either."

At the doorway, Blair appears again, now with a baby monitor clipped to her shirt and her hair pulled up into a messy bun.

She pulls me into a hug and holds on longer than usual. "It's going to work out," she says into my shoulder.

"I hope so," I say.

"I know so," she counters. "Just be patient with her. And with yourself. She's had less than a day to process something that's going to change her life. Same with you."

I nod, throat tight. "Yeah."

Outside, the air is cooler. The sky is washed out with city light, a few stars punching through anyway. I sit in my car for a second before starting it, the quiet wrapping around me.

I pull out my phone. No texts from Natalie. I didn't

expect any. I know she needs time. But that doesn't mean I can't do something.

I open my grocery delivery app, fingers hovering for a second. Then I start adding things without overthinking it. Fresh berries. Apples. Whole grain bread. Yogurt. Cheese. Eggs. Orange juice. I add some easy snack stuff. Nuts. Granola bars. Crackers. Things she can grab when she's tired and overwhelmed and doesn't want to cook.

My thumb hovers again.

Then I scroll to the vitamins section and add a bottle of prenatal vitamins. It feels big and intimate and slightly presumptuous and also exactly right.

I type in her address and, after a second of debating, open the little box for delivery instructions.

Just a few things to make sure you're taking care of yourself. Hope it makes your day a little easier. – Jake

I stare at the words for a long beat. It feels like a lot. It also feels like nothing at all compared to what she's carrying.

I hit order before I can talk myself out of it and set the delivery for tomorrow morning.

It's small. It might be too much. It might be not enough. She might roll her eyes. She might cry. She might text me. She might not.

But at least she'll know I meant what I said. I'm not going anywhere.

seven

. . .

Natalie

I WAKE up in my childhood bedroom and for three whole seconds, my brain does that blissful, blank thing where it doesn't remember anything bad. Then the word slams into me like a truck.

Pregnant.

I blink up at the ceiling, at the faint glow-in-the-dark stars my fourteen-year-old self stuck up there with a plan that included UCLA, writing TV shows, and zero babies.

The walls are still the same soft lavender I begged my mom to let me paint them. My old bookshelf is still crammed with dog-eared YA paperbacks, SAT prep books I pretended to study, and a row of yearbooks with my awkward braces era immortalized in glossy color. It's like the room is frozen in time, preserved in case I ever needed to crawl back into it and hide away from the grown up world.

Apparently I did.

I press my hand to my stomach. Still flat. Still the same as yesterday and the day before and the day before that. Twelve weeks, Dr. Patel said. Heading into the second trimester.

How did I not notice?

I drag my hand away and reach for my phone on the nightstand. The screen lights up with the time and a handful of notifications. Group texts from the writers' group. A text from my dad.

> **DAD**
> Good morning, kiddo. Glad you're feeling better. Let me know if you need anything.

I sent a text last night, told him I was fine, that the doctor said it was just low blood sugar. Made up something about stress and not eating enough. He didn't even question it.

I scroll past his message and land on one from a number I just added but already know by heart.

> **JAKE**
> Hope you're doing okay. Just a heads up that a grocery delivery is headed your way this morning.

I stare at the message for a long beat. Jake Reyes sent me groceries.

A tiny part of my chest warms at that and I immediately smother it. But the groceries are going to my apartment. Where I'm not. Which means I should probably get up and head home before everything melts on my doorstep.

The smell of coffee drifts under the bedroom door, warm and familiar. There's the faint sizzle of bacon in a pan, the low murmur of the morning news from the living room. My stomach growls like it's never been fed. Which is wild, because I haven't wanted to eat in days. Weeks. I thought it was stress.

I roll out of bed and pad down the hall in an oversized T-shirt and pajama bottoms. The photos on the wall are a walk down memory lane. One of me missing my front teeth, me holding a certificate from winning my first spelling bee, and me and mom on my tenth birthday at the beach, sunburned and grinning. It feels like walking through a museum of a girl who had no idea how complicated her life would get.

Mom's at the stove when I walk in, spatula in hand, steady and unflustered, already making breakfast.

"Morning," I say, my voice rough.

She looks over her shoulder and gives me that soft, assessing mom smile that somehow does not miss a single detail. "Good morning, sweetie," she says. "How are you feeling?"

I sink into one of the chairs at the kitchen table. "Tired," I say. "Confused. Pregnant."

One corner of her mouth lifts. "I meant physically. Any nausea? Cramping? Headaches? Or are we venturing into monster hunger phase yet?"

"No nausea," I say slowly. "Definitely hungry. Which is weird. I feel like I haven't wanted to eat anything in forever."

"That's good." She turns back to the stove, gives the pan a practiced flick. "Second trimester usually brings your appetite back. Scrambled eggs okay? With toast and bacon?"

"Yeah," I say. "That sounds amazing, actually. Thanks, Mom."

She slides fluffy scrambled eggs onto a plate, adds two

slices of toast, some bacon, then tosses a handful of berries on the side like she is plating something for a food blog. She sets it in front of me, pours a glass of orange juice, then tops off her own mug with coffee before sitting down across from me.

I pick up my fork, but before I take a bite, I look across the table at her. At the woman who raised me alone, who juggled law school and a toddler, who never once made me feel like I was a burden.

Last night, when I showed up on her doorstep, I thought she might panic. Or worse, be disappointed. Instead, she made tea, sat me down on the couch, and listened to the whole messy story without interrupting once.

When I finally stopped talking, throat raw from crying, she'd just pulled me into her arms and said, "Okay. We'll figure it out."

Not "We'll fix it." Not "What were you thinking?" Just "We'll figure it out." Like it was that simple. Like I wasn't about to derail my entire life. She's been steady ever since. Practical. I don't know what I'd do without her.

"Eat," she says simply, pulling me back to the present.

The first bite hits my tongue and my brain lights up. Salt and butter and actual flavor. My body, apparently, has decided it's done with the hunger strike.

Mom wraps her hands around her mug, watching me with that lawyer face she uses in court softened by pure mom-ness. "So," she says after a minute, voice gentle. "Have you thought at all about next steps?"

"You mean besides having a dramatic meltdown?" I ask around a bite of toast.

"Yes," she says, lips twitching, "besides that."

I put my fork down, push my plate back an inch, and stare at the condensation on my glass of orange juice. "I don't know, Mom," I say. "I just signed the biggest deal of my life. What if FlixPix decides I'm too much trouble? What if they replace me?"

"That's not going to happen," she says, no hesitation.

I look up. "How do you know that?"

"Natalie." She reaches across the table and lays her hand over mine. "Stop catastrophizing. Your career is going to be fine. You're talented, you're smart, and you have people in your corner who will fight for you if they have to. Being pregnant doesn't erase your talent."

"It feels like it might," I say, voice small.

"I know it feels that way," she says. "Because everything is fresh and loud and your brain is trying to protect you by preparing you for every possible disaster. But trust me." She squeezes my hand. "You can have a child and a career."

I study her face, the fine lines at the corners of her eyes that weren't there when I was in high school, the strength in her jaw, the way her presence has always seemed slightly too big for whatever room she's in.

"What made you believe you could do it?" I ask. "Back then. When it was just you and me. What made you think, *Yeah, I can be a mom and a lawyer and not explode?*"

Her thumb moves in slow circles on the back of my hand. "I didn't believe it at first," she says softly. "I was terrified. I thought I'd ruined my life, honestly. I thought I'd ruined his life, too. He had this big, shiny future mapped out, and I was young and pregnant and very certain I was going to derail everything if I told him. So I didn't. And that's something I'll always regret."

Pain flickers across her face for a second, there and gone. "But I believed I could do it because I wasn't alone. My parents helped with you. They encouraged me to go back to school when I was ready. I had friends who showed up with hand-me-down baby clothes and frozen meals and zero judgment. I had professors who let me bring you to class when childcare fell through. I had a village." She looks at me, eyes steady. "And so do you."

"Was it hard without him?" I ask. "Without Dad?"

"Yes," she says honestly. "And no. There were moments I wanted to tell him about something you did and I couldn't. There were nights I wanted to hand you to someone else and go stand outside and just breathe. And sometimes I wished I hadn't made that choice for him. Or for you."

She pauses, and I can see her deliberating over every word. "But I made that decision," she says. "I didn't give him the chance to step up. Your situation is different. Jake already knows and from what you told me last night, he wants to be involved."

I pull my hand back and wrap both arms around myself, palms pressing into my biceps like I can hold all the pieces of me in place. "What if I don't want him to be?" I say.

Mom tilts her head. She doesn't pounce on it. She just sits with it for a second. "Why wouldn't you want him to be?" she asks quietly.

"I don't know," I say, not entirely honestly. "I don't know what I want."

"Okay," she says. She leans back, gives me a little more

space. "Then don't pretend you do. Don't force yourself into some decision today because you think you should. But don't make this choice from fear either."

I stare at the little pile of scrambled eggs on my plate, now cooling. "I told him I don't do relationships," I say. "I told him it was one night. No strings. No complications."

"You need to talk to Jake," she says, voice firm but kind. "Not to make a forever decision today. Just talk. Figure out where he stands, what he's thinking, what he wants his role to be. You don't have to know all your answers yet but you can't make plans for the future by avoiding the person who's already part of it."

She's not wrong. Unfortunately. Because the truth is, when he put his hand over mine in that parking lot and said "I'm not going anywhere," there was this moment where I believed him. Where I wanted to lean my whole tired body into that promise and let someone else carry some of the fear. Which is the scariest part of this entire thing.

"I know," I say quietly.

"And who knows," she adds, taking a sip of her coffee, "maybe this will blossom into a wonderful relationship."

"Mom," I groan.

"What?" she says, feigning innocence. "It happens. People have surprise babies and fall in love all the time."

"I don't do relationships," I remind her. "I don't do hope or love or any of that. It's all a lie."

Her eyes soften in that way that makes me feel both seen and called out. "You're allowed to protect yourself," she says. "You're allowed to be careful. You've been through things that make that reasonable."

I wait for the but. It's coming. I can feel it.

"But," she says, "there's a difference between being careful and being so walled-off no one can reach you. You can't spend your whole life building fortresses just to keep the pain out. The same walls that keep the bad out keep the good out too."

It hits harder than I want it to. I look away.

"That's not fair," I say quietly. "You know what happened. You were there. You saw what he did to me."

Mom's face softens. "I know, baby."

"There were no signs," I continue, my throat tightening. "No red flags. Nothing that would have told me to run. And then he just..." I shake my head. "How am I supposed to trust my own judgment after that? How am I supposed to believe anything anyone says when I was so completely wrong about someone I thought I knew?"

"He made his choices," Mom says firmly. "That wasn't about you missing something. That was about him being a coward."

"But I didn't see it," I say. "That's the point. And now I'm supposed to, what, trust a guy I barely know because he made some promises in a parking lot?"

Mom reaches across the table and covers my hand with hers. "I'm not saying trust him blindly. I'm not saying forget what you've been through. I'm just saying don't let one person's betrayal convince you that everyone will do the same thing."

I don't answer because she's right and I hate it.

"I'm not saying fling the gates wide open," she adds. "Maybe just start with cracking a window."

I roll my eyes, because the alternative is crying again.

"And you need to tell your father," she adds, switching lanes smoothly.

"I know," I say, stomach dropping.

"Soon," she says. "He's going to find out, and it's better coming from you than from a medical chart or a gossip site or Jake accidentally saying the wrong thing in a meeting."

"I want to talk to Jake first," I say. "I want to know where his head is, what we're even doing, before I drop, 'Hey, I'm pregnant with your associate's baby.' I don't want this to blow up Jake's career."

"That's smart," she says. She rises and starts gathering our plates. "And honestly? Of all the people in Los Angeles, I can't believe you somehow managed to get pregnant by the guy who works for your father."

Despite everything, my mouth curves. "That's not funny."

"It's a little funny," she says, rinsing dishes.

"It's a disaster," I say.

"It's life," she counters, glancing at me over her shoulder. "Messy and inconvenient and rarely on schedule. And for what it's worth, getting pregnant by a man who is stable, employed, and apparently very invested in doing the right thing is not the worst outcome."

My phone buzzes on the table and saves me from responding to her.

> Your order is on the way.

I tap the notification. The delivery note pops up first.

> Just a few things to make sure you're taking care of yourself. Hope it makes your day a little easier. – Jake

I scroll down and see the list of healthy items and my throat tightens.

"What is it?" Mom asks, drying her hands.

"Jake sent groceries to my house," I say, staring at the screen.

Her smile is small but knowing. "That's sweet."

"It's ridiculous," I say, but my voice comes out softer than I intend.

Because the truth is, it doesn't feel ridiculous. It feels like relief. Like for the first time in longer than I can remember, someone noticed I needed something and just did it. No strings. No expectations. Just groceries and a quiet promise that I'm not doing this alone.

I've spent so long keeping people at arm's length, building walls so high I can't see over them anymore, that I forgot what this feels like. Someone caring. Someone showing up.

It's terrifying how good it feels.

I lock my phone and set it face down on the table before that warmth in my chest can spread any further.

"It's thoughtful," Mom corrects, watching me with those all-seeing eyes that miss nothing.

"I should get home," I say, standing.

She pulls me into a hug, arms wrapping all the way around me, and for a second I let myself lean in, really lean, like I did when I was little and she was the whole structure holding my world up.

"You're going to be okay," she murmurs into my hair. "I promise."

"I hope so," I say before I can stop myself.

She pulls back just enough to look at me. "Hope isn't a bad thing, you know. Even if you think it is."

The word lands like a stone in my chest. Hope.

People love that word. They wear it on bracelets. Tattoo it on their ribs in curly script. Throw it around in speeches and Instagram captions like it's some kind of magic spell.

Keep hoping.

Have hope.

Hope for the best.

The hope I know has never been soft or pretty like that. The hope I know is what you cling to right before everything explodes and you're left standing in the smoking crater wondering why you were stupid enough to believe this time would be different. Hope has only ever been the prequel to disappointment. The quiet drumbeat leading up to the fall.

Every time I've let myself want something out loud, every time I've let that fragile little spark light up in my chest, it's ended in the same place. Devastation. Hope is not a lifeboat. It's a trapdoor.

So no. I don't want to feel it. Not about my career. Not about Jake. Not about a baby I did not plan for and am terrified to want.

eight

...

Jake

A FORTY-PAGE LICENSING agreement is open on my screen and I've read the same sentence four times. I still couldn't tell you what it says because my brain is not here.

My brain is in a tiny exam room watching Natalie's face go white when the doctor said the word pregnant. My brain is replaying the feel of her hand under mine in the parking lot when she pressed her palm to her stomach. My brain is stuck on a loop thinking about one thing.

I'm possibly going to be a dad.

My phone buzzes on the desk. I grab it so fast I almost knock over my coffee.

> **NATALIE**
> Thanks for the groceries. Can we talk?
> Tonight?

The relief that hits is stupidly intense for such a short text. I feel like I've been holding my breath since I left her at her door yesterday.

> **JAKE**
> Of course. I can come to you. What time?

The dots appear, vanish, reappear. I have never in my life been so desperate for someone to finish composing a text.

> **NATALIE**
> Maybe around 7?

> **JAKE**
> Perfect. I'll bring dinner.

> **NATALIE**
> You don't have to do that.

> **JAKE**
> I know. See you at 7.

I set my phone down and blow out a long breath. I'm so relieved she wants to talk. She could have ignored me. Could have told me she needed space, or that she'd decided to handle everything alone.

"Jake."

I look up. Ryan is standing in my doorway, one hand on the frame, the other wrapped around a coffee mug. My stomach drops straight through the floor and keeps going.

Does he know? Did she tell him already? Is this the part where he fires me, sues me, or buries my body behind the building.

"Hey," I say, aiming for casual and landing somewhere in the neighborhood of mildly constipated. "What's up?"

He steps into the office and settles into the guest chair like he owns the place—which, to be fair, he kind of does.

"I just wanted to thank you again for yesterday," he says. "For taking care of Natalie."

Guilt punches me right in the solar plexus.

"I tried calling her last night," he goes on, "but I think she crashed as soon as she got home."

"Yeah," I say. "She was pretty wiped out."

Not technically a lie. Just not the whole screaming circus of the truth.

"What exactly did the doctor say?" He takes a sip of coffee, watching me over the rim of the mug.

I choose every word like it might be used as evidence later. "They said her blood sugar was a little low," I say. "She needs to eat more regularly. Rest. She'll be all right."

Ryan exhales, some of the tension leaving his shoulders. "Good. She pushes herself too hard."

"She's tough," I say.

"Thank you Jake. I really appreciate you taking her to get checked out. You're a good man."

I almost choke.

If you only knew.

"Thanks," I manage. "That means a lot."

He nods, and stands to leave. "I'll let you get back to it." He lifts the mug in a little salute and disappears down the hall.

I slump back in my chair, staring at the ceiling. This is a disaster. A hopeful disaster, sure. A disaster with a tiny heartbeat at the center of it. But still.

I force myself to work the rest of the afternoon. Contracts, emails, a quick call with a client. By six, though,

I'm done. I shut down my computer, grab my jacket, and head out.

In the parking garage, I sit behind the wheel for a minute, hands loose on the steering wheel, letting the quiet soak in. I unlock my phone and pull up a browser and type in "typical pregnancy cravings."

The results are endless. Pickles. Ice cream. Pickles with ice cream. Spicy food. Sour candy. Things that should never occupy the same plate. One result says meat. That I can do.

I put in an order at Five Guys for burgers and fries. It's way too much food for two people. While I wait in my car for the order to be ready, I let my head fall back against the seat and finally admit the thing I've been dancing around all day: *I want this.*

I want the baby. I want to be a dad. That part has always been there, humming under everything else like background music. Even at my lowest point after the divorce, when I was pretty sure the universe had stapled a "Do Not Resuscitate" sign to my love life, there was still this small, stubborn feeling that someday I'd have a family.

I just assumed there would be a more conventional route to that destination. Marriage, then kids. Not fireworks, champagne, and my boss's daughter breathing "This is one night only" in my ear.

Six months. That's roughly what we have before everything changes on a practical level. Six months to show her I mean what I say. Six months to earn her trust. Six months to figure out if we can be more than two people orbiting the same baby.

In my ideal version, yeah, we end up together. We raise

our kid under the same roof. We argue about paint colors for the nursery and names and who gets up for the middle-of-the-night feeding. We keep laughing the way we did that night, and she lets me see all the parts of her she keeps tucked away behind her walls.

But I can't say all of that to her tonight without sending her sprinting for the hills, so tonight is simple. Tonight is "I'm here." Tonight is "I'm not going anywhere." Tonight is "I will show you with a hundred small actions that I can be counted on, and if you never want anything more than co-parenting, I will still be all in as a dad."

I get a text that my order is ready and ten minutes later I'm pulling up in front of her house. The porch light is on. My stomach does a weird flip. I climb out of the car and head up to the door holding the bags of food in one hand and knock. When the door opens, whatever little speech I had queued up in my brain vaporizes.

She is beautiful. Barefoot in black leggings and an oversized sweater that hangs off one shoulder, dark hair down around her face in loose waves. No makeup. She looks softer than yesterday, less brittle around the edges, but there is still a tightness around her eyes that says she hasn't stopped thinking either.

"Hi," I say.

"Hi." Her voice is a little tentative, but she smiles, and something unclenches in my chest.

We stand there for a second locked in eye contact before she shifts back and opens the door wider. "Come in."

The house smells like sugar cookies and mint, and looks just as comforting as it smells. The living room has dark blue walls crowded with framed vintage movie posters, built-in shelves crammed with paperbacks and scripts and notebooks. There's a beat-up, overstuffed couch with a throw blanket crumpled in one corner and a half-empty mug on the coffee table. Her laptop is open on the small desk along the wall, surrounded by a perimeter of pens, sticky notes, and what looks like a stack of notebooks.

"Nice place," I say, setting the food on the kitchen counter. "It looks completely different from when Blair lived here."

"Thanks," she says, closing the door behind us. "I told her I appreciated the beige, but my soul needed color."

"Bold choice," I say. "But it suits you."

She eyes the bags in my hands. "Smells delicious."

"I hope it is," I say. "Google said meat, so I thought maybe burgers."

Her eyes light up in a way I did not see yesterday. "Seriously?"

"Yeah." I shrug, suddenly feeling self-conscious. "If you want something healthy I can go get something else."

She stares at me, then laughs, this surprised, real sound that hits me right under the sternum.

"That is exactly what I've been craving all day," she says. "Like, specifically Five Guys."

"Really?"

"Really. How did you—" She shakes her head. "Never mind. That's...that's perfect. Thank you."

"You're welcome."

We unpack the food together in her small kitchen, brushing elbows as we reach for napkins and plates. We sit at the little table against the window and for a minute all I do is watch her eat. She doesn't pick at it. She dives in like someone who finally remembered food tastes good. She hums under her breath at one bite and looks mildly embarrassed when she realizes I heard it.

"This is so good," she says around a mouthful, eyes closing for a second.

Her response is fucking turning me on. *Jesus.*

Eventually, she slows down and then sets the last bit of her food down. I can see the moment she switches tracks when her shoulders shift and her gaze sharpens. "So," she says.

"So," I echo.

She twists her napkin between her fingers, eyes dropping to her plate. "Tell me about yourself," she says suddenly.

I blink. "What?"

"I mean, I know some things," she says. "You work for my dad. You are terrifyingly good at predicting comfort food."

She's buying herself time. Keeping the spotlight on me instead of all the "what now" questions clanging around her head.

I recognize it because I do the same thing. In the conference room, in negotiations, when I need to control the pace of a conversation. Keep things where I want them until I'm ready to pivot.

Her eyes flick up to mine for half a second, and something passes between us. A flash of recognition. Of memory. The way I kept her exactly where I wanted her that night in July, slow and deliberate, until she was the one begging me to move faster.

Her cheeks flush, just barely, and she looks back down at her plate.

I clear my throat, pushing the memory aside before it derails me completely. "Okay," I say, deciding to play along, at least for a minute. "I grew up in Seaside, Connecticut. Moved out here for college. UCLA."

Her eyes brighten. "I went to UCLA."

"Small world." Something about that makes me smile.

"I met Wyatt freshman year," I say. "We were roommates in the dorms. We survived that and decided to stay roommates all through undergrad and law school."

"So he's been stuck with you a long time." She grins when she says it, eyes lighting up in a way that makes her whole face soften. It's teasing, not mean, and something in my chest loosens.

"Pretty much," I say, grinning back. "My mom still lives in Connecticut. My dad passed away a few years ago."

Her expression softens. "I'm sorry."

"Thanks." I feel that familiar ache in my chest—dull, not as sharp as it used to be, but still there.

She reaches out without seeming to think about it and lays her hand on my forearm. Her fingers are light, but the contact sends a jolt up my arm that sends electricity through my body and makes me want her hands on more of me.

"Do you have any siblings?" she asks.

"Nope," I say. "Only child."

"Explains a lot," she says, pulling her hand back, a hint of a smile on her lips. "And you were married, right? To Lauren?"

"See," I say. "You know more than you think."

"What happened?" she asks. The question is gentle, no prying edge, just curiosity.

I take a breath. I could tell her about the tabloid stories, about the betrayal, about waking up one day and realizing the person you built your life with has been using you as a stepping stone to better things. But that is not why I am here tonight.

"I'll tell you every detail of my marriage and divorce if you want," I say, "but not tonight. Tonight I want to talk about us."

She looks back down at her plate, jaw tight. The jokes and casual questions fall away. I can almost see her steel herself.

"I'm keeping the baby," she says, voice steady, like she practiced that sentence in the mirror. "I need you to know that."

The relief is immediate. "Okay," I say, and I mean it. "I'm glad."

Her head snaps up, eyes searching my face. "You are?"

"Yeah," I say. "This is not what either of us planned, I get that. But I've always wanted kids. And I want to be involved. If you'll let me."

She studies me like she's suspicious of my intentions. "I can do this alone," she says finally.

"I know you can," I say. "You seem like the most capable person in any room you walk into. I have no doubt you could do it alone."

Her gaze flickers, then drops to her hands. She twists her napkin again, the paper already soft from how many times she's done it. "Why?" she asks quietly. "Why are you so...

sure? About being involved? About this? You barely know me."

"Because I like you, Natalie. There was a connection between us, and I think you felt it too. And I know you said that night was supposed to be one time only, but now we have a reason to actually get to know each other. I'm not going to waste that."

She looks away. "I'm not interested in a relationship."

"Okay." I won't push her any more on the topic tonight.

"So what does co-parenting look like to you," she asks.

"I've never done this before," I confirm. "But in my head, it looks like doctor's appointments together. Both of us at the big stuff. Being in the room when the baby is born, if you're okay with that. A schedule we build together.'"

She nods slowly, like she's turning the idea over, checking it for cracks. "I have to tell my dad," she says quietly.

"I know," I say.

"Are you worried about your job?" she asks, looking up.

"A little," I say. "But I'm more worried about him being hurt that we didn't tell him sooner. "

"Me too," she says softly.

Silence settles between us for a moment.

"Okay," she says finally, like she's making a decision with herself as much as with me. "Co-parents. Doctor's appointments together. We figure everything else out as we go."

"That works for me," I say.

We clear the table together, moving in that careful dance people do when they're hyper-aware of each other's proximity. My hand brushes hers as we both reach for the same plate. I don't pull away immediately. Neither does she.

The contact lasts maybe two seconds, but I feel it everywhere. The warmth of her skin against mine. The way her breath catches, so quiet I almost miss it.

She pulls back first, fingers curling into her palm like she's trying to hold onto the feeling or push it away. I can't tell which.

We finish in silence, moving around each other in her small kitchen. Every time I pass behind her, I'm aware of how close I am. Close enough to catch her scent. Close enough to see the way her shoulders tense when I reach past her for a dish towel.

She's not unaffected. That much is clear.

When the last dish is put away, I walk over to the chair where my jacket hangs and shrug it on, taking my time. Letting the sleeves settle over my arms, the fabric stretching across my shoulders and chest.

I don't miss the way her eyes track the movement. The way they linger on my biceps, on the line of my shoulders, before she catches herself and looks away.

I straighten, letting the jacket fall into place, then meet her gaze and hold it for a beat longer than necessary. The air between us feels thick. Charged. Like we're both pretending this is just a normal visit.

She wraps her arms around herself. "Thank you," she says quietly. "For the groceries. For dinner. For being decent about all of this."

I take a step closer. Not crowding her, just closing some of the distance she's trying to maintain. "You don't have to thank me for being decent," I say, my voice dropping lower. Calmer. The same tone I use in negotiations when I need someone to actually hear me. "And you don't have to do any of this alone."

Her lips part slightly, like she's going to argue, but nothing comes out.

"I meant what I said," I continue, holding her gaze. "I'm here. Whatever this looks like, I'm in. You don't have to trust me right away, but I'm not going anywhere. And I'm not leaving you to handle this by yourself."

Something flickers across her face. Relief, maybe. Or surprise. For just a second, the walls come down and I see her. Really see her. The fear underneath all that armor. The exhaustion. The small, stubborn hope she won't let herself name.

Then she gathers herself again, shoulders straightening, chin lifting just slightly.

But her eyes linger on mine a heartbeat too long. And when she finally looks away, there's color in her cheeks that wasn't there before.

"Okay," she says softly.

I let myself smile, just a little. "Okay."

nine

...

Natalie

THE CIRCULAR DRIVEWAY in front of my dad's house is already occupied by Rachel's SUV and my dad's Mercedes, so I park on the street.

The house is massive. Spanish Colonial Revival with arched windows, terracotta tile roof, and perfectly manicured hedges that probably cost more to maintain than my monthly rent. It sits on almost an acre in Hancock Park.

I didn't grow up here. By the time my dad found out about me, he was already married to Rachel with a baby on the way. I was always welcome, but between his new family and my life with my mom across town, I just never ended up spending much time here. Different worlds, different routines.

Through the tall windows, I can see movement inside. The front door swings open, and my half brother Ethan comes barreling out with his soccer ball.

"Natalie!" He grins, all legs and arms and shaggy pre-teen hair.

"Hey, E."

Mia appears behind him, ponytail bouncing. "Will you be here later? I wanted to ask you about this assignment for AP Lit."

"I can't stay long, but text me later if you want."

She gives me a thumbs up and climbs into the SUV parked in the driveway as Rachel emerges with her purse and water bottles, keys already in hand.

"Natalie! So good to see you, honey." She gives me a quick hug. "Sorry to rush out, but I'm already running late getting these two where they need to be. Promise you'll come for dinner this week?"

"Definitely."

"Perfect. Your dad's inside." She calls toward the SUV. "Ethan, did you grab your water bottle? Mia, where are your shin guards?"

I watch them get settled, the familiar chaos of cleats and bags and half-shouted reminders, and then Rachel waves from the driver's seat as they pull away.

I stand there for a second, watching the SUV disappear around the corner. This is what normal looks like. Two kids, two parents, weekend soccer games and AP Lit assignments. The kind of family rhythm my mom and I never had because it was always just us.

I wonder what it was like for my dad, stepping into this version of fatherhood with Rachel when he'd missed it completely with me. If it hurt. If it felt like a second chance or a constant reminder of what he'd lost.

And I wonder what my own kid's life will look like. Will they grow up watching me build something with Jake, or will they be the one standing on the outside of someone else's tidy family picture?

My hand drifts to my stomach before I can stop it.

I head up to the front door where my dad is standing in the doorway, coffee mug in hand, still in his Yale Law hoodie.

"Finally, some peace and quiet." He grins, kissing my cheek. "Come in. I just made breakfast."

I follow him into the kitchen, the familiar warmth of their home settling around me. It's so different from how I grew up, but I love being part of this family, too.

"Tea?" Dad asks, already reaching for a mug.

"Just orange juice, actually."

He raises an eyebrow but doesn't comment, pouring me a glass instead. We settle at the kitchen island, and he leans against the counter with that calm lawyer energy that makes people confess things.

"So what's new, kiddo? How's the writing going?"

"Good. Really good. I'm meeting with the showrunner Rebecca next week to start talking about the writers' room."

"That's exciting. When do you officially start?"

"December. Production starts in the spring."

"And how are you feeling about all of it?"

"Terrified but excited." I take a sip of juice, then set it down. "Actually, there's something else I need to tell you."

His expression shifts slightly, lawyer instincts kicking in. He sets his coffee down and gives me his full attention. "Okay."

My pulse kicks up. I've been rehearsing this conversation in my head since I left my apartment, but now that I'm here, the words feel stuck somewhere between my chest and my throat.

"You know how I wasn't feeling well at your office the other day?"

"Yeah." His voice is careful now, measured. "You said everything was fine."

"It is. Sort of." I take a breath. My hands are shaking, so I press them flat against the cool granite countertop. "When we were at the clinic, they ran some tests. Blood work and everything."

He's completely still now, eyes locked on mine. Waiting.

"And they found something." My voice comes out steadier than I feel.

The air between us feels heavy. I can see him running through possibilities in his head, worst-case scenarios, his jaw tightening slightly.

I force the words out before I lose my nerve or give him a heart attack.

"I'm pregnant, Dad. About twelve weeks."

The words settle between us. My dad goes very still, his face cycling through surprise and concern before landing on something softer. "Pregnant," he repeats quietly.

"Yeah."

"As in, I'm going to be a grandpa?" His eyes light up as realization hits.

"Exactly that."

He is quiet for a moment, taking in this information. Then he asks, "How are you feeling about it?"

I relax at his genuine concern for me.

"Honestly? I'm still processing. It's a lot."

"I imagine so." He runs his hand through his hair. "Does the father know?"

"He does. He was actually there when I found out."

My heart is pounding so hard I can hear it in my ears. This is the part where I have to say Jake's name out loud to my dad. Where I have to connect the dots he hasn't connected yet. I brace myself.

"It's Jake."

My dad blinks. "Jake. Jake Reyes?"

"Yeah."

"I didn't even know you knew Jake. You didn't mention it when you met in the office?"

"We kind of run in the same circles. Entertainment industry people, mutual friends." My throat feels tight. I swallow. "We sort of hung out at his Fourth of July party."

He processes this, his lawyer brain working through the timeline. I can almost see him counting backward, putting pieces together. "And you just found out?" he asks.

"It was a complete surprise for both of us," I say. My hands twist together in my lap.

I watch his face carefully, waiting for anger or disappointment or something worse. But all I see is him processing, thinking, trying to understand. He walks to the other side of the kitchen and braces his hands on the counter. I watch his shoulders tense, waiting for whatever is coming next.

When he turns around, his voice is gentle. "How's Jake handling this?"

"Really well, actually. He wants to be involved. He's been supportive."

My dad nods slowly. "Good. That's important."

"You're not mad?"

"Mad?" He looks genuinely surprised. "Natalie, you're an adult." He moves back toward me, his voice catching. "I missed the first ten years of your life. I wasn't there when your mom was pregnant with you. I missed your first steps, your first words, all of it." He squeezes my shoulder. "If Jake wants to be there for you and this baby, I'm grateful. I know what it feels like to miss that."

My throat tightens. "What about work? Will this make things complicated between you two?"

"Not on my part. Although that explains why he was acting so strange yesterday." His mouth twitches. "Jake's one of my best attorneys. I trust him."

He pulls me into a hug, and I press my face against his hoodie. "You're going to be an amazing mom, Nat."

The tears come before I can stop them and I did not realize how tightly I had been holding myself together until that moment. Hearing him say "amazing mom" cracks something open. I have spent days braced for judgment, for someone to tell me I ruined everything I have worked for, that I should have been more careful. Relief hits so hard it almost hurts.

When we pull apart, we are both wiping our eyes.

"Okay." He clears his throat. "Now that we've settled all that. You hungry? Feels like we should make some pancakes now, too."

"That sounds perfect."

We spend the next hour cooking and eating breakfast together, talking about the show and his work and Rachel's new obsession with pickleball. Normal things. Easy things. When it's time to go, he walks me to the door.

"Come to dinner this week. I'll ask Rachel to make that curry you love."

"I will. Promise."

He hugs me one more time. "I am proud of you, kiddo. And I am here for whatever you need."

"Thanks, Dad."

I am still wiping my eyes when I get to my car. My phone buzzes.

> STELLA
> Porto's at 2? We need to celebrate!!!

Right. The celebration she has been planning since I told her about FlixPix.

I stare at the text for a long moment. The last thing I want to do right now is sit in a crowded bakery and pretend everything is normal when my entire life has turned upside down in less than a week.

But Stella has been so excited about this. She's been my biggest cheerleader since I finally confided in her when I sold the pilot. And I bailed on her the day of my contract signing. And maybe I need to be around people who know me. People who will support me no matter what mess I've gotten myself into.

> ME
> See you there.

ten
...
Natalie

PORTO'S IS PACKED when I arrive, the smell of cheese rolls and café con leche making my stomach rumble. I spot Stella immediately, practically bouncing in her seat near the window. Blair, Sophia, and Jess are already there, pastry boxes stacked in the center of the table.

Stella sees me and leaps up, wrapping me in a hug that nearly knocks me over. "Finally! I have been dying to celebrate with you properly."

"I missed you too," I laugh.

They all stand, pulling me into hugs. Jess squeezes my shoulder. Sophia kisses my cheek. Blair gives me a longer hug, and there is something knowing in her eyes when we pull apart.

"Sit," Stella commands, pushing me into a chair. "We got you a potato ball and a cheese roll."

I grab the potato ball immediately, taking a huge bite. "You are my favorite people."

"So." Sophia leans forward, grinning. "What is this big news Stella keeps hinting about?"

Stella is practically vibrating. "Tell them. Tell them now!"

I look around the table at these women who have become my closest friends over the past few years. "I sold a show. To FlixPix."

The table erupts. Sophia shrieks. Jess's jaw drops. Blair is grinning, her happiness genuine even if it's not a surprise, as I suspect it isn't. They all jump up at once, another round of hugs and squealing that makes half the bakery turn to look at us.

"When did this happen?" Jess demands as we all settle back down.

"Couple weeks ago."

"What is the concept?" Sophia asks.

"Three estranged sisters who inherit their grandmother's witch powers and have to deal with family trauma while fighting supernatural threats. Think *Charmed* meets *Practical Magic* meets *Supernatural*."

"That sounds amazing," Blair says warmly. "Congrats to you."

"Wait." Jess sets down her iced coffee. "Have you been a writer this whole time we have known you?"

Heat creeps up my neck. I feel guilty that I have kept this a secret for so long. "Yes. I have been working on it while teaching yoga."

"And you didn't tell us?" Sophia looks genuinely hurt.

I take a breath. This is the part I have been dreading. "I didn't tell anyone except Stella, and she only found out a few weeks ago when I got the call." I look around the table. "The thing is, my dad is Ryan Cole."

The table goes quiet. They all know that name.

"Ryan Cole," Sophia repeats slowly. "Ryan Cole...from Hays & Cole?"

"Yeah."

"Ryan Cole who has worked on half of Hollywood's biggest deals?" Jess adds.

"That's him."

"Holy shit," Sophia breathes. "You are Ryan Cole's daughter?"

"Nobody knows. I've kept it private for years." I tear apart my cheese roll. "I wanted to do this on my own. No connections, no favors, no 'Ryan Cole's daughter sold a show.' Just me and my work."

Blair is watching me with soft eyes. "That's why you kept it so quiet."

"Yeah. I needed to prove to myself I could do it without anyone knowing who my dad is."

"That is very you," Jess says. "Independent to a fault."

"But incredibly impressive," Sophia adds. "You sold a show to FlixPix on merit alone. That is huge, Nat."

"I still can't believe you kept this from me for so long," Stella mumbles.

"I'm sorry. I just, I needed to keep it separate."

Blair leans forward slightly. "Jake mentioned he helped with the contract signing at your dad's office." There is something in her tone, in the way she is looking at me, that tells me she knows more than she is saying.

My stomach flips. Of course Jake told Wyatt. And of course Wyatt told Blair.

"Yeah," I say carefully. "He was there."

"He said it went well," Blair adds, and the knowing look she gives me is gentle and supportive.

"We should celebrate properly," Jess announces. "I'll grab us a bottle of champagne!"

"Oh, I'll just stick with water," I say quickly.

Everyone pauses, looking at me.

"Water?" Sophia frowns. "Nat, you just sold your first show."

"I know. I just can't drink right now."

"Why not?" Stella asks.

I hesitate for a second. I didn't want to share this news with everyone yet, but these are my people. And I may need their support. My hands are clammy where they're pressed against my thighs under the table.

"I'm pregnant."

The words come out quieter than I intended, but they land like a bomb anyway. Stella gasps so loud the entire bakery turns to stare again. Sophia's mouth falls open. Jess very carefully sets down her coffee cup.

"Pregnant?" Stella's voice climbs an octave. "You're pregnant?"

Heat floods my face. My pulse is racing. "About twelve weeks."

"Twelve weeks?" Jess's journalist brain kicks in. "How long have you known? Why didn't you tell us?"

"I just found out a few days ago. I didn't know before that."

"Who is the father?" Sophia asks.

My stomach flips. Here comes the moment of truth.

"Jake."

Just saying it does something to me. My skin feels warm. My heart kicks against my ribs. Because saying Jake's name out loud to my friends makes him real in a way he hasn't been yet. Makes the night we spent together something I can't pretend didn't happen.

"Jake?" Stella's eyes go wide. "Jake Reyes? Our Jake?"

"Yes."

"Wyatt's Jake?" Jess leans forward. "Wait. When did you and Jake hook up?"

"His Fourth of July party. Remember when you guys went out of town?" I look at Stella. "You texted me the address. I figured, *Why not check it out?*"

"Oh my God." Stella is staring at me like I have grown a second head. "You hooked up with Jake and didn't tell us? I feel like I don't even know you."

"Jake told us he was with you when you found out," Blair says. She reaches under the table and squeezes my hand. A silent show of support. "How are you feeling about it?" she asks.

The whole table grows quiet, waiting for me to answer.

I take a breath. "Terrified. I just sold my first show, and now I am going to be visibly pregnant during production. What if FlixPix decides I am too much trouble?"

"They can't do that," Stella says immediately. "It's illegal."

"They can find other reasons. Creative differences. Wrong vision for the show."

"Over my dead body." Jess's voice has that dangerous edge. "If anyone at FlixPix even thinks about sidelining you because you are pregnant, I will personally destroy them."

"Same," Stella adds. "Blair and I know everyone in this town. We'll make sure the right people know what's up."

Sophia squeezes my other hand. "I've been in this industry a long time. I've watched them try to sideline women for way less. But things are changing." Her voice softens. "They're not going to throw away a good show because the creator is pregnant. That would be incredibly stupid."

"How's Jake handling everything?" Stella asks gently.

"He's been really supportive. He wants to be involved."

"Of course he does," Jess says, and there is genuine warmth in her voice. "That is so Jake."

"He's probably already bought out half of Kidsland," Sophia adds with a grin. "Jake has wanted to be a dad forever."

I think about the groceries he ordered without being asked. The food he brought over. "Yeah. He's definitely excited."

"And you?" Jess asks carefully. "How are you feeling about Jake specifically?"

My throat goes dry. I reach for my water, buying myself a second.

"We're going to co-parent. Figure it out as we go."

They all exchange glances. I can feel them silently communicating, deciding who's going to push me on this.

"Co-parent," Jess repeats, one eyebrow raised.

"That's the plan." I tear off a piece of my cheese roll, not because I'm hungry but because I need something to do with my hands. "I mean, we barely know each other."

"But Jake is a really good guy," Stella says gently. "Like genuinely one of the best people we know."

"He's also hot," Sophia adds. "Like objectively hot."

An image flashes through my mind before I can stop it. Jake's hands on my hips. His mouth on my neck. The way he looked at me in the dark like I was the only thing that mattered.

Heat crawls up my chest.

"I'm aware," I manage.

Jess leans forward, eyes sharp. "So, did you not like being with him?"

My face is on fire now. "I didn't say that."

"So you did like it," Sophia says, grinning.

Heat floods my body. Because the truth is, I haven't stopped thinking about that night. About the way he made me feel seen and wanted and safe all at once. About the way my body responded to his like we'd done this a hundred times before.

"We agreed to one night. And I don't do relationships."

"But was it a good night?" Jess presses.

I take a long drink while I decide how much to admit. My pulse is hammering. My hands are shaking slightly.

"Yes," I say finally.

"How good?" Stella is practically bouncing.

"I'm not giving you details."

"Come on," Sophia whines.

I close my eyes for a second, and there he is again. The weight of him above me. The sound of my name in his voice, rough and needy. The way he took his time like he had all night and wanted to use every second of it.

My stomach flutters.

"Fine. It was really good. Like really, really good. Happy now?"

"Very," Jess says, smirking. "So you're attracted to him, sounds like you have amazing chemistry, and he is a great guy who wants to be there for you and the baby."

Everything she's saying is true, and that's the problem. Because the more I think about Jake, the more I remember how it felt to be with him, and the harder it is to keep my walls up.

"We don't want to complicate anything right now," I say, but my voice sounds uncertain even to my own ears. "Co-parenting is something we both agree on."

Blair squeezes my hand again. "You don't have to figure everything out right now. Just see what happens."

I look down at our joined hands, then back up at the faces of my friends. They're not pushing, exactly. Just opening a door I've been trying to keep closed.

But the truth is, Jake's already halfway through it. With his groceries and his dinner and his calm certainty that he's not going anywhere.

And I'm terrified of how much I want to let him in.

"Maybe," I say. And this time, I almost mean it.

"You never know," Sophia says softly. "Sometimes the best things are the ones we don't plan for."

eleven

...

Jake

THE EMAIL COMES through at seven forty-five Monday morning, before I have even finished my first coffee.

From: Ryan Cole
Subject: My office – 8:30 AM

That's it. No message in the body of the email. No pleasantries. No agenda. Just a summons. My stomach drops. *He knows.*

Of course he knows. Natalie said she was going to tell him this weekend, and clearly she did.

By eight twenty-five, I am outside his office, because somehow showing up early feels less risky than walking in right on time. His assistant looks up from her computer and gives me a quick, tight smile.

"He's expecting you. Go on in."

Ryan is standing at the window when I walk in, hands in

his pockets, looking out over downtown LA like he owns it. He might.

"Close the door," he says.

My heart starts hammering so hard it feels like the only sound in the room. I close the door. He doesn't turn around right away. When he does, his expression is unreadable. Not angry. Not smiling. Just serious. The kind of serious that makes opposing counsel fold during depositions.

"Sit."

I sit. He doesn't take his chair. He leans against the front of his desk instead, arms crossed. It's a power move, subtle but deliberate. I've seen him do it in negotiations. The physical positioning, the controlled stillness. He's establishing the terms of this conversation before it even starts.

I settle back in my chair, let my shoulders relax. I'm not going to play small here. Whatever he needs to say, I can handle it.

"Natalie told me," he says.

I nod.

"She told me how you met. That you've run into each other at events over the years. That she attended your Fourth of July party." His voice is calm. Measured. "She also told me neither of you had any idea she was pregnant until you took her to the clinic."

"That's all true," I say evenly. "I didn't know she was your daughter, Ryan. If I had, I never would have put either of you in this position."

He watches me for a beat, then nods. "I know. She made that clear."

The tension in the room shifts slightly. Not gone, but different. He believes me. That's something.

"What I need to know is this." He uncrosses his arms, plants his hands on the edge of the desk. "Are you planning to be involved? With the baby."

I don't hesitate. "Absolutely. If she'll let me, I'm all in."

"And if she doesn't?" His gaze doesn't waver. "If she decides she wants to handle this on her own."

I hold his eyes. "I want to be part of my child's life. If Natalie doesn't want me in her life romantically, I'll respect that. But I'm going to show up for this baby however she'll let me. Every appointment. Every decision. I'm not going anywhere."

Ryan studies me for a long moment. The silence stretches. I've had easier cross-examinations.

Finally, he nods once. "Good. Because I missed ten years with her." His voice drops a notch. "Ten years I can't get back. I wasn't there when her mom was pregnant. I missed her firsts. All of them. I know exactly what that feels like, and I wouldn't wish it on anyone. Not even an opposing counsel I hate." A corner of his mouth twitches.

My throat tightens. "I won't miss any of it," I say. And I mean it.

"I'm glad to hear that." His expression softens just a fraction. "She needs people who are going to show up. People who do what they say they will do."

"I will."

He uncrosses his arms. "Which is why I'm not firing you, in case that's been keeping you up at night."

The laugh that escapes me is half relief, half disbelief. "It crossed my mind."

"You are one of my best attorneys, Jake. I'm not losing you because you got my daughter pregnant." He pauses. "Although maybe we don't talk about that fact in a client meeting."

"Noted." The knot in my stomach finally unwinds.

Ryan walks around the desk and sinks into his chair. Then his expression hardens again, and the dad side of him tags the lawyer back in. "That said," he says, voice quieter but sharper, "if you hurt her, I will make your life miserable in ways that are both creative and fully legal."

"Yes sir."

"You break her trust, you disappear on her, you turn this into one more story she has about men who do not show up, and I will spend the rest of my career making sure every contract you touch feels like penance. Do we understand each other?"

"Perfectly," I say. "I'm not going to disappear on her. I'm not going to hurt her. That's not who I am."

He holds my gaze for another long moment, and I don't flinch. I mean every word, and I need him to see that.

"Good." He leans back, watching me for another beat. The intensity eases, just a hair. But his look lingers for a long moment like he is weighing something. Then he nods, slowly. "Natalie has walls," he says. "You've probably noticed."

"A little," I say.

"They're there for a reason," he continues. His voice is not sharp now, just tired. "She's had people let her down. More than once. It's not my story to tell, and I'm not going to stand here and give you a play-by-play of her worst moments." He holds my gaze. "But if you are serious about being in her life, you need to understand that pushing her is the fastest way to lose her."

"I hear you," I say. "I don't need easy. I just need time. And the chance to prove I mean what I say."

Something like approval flickers across his face. "Then here's my advice," he says. "Show up when you say you will. Don't make promises you cannot keep. Don't try to fix her. She doesn't need fixing. She needs consistency." He taps his pen against the desk once. "And for God's sake, don't try to turn this into some grand romance before she's even caught her breath. Let her be freaked out. Let her be angry. Stay anyway."

"I can do that," I say. "I will do that."

He studies me one more time, then nods, like he has come to a decision. "All right." He stands, signaling that the meeting is over. "In that case, consider this your official welcome to whatever version of the family we are building here."

The word lands heavier than I expect. Family. We haven't defined what Natalie and I are to each other yet, but we are connected now, permanently. Through this baby. Through every choice we make from here.

"Thank you," I say, standing too. "For not firing me. For being understanding about all of this."

As I walk back to my office, I replay what he said about Natalie. That wasn't just my boss giving me a warning. That was Natalie's father trusting me with something precious.

I'm not going to let either of them down.

twelve

...

Natalie

THE WAITING room is exactly what I expected. Pregnant women everywhere. Some alone with their faces buried in their phones, some with partners who look either excited or terrified or both. Parenting magazines are scattered across side tables. A water cooler in the corner with those tiny paper cups that hold approximately three sips.

I spot Jake immediately.

He's standing near the reception desk in dark jeans and a button-down with the sleeves rolled up, and my eyes do a full sweep before my brain even pretends to be polite. There's no denying Jake is good looking. What really kills me are the creases that bracket his mouth when he smiles. Not exactly dimples, but they up his hot factor by at least a hundred.

When he sees me, his whole face lights up. It's that right there that worries me. The way he looks at me, like I'm not a walking complication. As much as I love the way his expression softens when I show up, I know I can't give him what he wants. He has this stable, normal life, and mine is about to be the opposite of that. He'd get tired of it eventually. He's too nice and I know myself. I can be a lot. I don't want to be the one who eventually breaks his spirit.

"Hey." He crosses the waiting room in a few easy strides. "How are you feeling?"

"Nervous."

"Me too."

That comforts me more than I want to admit. "Really?"

"Yeah." He runs a hand over his head, gaze flicking toward the hallway like he can see the exam rooms from here. "I'll feel better once we hear the heartbeat and everything looks okay." He gestures toward the reception desk. "Have you checked in?"

"Not yet."

We walk up together, and the receptionist slides a clipboard toward me, stacked with forms. Insurance information. Medical history. Emergency contact. There's a whole section labeled "Father's Information" with blank lines staring at me.

Jake leans one forearm on the counter next to me, close enough that I can smell his cologne. Something clean and masculine and annoyingly comforting.

"Need a pen?" he asks quietly.

"I've got one."

We find two seats in the corner, tucked a little away from everyone else, and I start filling everything out. Name. Date of birth. Address. Easy things. Things that don't require a full mental spiral.

When I get to the emergency contact section, I hesitate. My mom is the automatic answer. She's always been my emergency contact. But I'm having a baby now. Things are different, and the lines on this page feel heavier than they did five minutes ago.

Jake notices the pause. "You okay?"

"Just thinking."

He doesn't push. Just waits, ankle resting on opposite knee, fingers tapping lightly against his knee like he's giving all that lawyer energy something to do besides hover.

After a moment, I write my mom's name and number in the first line. The familiar choice. The safe one. Then I glance over at him.

"Can I put you as my second emergency contact?" I ask.

His expression shifts. Surprise, then this warm, almost shy kind of pleased. "Yeah," he says. "Of course."

I write his name and number on the second line. Seeing it there makes something low in my chest loosen and tighten at the same time. We're tied together now in more ways than just biology.

When I finish the forms, I slide the clipboard toward him. "Can you fill out the father's section?"

He takes the clipboard like it's an actual contract that might go before a judge, eyes scanning each line with that focused, careful attention that made him one of my dad's favorite attorneys before any of this.

"Here you go," he says finally, handing it back.

We sit in companionable silence for a few minutes before a nurse appears in the doorway, clipboard in hand.

"Natalie?"

Jake stands immediately. When he places his hand on the small of my back to usher me through the doorway, my stomach flips. I'm not sure if it's from the nerves or him. I hand the completed forms to the receptionist as we pass, and decide it might be a bit of both.

The nurse leads us down a hallway lined with exam rooms, the floor a little too shiny under the fluorescent lights. "Right in here. I'm going to get your weight and blood pressure, then the doctor will be in shortly."

She glances at Jake and smiles. "Dad, you can have a seat right there."

Jake sits in the chair by the window, phone in his hand, knuckles white around it like it's some kind of grounding device.

"You can go ahead and change into the gown. Opening in the front," the nurse says, heading for the door.

"Do you want me to step out?" Jake asks immediately, already half rising.

"No." I shake my head. "Just...turn around for a second."

I change quickly, the gown thin and drafty and making me feel far more exposed than I'd like. My bare legs dangle off the side of the table.

"Okay," I say.

He turns back around, eyes firmly on my face. I can literally see him make a conscious decision not to allow his gaze to drop below my shoulders, which is both sweet and slightly ridiculous.

"You okay?" he asks.

"I'm great," I lie, swinging my foot once.

This is so awkward.

A knock sounds, then the door opens and a woman in a white coat steps inside. "Hi there." She smiles as she checks the chart on her tablet. "Natalie? I'm Dr. Nelson."

"Hi," I say, forcing my voice not to squeak.

"And you must be Dad." She shifts her smile to Jake and offers her hand.

"Jake Reyes," he says, shaking it. Lawyer charm activated.

"Nice to meet you both." She pulls up a little stool and taps on her tablet. "Looks like you're about fourteen weeks now. How are you feeling?"

"Good," I say. "Hungry."

"That tracks." She smiles. "Energy levels?"

"Totally normal."

"Excellent." More tapping. "Any bleeding? Cramping? Anything out of the ordinary?"

"Nope."

"Great. And you're taking prenatal vitamins?"

"Every day." I flick a glance at Jake. I have him and his grocery delivery to thank for that.

"Perfect." She stands, rolling the ultrasound machine a little closer. "All right, let's take a look and see how baby's doing. We'll get some measurements and make sure everything's on track."

My heart rate kicks up so fast I'm pretty sure she can see my pulse in my neck. Jake gets up, hovering, clearly uncertain where he's supposed to be. Dr. Nelson glances up and nods toward me.

"You can stand next to her," she says. "Most dads like to watch the screen."

He moves to my side, close enough that I can feel the heat of him through the gown. His arm is right there if I need to grab onto something.

"This is going to be cold," Dr. Nelson warns as she squirts gel onto my stomach.

She's not exaggerating. I flinch when the wand hits my skin, teeth almost chattering from the unexpected chill. Then the monitor flickers on.

And there it is.

My baby.

There's a clear curve of a head, a spine like a string of tiny pearls, little limbs moving. Arms. Legs. A profile that looks like something you'd recognize if you saw it again.

The air leaves my lungs in a rush. That's a person. A tiny, impossible person who's been growing inside me this whole time while I taught yoga classes and rewrote scripts and pretended everything was normal.

My throat goes tight. I want to reach out and touch the screen, trace the outline of that perfect little head, but my hands are frozen at my sides. There's this overwhelming surge of something I can't name. Protectiveness, maybe. Or terror. Or both at once, fighting for dominance in my chest.

This is real, moving, living proof that in a few months, I'm going to be responsible for another human being.

"Oh my God," I whisper.

"There we go," Dr. Nelson says, adjusting the angle. "Baby is measuring right on track for fourteen weeks."

She clicks a few buttons. The image sharpens, and I swear I see a hand flicker near its face like an accidental wave.

"Let's get that heartbeat," she says.

She moves the wand, and then the room fills with sound. Fast, steady, impossibly loud for something so small.

Whoosh whoosh whoosh whoosh.

"That's the baby's heartbeat," she says. "Nice and strong. About one-fifty beats per minute. That's exactly what we like to hear at this stage."

I can't look away from the screen. The baby moves again, a little twist, a flex of tiny arms. It's so small and yet so very clearly there. Not theoretical. Not maybe someday. Right now.

I risk a glance at Jake. He is staring at the monitor like he's hypnotized. His eyes are shiny, and when he realizes I'm looking at him, he doesn't bother to even hide his emotion.

"That's our baby," he says, voice rough.

I hold his gaze for a moment and then turn away, overwhelmed by all the feelings happening in this room.

"Everything looks great," she says finally, wiping the gel away with a towel. "Baby is growing beautifully. Any questions?"

Jake pulls out his phone and opens his notes app. "I have a few," he says. "When can we find out the sex of the baby?" He pauses and turns to me, "I mean if that's something you want to know?"

"I do."

"Around twenty weeks," Dr. Nelson says. "We'll get that scheduled before you leave today."

"And movement? When will she start feeling the baby move?"

"Usually between sixteen and twenty weeks for first-time moms."

He types furiously. "Are there any specific activities she should avoid?"

"No high-impact or contact sports," Dr. Nelson says, smiling. "But yoga, walking, swimming are all excellent. I see here you're a yoga instructor?"

"I am," I say.

"Then you're already very in tune with your body. Listen to it. If something feels off, stop and call us. Otherwise, you can keep moving."

Jake asks about sleep positions and what qualifies as a real emergency and which symptoms are normal versus "call us immediately." He's thorough without being obnoxious, and by the time he's finished, Dr. Nelson looks genuinely delighted with his level of investment.

"Those are all great questions," she says. She prints several ultrasound photos and hands them to me. "We'll see you next month, but call if anything worries you in the meantime."

"Thank you," I say.

Once she's gone, Jake offers me his hand to help me sit up. I take it, and together we look down at the glossy black-and-white images in my lap. There are three. In one, the baby's hand is right up near its face.

"I still can't believe that's real," he says quietly.

"I know."

"Can I..." He hesitates for the first time all morning. "Can I have one of these? If that's okay?"

Something in my chest cracks. The way he's looking at the photos, like they're the most precious thing he's ever held, makes my defenses wobble. I've been telling myself this is just a partnership. Just logistics and doctor's appointments and figuring out how two strangers raise a baby together.

But Jake's not looking at these pictures like logistics. He's looking at them like he's already in love.

And that terrifies me. Because it would be so easy to let myself believe in this. In him. In the idea that maybe I don't have to do everything alone.

I can feel my walls trying to slam back into place, that familiar instinct to protect myself from disappointment. But then I look at his face again, at the genuine wonder there, and something in me softens despite my best efforts.

"You want one?" I ask, keeping my voice neutral even though my heart is pounding so loud I'm sure he can hear it.

"Yeah." He gives a small, almost sheepish smile.

"Of course." I pass him the "waving" one. "Take this one."

He takes it carefully, then pulls out his wallet. He slides the picture into one of the clear slots, right where a photo ID would go, and holds it up for me to see.

"Perfect," he says, grinning.

Jake Reyes is standing there with an ultrasound photo tucked into his wallet, looking like someone just handed him the moon, and it's threatening to make me feel hope. Which is exactly why I shut that feeling down. Hope is a liar. Hope is the thing that shows up with confetti and then forgets to stick around when the mess hits. I know better.

"Uh, I'll give you a minute to change," he says, clearing his throat and backing toward the door. "I'll be right outside."

"Okay."

He steps out, and I peel off the gown, pulling my clothes back on. We check out at the front desk, schedule the next appointment, and Jake walks me to my car.

"Thank you for letting me be here," he says.

"You're the father, Jake." I unlock my car. "Of course you should be here."

"Still." He shifts his weight, one hand in his pocket, the other fidgeting with his keys. "I know this isn't easy. Any of it. But I really appreciate you including me."

I don't have a neat, emotionally healthy response for that, so I just nod. We stand there for another beat, the late-afternoon sun warm on my face, the reality of everything sitting between us like a third person.

"I should go," I say finally. "I have a class to teach at five."

"Right. Yeah." He slips his wallet back into his pocket. "Do you need anything? Groceries, more vitamins, anything? I'm happy to help with whatever."

"I'm okay for now," I say. "But I'll let you know."

"Good." He nods, like that was the answer he was hoping for. "Text me when you get home tonight?"

"Why?"

He shrugs, a tiny lift of one shoulder. "Just so I know you got there safe."

It's such a boyfriend thing to say that my first instinct is to bristle. But there's nothing possessive in it. Just genuine concern.

"Okay," I say.

I reach for my car door but before I get there, Jake steps closer. Close enough that I have to tilt my head back to look at him. Close enough that I catch the scent of his cologne, the smell that makes me think of his hands on my skin three months ago.

He reaches past me to open my door, his arm brushing

mine as he pulls the handle. The contact is brief, barely there, but it sends heat racing up my arm. I'm suddenly aware of how tall he is, how solid he feels standing this close. How if I leaned forward just slightly, just a fraction of an inch, I could rest my forehead against his chest.

I look up instead. His eyes are hypnotizing. His lashes are longer than mine, dark against his skin, and I notice again that small scar near his left eyebrow that I have the urge to place my lips on.

For half a second, I let myself wonder what would happen if I closed the distance. If I pushed up on my toes and pressed my mouth to his. Would he kiss me back? Would it feel the same as it did in July, all heat and urgency, or would it be different now that there's something between us besides chemistry? The thought hits me so hard I have to look away.

"Drive safe," he says, his voice rougher than it was a second ago.

I slip into the driver's seat before I can do something stupid. "Thanks."

He closes the door gently, then steps back, hands sliding into his pockets. Through the window, I can see him watching me, waiting to make sure I'm settled before he walks away.

I start the car and buckle my seatbelt, hyper-aware that he's still standing there. When I shift into reverse, he lifts a hand in a small wave. I wave back, then pull out of the spot.

In my rearview mirror, I watch him head toward his own car. I force my eyes back to the road, and as I pull out of the parking lot with the ultrasound photos on the passenger seat beside me, I catch myself smiling.

thirteen

. . .

Jake

I REWRITE for the third time the text I'm about to send, my thumb hovering over the screen.

> **JAKE**
> I got something for the baby. Can I bring it over?

It's Thursday night. I haven't seen Natalie since the doctor appointment, since the ultrasound, since we watched that tiny body wiggle on the screen and listened to the heartbeat fill the room. A week is not actually that long, but it feels like I have been stuck in a holding pattern for months.

I hit send before I can talk myself out of it and her response comes faster than I expect.

> **NATALIE**
> You don't have to buy things yet.

> **JAKE**
> Too late.

I grin at my phone while she types. The dots appear, disappear, appear again.

> **NATALIE**
> Fine. Come over. But if you bought something ridiculous, I'm returning it.

> **JAKE**
> See you in 20.

I grab my keys and head out to the garage, where the unassembled crib sits in the back of my SUV next to a bag from the pharmacy. The crib is top rated, convertible, all the safety features. The kind of thing you end up buying after two hours of reading reviews you did not know you cared about until you suddenly do. I already built the one for my house last night, so at least I know what I'm doing.

Traffic is light for a Thursday, so it only takes fifteen minutes. I haul the flat-packed crib box up the walk, and before I can knock, the door swings open. Every thought in my head flatlines.

She's wearing my shirt. The gray one she took from my bedroom that night. It's faded and soft-looking, hanging off one shoulder, paired with shorts that show off her long, tanned legs. Her hair is down, loose waves falling past her shoulders, and her skin looks like it's glowing in the moonlight.

She's stunning. I'm staring. I know I'm staring, but I can't stop. All I can think about is how badly I want to peel that shirt off her. How easy it would be to step inside, close the door behind me, and kiss her until neither of us can remember why we're supposed to be keeping our distance.

I'm in so much trouble with this woman.

"You bought a crib." Her voice is flat, but her eyes give her away. There's amusement there, threaded through the disbelief.

I force myself to focus. "I bought a crib," I confirm, clearing my throat.

"Jake, I'm barely in the second trimester."

"Never too early to prepare."

She steps aside to let me in, shaking her head. "You're insane."

"Practical," I correct, maneuvering the box through the doorway without taking out a plant in the process. "Where do you want it?"

She pauses, and looks unsure. "I guess the guest room?" She says it like she is trying the words on. "I haven't really thought about this yet. Where things are going to go."

"That's okay. We have time to figure it out."

She gestures down the hall. "Second door on the right."

I carry the box through the living room, past the cozy couch and the built-ins packed with novels and scripts, past a coffee table littered with notebooks and highlighters.

The guest room is small but bright, hardwood floors and a window that looks out over the side yard. There is a futon, a small desk buried under notebooks and pens, and several stacks of books that look like they are mid-organization.

"When you are ready, I can help you move things around," I say, setting the box down. "I can put it next to the futon for now."

She leans against the doorframe, arms crossed over her chest. "I can't believe this."

"Believe what?"

"You bought me a crib."

"Technically it's for the baby," I say. "And yeah, I bought one for my place too. I put it together last night, so this one should go pretty quick."

Something flickers across her face. "You already have a nursery?"

"Working on it." I pull out my phone and swipe to the picture. "This is what it looks like."

She studies the photo, quiet for a moment. I try not to read too much into it, but there is something careful about the way she looks at the screen, like she is seeing more than just wood and rails.

"I'm going to make some tea," she says. "You want some?"

"Sure. Thank you."

She disappears down the hall, and I hear cupboards opening, the clink of a mug, the soft whistle of the kettle. I open the box and start laying out all the pieces on the floor, grouping parts together, lining up screws. By the time she returns, I already have the base of the crib started.

She hands me a cup of tea and drops onto the futon, one leg tucked under her. For the next twenty minutes I work while she watches. I can feel her eyes on me in that way you always can when someone is paying quiet attention. I glance over. She is holding her mug with both hands, gaze thoughtful.

"How's work?" she asks, like the question has been hovering for a while. "My dad. Everything. Did he freak out?"

"About the baby?" I tighten a bolt and sit back on my

heels. "He emailed me first thing that Monday after and asked me to come to his office."

Her eyes widen. "That sounds ominous."

"It felt ominous," I admit. "But he was actually great. He asked if I planned to be involved, and when I said yes, he looked relieved, I think."

Her throat works like she has to swallow that down. "He told me he liked you," she says quietly. "When I told him you were the father. Said you were one of his best."

The statement hits somewhere deep. I clear my throat and pick the wrench back up. "That means a lot."

The room starts to feel hotter as I work, or maybe it's just the combination of physical effort and the way she keeps watching me. I set the wrench down and pull my button-down off, leaving me in my white T-shirt.

When I straighten, I catch her looking. Her eyes track my arms, then jump to my face when she realizes I noticed. A flush creeps up her neck.

I feel it. Whatever lit up between us that night. And right now, in this little room full of crib parts, it feels like it's still there, glowing under the surface.

I lock the last piece into place and tighten the final screw.

"There," I say, straightening up. "It looks good, right?"

"Yeah." She unfolds from the futon and walks over, stopping beside me at the foot of the crib. "It's perfect," she says softly.

We're standing close enough that I can smell her shampoo, something citrusy and fresh. Close enough that when I glance over, I can see where my shirt has slipped further off her shoulder, exposing the slope of her chest.

I shouldn't be thinking about how good she looks in my clothes. How her breasts have gotten fuller, straining against the soft fabric in a way that's making it impossible to think straight. But I am. I'm thinking about all of it.

She shifts her weight, and I catch her eyes tracking across my chest, lingering on my arms. It's not the first time today. She's been watching me work for the last twenty minutes, and every time I've glanced over, her gaze has been somewhere it shouldn't be if we're really just co-parents.

The thing is, I haven't touched her in three months. And none of this has faded. Not the attraction. Not the pull. If anything, it's gotten worse. More intense. Like spending time together is only making it harder to ignore what's still burning between us.

"I think I need more tea," she says suddenly, her voice a little too bright. "You want a refill?"

She's already moving toward the door before I can answer, putting distance between us like she needs the space to breathe.

I hear her in the kitchen, the sound of the kettle refilling, cupboards opening and closing. I crouch down and start gathering the leftover nuts and bolts, tossing them back into the plastic bag, breaking down the box.

When she comes back, she pauses in the doorway, watching me clean up the mess. She sets the mugs down on the windowsill. "Oh, I can clean that up."

"I've got it," I say, but she's already moving toward me.

I stand just as she drops to her knees in front of me to reach for a stray screw. The position is awkward and charged all at once. She's kneeling right there, eye level with my crotch, and when she looks up at me, it takes every shred of restraint to keep my dick in check.

I watch her throat work as she swallows and her lips part slightly. I drop back down on my knees to help her, our faces suddenly close, her eyes wide.

"I can help," I say, my voice rougher than I mean it to be.

She doesn't move. Just stares at my mouth like she's forgotten how to speak. "Okay," she whispers.

Then her hand lifts, fingertips brushing the small scar near my eyebrow. The touch is feather-light, tentative, and my eyes close instinctively. When I open them, she's still looking at me, her hand trembling slightly against my skin.

I lean in slowly, giving her every chance to change her mind, and brush my lips against hers. Testing. Soft at first, letting her respond. She melts into me with a sound that goes straight to my cock.

I deepen the kiss, and her hands twist in my shirt, tugging me closer, pulling me fully into her. Every inch of her is heat, every gasp, every tiny shift of her body against mine sending fire straight through me.

I stand, pulling her up with me, and walk her backward until her back hits the wall. She gasps against my mouth, and I hold her there, letting the kiss stretch, letting her feel what she does to me, giving her every chance to slow things down.

"Bedroom," she breathes against my jaw.

I scoop her up, and her legs lock around my waist like this is muscle memory. She kisses along my neck as I carry her down the hall, and it takes every ounce of coordination I can summon not to run us into a wall.

Her bedroom is cozy and dark. Deep purple walls, plants

on every surface, pools of warm light from lamps instead of the overhead fixture. The bed is unmade, sheets tangled, like she left in a hurry this morning.

"Are you sure?" I ask. "We don't have to—"

"I'm sure." She pulls back to look at me. "Are you?"

"Fuck yeah."

I lay her down, and she sits up right away, pulling my T-shirt over her head. *Fuck.* No bra. Just skin and that delicate tattoo along her ribs.

"You're staring," she says.

"Can you blame me?"

She gestures at my shirt with a wave of her hand. "Off."

I strip my shirt in one motion and toss it aside. Her hands are on me immediately, fingers tracing across my chest, down my stomach, like she is reacquainting herself with every line.

"I forgot how amazing your body is," she murmurs.

"I didn't forget anything about you," I say before I can stop myself.

Her gaze flickers up, something unguarded passing through it, then she drags me down into another kiss, and any chance for deeper conversation goes out the window.

My hands find the waistband of her leggings. "Okay?" I ask.

"Yes."

I slide them and her panties down together, and she lifts her hips to help, all business, no shyness. When she is naked beneath me, heat floods my system like a shock.

I reach for my belt, then freeze. "I don't have a condom."

She lets out a breathy, disbelieving laugh. "I'm pretty sure that ship has sailed."

"Right," I say. "I should still say I got tested after July. I'm clean."

"Me too. And there hasn't been anyone else. Since you."

Is it wrong that I love that fact? I look down at her, and there's something in her expression I haven't seen before. A softness. A flicker of vulnerability that makes my breath catch.

"Same," I say, my voice rougher than I mean it to be. "No one else."

Her eyes search mine for a long moment, and I swear I can see her walls wobbling. Not falling, but shifting. Like maybe she's starting to believe this could be more than she's letting herself admit.

"Okay then," she says. She plants her palms on my shoulders and tries to guide me down to the bed. "Lie back."

"Wait, I want to taste you first. Savor this gorgeous body."

She gives me sly smile, and I love that she hasn't lost her edge either. "Next time. I'm too horny right now. Every time your skin brushes mine I feel like I'm going to explode."

I let go and fall back on the bed. She swings a leg over my hips, settling on top of me like she has been waiting for this since the second we walked into the room. Her hands slide along my sides as she leans down to kiss me, then she sits up, reaches between us, and wraps her fingers around me.

"Natalie," I grit out, hands locking on her hips.

She lifts herself, guides me to her, and sinks down in one slow, deliberate motion.

My vision actually blanks for a second.

She closes her eyes, head tipping back, a quiet moan

escapes her. I force my hands to stay on her hips instead of dragging her down faster, letting her set the pace.

"Look at me," I say, voice rough.

Her eyes open, and something in my chest pulls tight.

She starts to move, rocking against me, finding a rhythm that is all urgency and no hesitation. Her hands brace on my chest for leverage, and it is messy and hot and real in a way that feels like that first night.

"God, Jake," she breathes.

My fingers flex on her hips and I thrust up into her, matching her tempo. The room fills with the sounds of us, the creak of the bed, the catch of her breath every time she grinds down just right. I slide one hand between us, finding her clit, and the way she reacts nearly undoes me on the spot.

"Don't stop," she gasps. "Right there."

"Take what you need," I say.

She rides me harder, chasing what she wants, and it takes everything I have to hold my own orgasm back. Her nails dig into my shoulders, her movements start to stutter, and I feel the shift in her body right before she shatters around me.

"Oh fuck, Jake," she cries out, and then she is gone, coming apart above me, body tightening, head thrown back.

The sight and feel of it rip me open. I drive up into her one last time and follow her over, every muscle locking as I spill inside her.

We just stay there, connected and lost in the moment, both of us breathing like we ran a race, her head pressed to my chest, my hands smoothing down her back as if that might slow my heartbeat. The corner of her mouth curves in the faintest, sweetest smile. It's there for just a heartbeat, but I catch it.

Then, just as quickly, it's gone. I can feel the tension starting to creep back into her muscles and the wall slides back into place.

She finally exhales against my shoulder, her voice muffled. "This can't happen again."

The words land like a bucket of cold water, but she doesn't move. Her body is still wrapped around mine. My hand is still on her spine.

I swallow and try to keep my tone even. "Okay."

"What just happened doesn't change anything. It's just—I don't do relationships," she says, like it's her mantra.

I want to tell her it does change things. It makes me want her even more. But I keep my hand on her back, keep my voice steady, and give her what she needs to hear.

"Okay."

fourteen

. . .

Natalie

I CAN'T STOP THINKING about what happened with Jake.

My mind keeps circling back to him assembling the crib in my guest room. To what happened after.

The way he looked at me when I grabbed his shirt. The roughness in his voice when he said my name. The moment right before he kissed me, when I could have stopped it but didn't want to.

I told him it couldn't happen again. And I meant it.

Except I can't stop replaying every detail. The heat of his skin under my palms. The sound he made when I sank down on him. The way he held me after, like I was something precious instead of just a complication he's stuck dealing with.

I really like him.

The thought hits me hard enough that I have to grip the edge of the counter. I like Jake Reyes. Not just the sex, though that's admittedly incredible. I like the way he shows up. The way he remembers things. The way he looks at our baby on the ultrasound screen like it's already the center of his universe.

And that terrifies me.

Because three years ago, I liked someone else. Liked him enough to say yes when he proposed. Liked him enough to plan a wedding, buy a dress, believe him when he said forever.

And he liked me back, too. I thought. That's the part that still messes with my head. There were no signs. No obvious red flags. No evidence that something was wrong. Until he didn't show up at the altar.

No phone call. No explanation. Just gone. I stood there in that stupid white dress and pretended my heart wasn't shattering into a thousand pieces.

How am I supposed to believe what I'm feeling with Jake is real, when I was so sure before and ended up humiliated in front of everyone?

But Jake is different whispers a traitorous voice in my head.

I shove the thought away and arrange crackers on a plate with more force than necessary. It doesn't matter if he seems different. My instincts can't be trusted.

The front door opens without a knock.

"It's just me!" Jonah calls, appearing in the doorway with his signature container of homemade dumplings. "These are fresh. Still warm."

"You're a saint."

"I know." He kicks the door closed with his foot and

makes himself at home on the couch, already pulling out his notebook.

This is how it always is with our writers' group. We've been meeting for five years, so we're long past pretending we're guests. We just walk in and start talking.

Wren arrives next, blonde and eternally optimistic, color-coded notebook already open, chattering about some meet-cute she witnessed at the talent agency where she works. Then Eric, rumpled from whatever set he just came from, former journalist turned screenwriter with an obsession for structure. Iris in all black, quietly brilliant, carrying a box of fancy tea like an offering. And finally Brody, the youngest at twenty-four, clutching his latest draft like he's afraid someone's going to snatch it away.

Eric and Jonah started this group six years ago. The rest of us found our way in through various connections, industry events, and one desperate post on a UCLA alumni board. Now we're family.

I wish they were working with me on *Spellbound*. But someday, when I'm actually in charge of something, I'll bring them along. That's the dream anyway.

"All right," Jonah announces once everyone's settled around my living room. "Before we do anything else, let's celebrate!"

"We really don't need to—"

"Yes, we do." Wren produces a small cake from her oversized bag like a magician. "You sold a pilot to FlixPix. That's huge!"

"The first one of us to actually make it," Eric adds, raising his coffee mug in a toast.

"I haven't made it yet," I protest. "The show still has to get produced."

"You will," Iris says quietly from her spot on the floor, teacup balanced on her knee. "Your writing's too good not to."

My throat tightens. These people have seen every draft of *Spellbound*, every rejection, every almost-deal that crashed at the one-yard line.

"Speech!" Brody grins.

"Absolutely not."

"Come on," Jonah pushes.

I sigh. "Fine. Thank you for reading all my terrible early drafts and telling me not to give up."

"They were never terrible," Wren says loyally.

"That first draft of the pilot was rough," Eric says.

"Okay, yeah, that one was bad." Iris laughs.

"But you all helped me make it better. So thank you. For everything," I say.

We cut the cake, and Wren pours wine for everyone except me. I tell them I'm doing a cleanse, and no one questions it. Perks of having friends who try all the wellness trends.

"So when do you start?" Eric asks.

"Writers' room starts in December. Pre-production in the spring."

"That's soon," Jonah says. "Nervous?"

"Terrified."

"Normal," Eric assures me. "First room's always scary. But you know your show better than anyone. Trust that."

We talk about what it'll be like, the group peppering me with questions about the deal, the timeline, whether I've heard anything about who else might be staffed. It feels surreal, sitting cross-legged on my own rug talking about *Spellbound* as a real show instead of a document I quietly tinkered with for years.

Eventually we transition into notes. Tonight is Brody's turn, and he's brought pages from his multi-cam pilot about friends working at a failing arcade. It's funny and surprisingly heartfelt, with the kind of sharp dialogue that makes you mad you didn't write it yourself.

"This is really good," I tell him when it's my turn. "The banter between Luke and Jessica in scene three is perfect. But I think you're burying your emotional beat in scene seven. When Marcus talks about his dad? That should land harder. Right now it reads like a throwaway line."

Brody scribbles notes frantically. "You're right. I was worried about it getting too sappy."

"It's a comedy," Jonah says, "but comedy works best when we care about the characters. Let us feel something, then make us laugh. That's the magic."

We spend the next hour digging into Brody's pages, everyone pitching fixes and alt jokes, cutting the lines we love but know don't belong. This is what I love about this group. We make each other better. We call each other out when we're playing it safe.

When we finish, conversation drifts to industry gossip. Who's staffing where, what shows got picked up, which ones are quietly circling the drain. Jonah hints he's close on another deal, knocking on the coffee table for luck.

"Same time in two weeks?" Jonah asks, pulling on his jacket.

"My place," Eric offers. "I'll send out pages by the end of the week."

We say our goodbyes at the door, hugs all around. Wren squeezes me extra tight.

"I'm so proud of you," she whispers.

"Thanks, Wren."

I stand on the porch for a second, watching them pile into their cars, waving as they drive off. The street settles into that quiet, late-night hum. Distant traffic. A dog barking down the block. The soft whoosh of sprinklers kicking on somewhere. I'm closing the door when I hear footsteps on the porch.

"Forget something?" I call, pulling it open without looking, but it's not one of my writers' group friends.

It's Jake.

fifteen

. . .

Natalie

HE'S STANDING on my porch in athletic shorts and a fitted gray T-shirt, holding a bag from Mendocino Farms.

"Hey," he says, suddenly looking almost uncertain. "I was at the gym near here and thought I'd take a chance you'd be home."

My stomach does a stupid flip. He looks good. Too good. All lean muscle and easy smile and those gorgeous eyes.

"What's in the bag?" I ask, because letting him see the effect he has on me feels dangerous.

"Sandwich. That turkey cranberry one with the Brie. And the butternut squash soup."

I step aside. "Come in."

He follows me to the kitchen, setting the bag on the counter while I grab bowls. The soup smells incredible, all roasted and creamy, and suddenly I'm starving even though I just inhaled cake.

How am I supposed to guard myself against this? Against a man who shows up at my door with exactly what I'm craving before I even know I'm craving it? Who looks like that in a gray T-shirt that clings to every muscle he's earned at that boxing gym? It's not fair.

"How was your writers' group?" he asks, sliding onto one of my counter stools like he's done it a hundred times.

Even that. The easy way he fits into my space, into my life, like he belongs here. I'm in so much trouble.

"Good. They threw me a surprise celebration. Wren brought a cake."

"That's nice."

I hand him a spoon. "They've been reading my pages for at least five years. I wouldn't have sold *Spellbound* without them."

"Tell me about them."

So I do. Jake listens intently, asking questions, laughing in the right places. He has this way of listening that makes you feel like the only person in the room.

"They sound great," he says. "I'd love to meet them sometime."

The comment's casual, but it lands heavy. Meeting my friends feels like a capital-R Relationship step. A step we're definitely not taking.

"Maybe," I say, noncommittal, and take a bite of soup.

We eat in comfortable silence for a few minutes. Then he asks about my week, and I tell him about the yoga class where someone fell asleep in savasana and started snoring.

"That happened to me once," he admits.

"In yoga?"

"The gym. I was so exhausted after a workout I lay down on the mat and totally passed out. Wyatt had to wake me up."

I laugh, trying to picture it. Jake always seems so put together, so in control. The image of him drooling on a gym mat is unreasonably endearing.

"What?" he asks, grinning.

"Nothing. You're just...not what I expected."

"What'd you expect?"

"I don't know. More buttoned-up, I guess. You're this successful attorney, you work for my dad, you drive a nice car and live in the hills."

"And?"

"And you're kind of a dork."

He laughs. "Guilty. I make dad jokes even though I'm not a dad yet. I can't watch horror movies because I get too invested in the characters. And I definitely cried at the end of *Toy Story 3*."

"Everyone cried at the end of *Toy Story 3*."

"Did you?"

"No."

"Liar."

"I'm a writer. I don't have feelings, I just observe them in others."

"That's the biggest lie you've ever told me."

He's smiling at me, and I can feel the ground start to tilt under my feet.

I should send him home. That's the smart thing to do. The safe thing. Every time he's here, every conversation we have that isn't about the baby, I can feel myself getting attached. And attachment leads to hope, and hope leads to heartbreak.

But I don't want him to leave.

The realization hits me hard. I like having him here. I like the way he makes me laugh. The way he listens like what I'm saying actually matters. The way being around him feels easy in a way nothing else in my life does right now.

I'm supposed to be keeping my distance.

Instead, I stand abruptly, grabbing our empty bowls, and hear myself say, "Want to watch something?"

His eyebrows lift slightly, surprise flickering across his face. "Sure."

There's something in his expression that warms my heart. Like he wasn't expecting me to ask. Like maybe he thought I'd usher him out the second we finished eating. And maybe I should have. But I don't.

We migrate to the couch, and I pull up FlixPix, not really caring what I click. I land on some action movie I've seen before. Plenty of explosions, zero emotional investment. Perfect.

Jake settles beside me, not quite touching but close enough that I can feel the heat radiating off him. Close enough that if I shifted just slightly, our legs would press together. I don't shift. But I don't move away either.

Ten minutes in, I couldn't tell you what's happening on the screen. I'm too aware of him. The way his arm rests along the back of the couch. The way he smells, clean and woody. The memory of his hands on my skin, the feel of his mouth on my neck.

It's just hormones, I tell myself. Pregnancy hormones. Chemistry plus proximity plus everything being heightened right now. That's all this is.

On screen, something explodes. I barely register it. Jake

shifts beside me, his thigh pressing against mine for just a second before he adjusts. The brief contact sends heat racing through me.

This is a bad idea. Letting him stay. Sitting this close. Pretending I can keep things casual when every cell in my body is screaming at me to close the distance. I should ask him to leave.

Instead, I let my head tip back against the couch, exhaustion pulling at me. The combination of pregnancy fatigue and the emotional whiplash of the last few weeks is catching up. My eyelids feel heavy.

"Tired?" Jake asks quietly.

"A little."

"We can turn this off if you want to sleep."

"No, it's okay. Just resting my eyes."

But the next thing I know, I'm waking up to darkness. The TV has gone into screensaver mode, casting flickering light across the room. And I'm not where I fell asleep.

I'm curled into Jake's side, my head on his chest, his arm wrapped around me. Our legs are tangled together, and one of my hands is resting on his stomach, fingers spread over the hard muscle beneath his shirt.

His heartbeat is steady under my ear. Slow and strong and impossibly comforting. I should move. Pull away. Put space between us before this becomes something I can't take back. But God, he's warm. And he smells so good. And I can't remember the last time I felt this safe.

My fingers trace lightly over his forearm following the line of muscle and vein, the dusting of hair. His skin is warm under my touch, and I feel his breathing change. Not asleep anymore.

I should stop. I should pull away. I tilt my head up instead, and his gaze is already on me. Intense. Focused. Like I'm the only thing in the world that matters.

The air between us ignites. I can see the restraint in his expression. The way he's holding himself still, letting me decide. Giving me every chance to back away. But I don't want to back away.

I know I told him this couldn't happen again. I know I'm the one who set the boundaries. I know he deserves better than me constantly changing the rules, pulling him close and then pushing him away.

But right now, with his arm around me and his heart beating under my ear and his eyes on mine like that, I can't remember why I thought I could resist this.

I rise up slightly, bringing my mouth close to his, and kiss him.

He responds instantly, like he's been waiting for permission. His hand comes up to cup my face, thumb brushing my cheek. The kiss deepens, and I swing my leg over to straddle him.

His hands slide up my sides, under my shirt, pulling it up until I break the kiss long enough to tug it over my head. I'm in just my bra, and his eyes hit my chest before coming back to my face, checking.

It's all very, very okay.

I hook my fingers in the hem of his T-shirt and pull it off. His skin is warm under my palms, muscles tightening when I slide my hands over his chest. He works my shorts down over my hips, leaving me in my panties, then pulls my bra down so my breasts spill free.

"Fuck, these tits are perfection," he says, voice low, before his mouth closes around my nipple. His tongue circles the tight bud, then he bites lightly and sucks, and heat flashes through me so fast it almost hurts. He moves to the other side, giving it the same attention while I reach between us, pushing his shorts down and slipping my hand into his boxer briefs. He's already hard, thick and smooth in my palm, and he groans when I wrap my fingers around him.

His hands know exactly where to touch me. Mine know exactly what makes him swear. It should probably worry me how easy this is now, how fast we find the rhythm of each other again. How right it feels.

I shove that thought away and shift on his lap, lifting up on my knees. I push my panties to the side and guide him to me, sinking down in one slow, greedy slide.

"Fuck, Natalie," Jake says, head falling back for a second. "You feel so goddamn tight, so warm and wet. I could do this forever."

A bolt of fear cracks through me at that word, forever, but it dissolves under the next thrust of his hips. I can't think when we're like this. When he's this deep inside me. When every drag of his hands over my skin feels like worship and possession and home all at once.

"You're so deep," I breathe. "God, that feels so good."

"Tell me what you need, Nat."

"Touch me."

His hand slides between us, fingers finding me with a certainty that makes my eyes slam shut. Within minutes, everything tightens, the world narrowing down to his body under mine, his thumb circling just right, the rough edge in his voice when he says my name.

We both fall hard and fast together, collapsing together on each other afterward. We stay tangled, and I can feel him starting to soften inside me, my chest still pressed to his as his arms wrap around me, holding me in place. My body feels loose and heavy, boneless. My mind is blissfully quiet for the first time in days.

But reality is already creeping back in.

"I should probably go," he says, voice roughened by sex and the time of night.

The words land like a punch, even though I know he's right. Even though I'm the one who created this situation. I'm the one who told him it couldn't happen again and then kissed him anyway. I'm the one who keeps pulling him close and pushing him away, changing the rules every time he thinks he understands them.

He thinks this is what I want. He thinks leaving is what I need. And maybe it is. Maybe I should let him go, let him protect himself from the mess I'm making of this. But something in my chest cracks at the thought.

"Okay," I whisper.

I slide off his lap, suddenly shy, and grab my shirt and shorts from the floor. I pull them on quickly while he tugs his boxer briefs and shorts back up and pulls his T-shirt over his head.

I walk him to the door, fingers twisting the hem of my shirt, guilt sitting heavy in my stomach.

"Text me when you get home?" I say, then immediately

want to take it back. That's too girlfriend-y. Too much like I care.

But Jake just smiles. "I will."

He kisses my forehead and I watch him walk down the path and climb into his car. He looks up, like he's checking I'm still there, then pulls away from the curb.

I close the door, lean my back against it, and let my head thump lightly against the wood.

What are you doing, Nat?

I thump my head against the door again, harder this time.

If you aren't careful you're going to push away a great guy who actually wants to raise this kid with you.

My chest tightens at the thought. What if he gets tired of this? Of me? What if one day he decides it's not worth the whiplash and just stops trying?

I'd deserve it. I know I would.

But the thought of Jake giving up on me, on us, makes something painful twist in my stomach.

I push off the door and clean up the kitchen with sharp, angry movements. Shove the bowls in the dishwasher. Wipe down the counter. Try to wipe away the guilt that's clinging to my skin.

I brush my teeth and climb into bed, pulling the covers up to my chin, willing myself to stop spiraling.

My phone buzzes.

JAKE
Home safe. Sleep well.

My heart aches. Actually aches. Because all I want right

now is for him to be here, in this bed, his arms around me, making me feel safe in a way I haven't felt in years.

I smile despite myself, something warm flooding my chest.

NATALIE

You too.

I set the phone on my nightstand and close my eyes. I have to do better. I have to figure this out. Before I lose him completely.

sixteen

...

Jake

I'VE BEEN COMING to the gym more than usual lately, but mostly late at night, when I can't sleep, when the buzzing under my skin won't quit. Today, I'm here early, trying to make sense the whiplash of the last few weeks.

I'm on the treadmill, headphones in, not really hearing the playlist, when a hand taps the front bar.

"Look who made it to the gym today," Wyatt says, stepping next to my treadmill with a grin pasted across his face.

I hit the button to slow my pace down to a walk. "Yeah, sorry man. I've been coming at night after I leave Natalie's place. Burning off some excess energy."

"Things going well there?" Wyatt asks, and there's something knowing in his tone.

I blow out a breath and hit stop. The belt slows underneath my feet. "Kind of. It's...complicated."

"How?" he asks.

I step off the treadmill and grab my towel. "You done with cardio? Spot me?"

"Sure, man."

We move over to the benches. I rack the bar, lie back, and take a breath, trying to line my thoughts up with the reps.

"So you gonna tell me how it's complicated? Or should I guess?" Wyatt asks.

"We've been spending more time together," I say. "I bring her dinner. We talk. And..." I trail off.

"Are you sleeping together?" he asks.

"Yeah."

He doesn't say anything for a beat. I knock out a set, rack the bar, and he's still quiet, which is not a great sign.

"Okay," he says finally. "Do you have feelings for her?"

I laugh once, but there's no humor in it. "I've had feelings for her since before my party."

"Really?"

"Yeah." I sit up, forearms on my knees. "I've noticed her at events for a while. She'd show up with Stella or I'd see her with other people, and I don't know...there's just something about her. She makes a room feel different. At my party we actually talked, and it just clicked. I wanted more even then, but she was very clear it was one night."

"And now?"

"Now she keeps saying she doesn't do relationships. That it doesn't mean anything."

"But you want it to mean something," he says.

"Yeah," I admit. "I do."

He nods like that tracks with the version of me he knows.

"There's work too," I say. "Her career's just taking off, and now she's pregnant and terrified it's all gonna blow up in her face."

Wyatt studies me. "So what's the plan?"

"Good question," I say. "The plan is to keep showing up. Be there for her and the baby. Be patient."

He lets out a low whistle and nods. "That's good. But Jake..." He hesitates. "You might want to know where you stand before the baby comes."

I flop back on the bench and stare at the ceiling for a second. "Yeah. I know. We've got time, though."

"Sure," he says.

He helps me through another set. When I rack the bar, my chest is burning in a good way. The rest of me, not so much. We hit the mats to stretch, then make our way toward the locker room. My phone buzzes in my pocket, and I pull it out immediately. The pregnancy app I downloaded flashes across the screen.

Your baby is now the size of a lemon! This week, baby can wiggle fingers and toes.

I just stare at it. My throat tightens.

Wyatt leans over my shoulder. "Already on the apps, huh?"

"Yeah," I say, huffing out a laugh. "Didn't realize getting emotionally attached to produce was part of the journey."

"Wait until it's 'your baby is the size of a pineapple,'" he says. "You'll walk through the grocery store and get weirdly choked up in the fruit aisle."

"Does it ever stop feeling huge?" I ask.

He thinks about that. "Honestly? No. It just changes. With Ruby, it felt like every week there was something new. First heartbeat, first kick, first time she grabbed my finger. Every one of those felt big. Still does."

I look down at the lemon notification again. "I'm really excited," I say quietly. "Like, stupid excited. This is what I've always wanted. To have a family. A kid. The whole thing. It just didn't look like this in my head."

He laughs, but then his face softens. "You scared at all?"

"Yeah," I admit. "I'm scared she's gonna wake up one day and decide I'm a complication she doesn't need. I'm scared she'll put up those walls and lock me on the outside and I'll still be in love with her."

He goes quiet at that.

I hadn't said that part out loud yet.

"You're in love with her?" he asks, voice low.

I drag a hand over my face. "I don't know if that's exactly what it is yet. It feels big. But I'm on that road. And I'm definitely further down it than she is."

We step into the locker room. It's quieter here, the usual gym sounds muffled by lockers and doors and the low murmur of other guys talking.

Wyatt grabs his bag from the locker and sits next to me on the bench. "Look, man. I get it. You don't want to push. That's good. But you also don't have to pretend this is casual in your own head. You're allowed to want the whole thing."

"I do," I say. "In my ideal version, we end up under the same roof. We fight about baby names instead of visitation schedules. We argue over whose turn it is for the middle-of-the-night feeding and then both get up anyway."

He smiles. "So you're already living in the sequel."

"I'm already living in every possible ending," I say. "Best case, we get there. Worst case, she never wants more than standing at opposite sides of the crib doing the handoff. I'm trying to be okay with both outcomes. My heart's not exactly on board with worst case."

"Yeah," Wyatt says softly. "That part's rough. I get it."

I look at him. "Did you ever worry about that? With Blair?"

"Sure," he says. "Back when we were trying to figure us out, I was terrified I'd screw it up. Or that I wanted more than she did. But I decided I'd rather risk getting my heart wrecked than sit on the sidelines of my own life."

I snort. "Since when did you become a feelings guru?"

"Since I started sleeping more than four hours a night," he says. "The clarity is wild."

I laugh, but the truth of it lands.

"Have you told your mom?" he asks after a beat.

"Yeah," I say, a little smile pulling at my mouth. "She cried happy tears and immediately asked when she could meet Natalie. Then asked if she should start a college fund. I had to remind her we don't even know the gender yet."

"Good ole Linda."

We finish getting changed and head out into the parking lot. The morning sun's already warm, the sky that perfect LA blue that looks fake on TV but somehow is real when you're standing in it.

"Well, the only advice I have is keep doing what you're doing. Show up. Be patient. Let her see you're not going anywhere," Wyatt says.

"And if she doesn't come around?" I ask.

Wyatt's quiet for a moment. "Then you'll still be an amazing dad," he says. "You'll still have this kid who knows you chose them every single time. But honestly? I don't think that's how this goes."

"You sound pretty confident."

"That's because I know you," he says. "When you want something, you don't half-ass it. And Natalie would have to be out of her mind not to see what a good guy you are."

I want to believe that. I do. But I also know you can show up for someone who doesn't want you there. You can give everything and still not be enough.

Lauren taught me that.

But I know Natalie's not Lauren. She's not using me for a stepping stone or a safety net. She doesn't want anything from me except that I show up for this baby.

"Thanks," I tell Wyatt. "I needed to say some of that out loud."

"Anytime," he says. "That's what I'm here for. Gym, beers, emotional support. Full-service best friend package."

My phone buzzes again.

> **NATALIE**
> Yoga class tonight. Should be home by 8 if you want to come over for dinner.

My heart does a stupid little jump. She's inviting me over casually, like it's normal. Maybe I am making progress.

> **JAKE**
> I'll be there. Any cravings?

> **NATALIE**
> Something with carbs. Lots of carbs.

> JAKE
> Got it. See you at 8.

I look up to find Wyatt watching me with a knowing smirk.

"That her?"

"Yeah."

"You're smiling like an idiot."

"Yeah."

He laughs, unlocking his car. "Text me later. Let me know how it goes."

seventeen

. . .

Natalie

I ADJUST the pointed black hat on my head for the third time, checking my reflection in the rearview mirror. The classic witch costume felt like a safe choice when I ordered it two weeks ago. Now, sitting in the Wonderland Studios backlot parking lot, I'm second-guessing everything.

The hat is crooked, my dress is too tight across my chest thanks to pregnancy boobs, and I'm about to walk into a party full of Hollywood's finest while stone-cold sober and pregnant. This should be fun.

Maybe it will be. I haven't been to a real party in months, and getting dressed up for Halloween and going out to a party sounds like exactly the kind of distraction I need.

My phone buzzes.

> **STELLA**
> Where are you??? We're already inside and it's AMAZING.

NATALIE

> Parking. Be there in a sec.

I grab my purse and climb out of the car, smoothing down the black dress. At least it's flowy enough that my tiny bump isn't obvious.

The night is warm, typical for LA, and I can hear music thumping from somewhere deep in the backlot. The entrance is marked by an archway of orange and purple lights, fake cobwebs stretched between vintage lampposts. A security guard checks my name off a list and waves me through, and suddenly I'm in the middle of a Halloween wonderland.

String lights crisscross overhead. Fog machines pump out a low mist that swirls around everyone's feet. There are food trucks lined up along one side, a DJ booth set up near what looks like an old Western saloon facade, and everywhere I look, people in elaborate costumes are laughing, drinking, dancing.

I spot Stella almost immediately. She's dressed as a flapper, all fringe and feathers, hanging on her boyfriend Brandon's arm. He's in a pinstriped suit with a fedora looking like the perfect gangster to her Gatsby girl.

Stella squeals when she sees me, rushing over to hug me. "You look amazing! Very *Practical Magic*."

"Oh, this old thing?" I say, striking a pose with my hat. "You look fantastic."

She laughs and does a little spin, fringe flying everywhere. "It does look kinda cool, doesn't it?!"

Brandon steps up, pulling me into a quick hug. "Looking good, Nat. Love the witch vibe."

"Thanks. You two look like you've come straight out of a speakeasy."

"That's the idea," he says, adjusting his fedora with a grin.

"Come on," Stella says, linking her arm through mine. "Everyone's over by the bar."

She drags me through the crowd, and I spot the rest of the group clustered near a tiki-themed bar that's been decorated with plastic skeletons and jack-o-lanterns.

Blair is dressed as a perfect 1950s housewife, complete with a string of pearls, victory rolls in her hair, and a retro apron tied around her waist. Wyatt matches her in a cardigan and slacks, his hair combed to the side, looking like he stepped straight out of *Leave It to Beaver*.

Jess and her husband Lucas committed fully to their couples costume, dressed as Barbie and Ken in matching hot pink and neon. Jess even has the blonde wig, and Lucas is rocking a spray tan that's bordering on ridiculous.

Sophia looks absolutely stunning as some kind of warrior princess, all leather and armor with intricate braiding in her hair. Grant stands beside her in a matching medieval king costume, complete with a crown and cape.

And then there's Jake.

He's wearing all black. Black dress pants that fit him perfectly, a black shirt with the collar popped and sleeves rolled up to his forearms, and a dramatic black cape. His eyes are focused on me, and when he smiles, I catch the glint of fake fangs.

Dracula. He's a sexy Dracula.

Our eyes meet across the group, and the air shifts. He

pushes off the bar and crosses to me in a few easy strides, his gaze never leaving mine.

"You look incredible," he says, voice low enough that it feels like the words are just for me.

My brain short-circuits for a second. He looks...I don't even have words. Devastating. Unfairly hot. Like every vampire fantasy I've ever had come to life.

"You too," I manage, then clear my throat. "Dracula?"

His mouth curves into a slow smile, and he just nods.

I wonder if he chose his costume knowing I'd go traditional Halloween. Or is he drawn to the dark and supernatural the way I am? There's something about not quite knowing his reasoning that makes him even more intriguing. I get tingles all over my body, but I try to play it cool.

"How very coordinated of us."

Blair appears at my elbow, pressing a drink into my hand. "Virgin mojito. Extra lime, just how you like it."

I could kiss her. "Thank you."

We fall into easy conversation, the group swapping costume compliments and party observations. I catch Stella whispering something to Blair, both of them glancing between me and Jake with matching grins.

Brandon suggests checking out the poker tables and the guys peel off, while Blair, Stella, Jess, and Sophia immediately close in around me like a coven.

"Okay," Stella says. "So. You and Jake."

"We're co-parenting."

The girls go silent. Is it getting chilly out here?

"What?" I ask.

"Oh, Nothing," Stella says. "Just that Jake literally hasn't taken his eyes off you since you walked up."

Heat creeps up my neck. "Stop."

"It's true," Jess chimes in. "He was watching the entrance like a hawk until you showed up."

I take a long sip of my mocktail. "We may have accidentally slept together. Again."

All four of them light up like I just announced I won the lottery.

"I fucking knew it," Jess says.

Stella grabs my arm. "Nat, this is amazing."

"Is it though?"

"Yes," all four of them say in unison.

"He's clearly into you," Sophia says. "Like, really into you."

"And you're into him?" Blair asks.

I don't deny it because what's the point? They all saw my face when I walked up and spotted him in his costume.

For just a second, I let myself imagine it. Jake and me and our baby. Holidays where we're all together, not split between houses. Birthday parties where we're both there, not taking turns. Lazy Sunday mornings tangled in bed while the baby naps.

It's terrifying how badly I want that. How easy it is to picture. How right it feels.

"Earth to Natalie," Stella says, waving a hand in front of my face.

I blink. "Sorry. What?"

"I said, are you going to do anything about it?"

"I don't know. Maybe. We'll see."

It's the most honest answer I've given in weeks, and judging by their faces, they know it. Before anyone can press further, the DJ switches to a throwback Halloween song, and the energy on the makeshift dance floor kicks up.

"Come on," Stella says, grabbing my hand. "Let's dance."

I let myself be pulled into the crowd, and for the next hour, I forget about everything except moving to the music. Stella spins me around, Jess teaches me some ridiculous TikTok dance, and Sophia joins in with surprising enthusiasm for someone dressed like royalty.

I'm laughing. Actually laughing. The kind of deep, unguarded joy I haven't felt in months.

When I finally step off the dance floor, breathless and grinning, Jake is waiting with a fresh mocktail.

"You looked like you were having fun," he says, handing me the drink.

"I was." I take a long sip, grateful for the cold sweetness. "I forgot how much I love dancing."

"You're good at it."

"You didn't dance?"

"I was enjoying the view."

Heat flashes through me at the way he's looking at me, and I have to glance away. "That's very smooth, counselor."

"I have my moments."

The DJ shifts to a slower song, something vintage and crooning, and couples start pairing off on the dance floor.

Jake extends his hand. "Dance with me?"

I don't hesitate. I set down my drink and take his hand.

He leads me onto the floor, one hand settling on my waist, the other holding mine. We sway together, and I'm acutely aware of how close we are. How good he smells. How his thumb is tracing small circles on my lower back.

"This is nice," he says quietly.

"Yeah. It is."

"I like seeing you like this. Happy. Carefree."

"I can be fun, you know."

"I'm learning that." His eyes catch mine, and there's something playful there. "You're full of surprises, Natalie Cruz."

"Good surprises?"

"The best kind."

We spin slowly, the fog swirling around our feet, lights twinkling overhead. For a moment, it feels like we're the only two people here. Like this is exactly where we're supposed to be.

"Thank you," I say.

"For what?"

"For this. For the costume. For making tonight fun."

His hand tightens slightly on my waist. "Anytime."

The song continues, and we keep swaying. I let my head rest against his chest for just a second. I can hear his heartbeat, steady and strong, and something in me settles.

This feels right. I tilt my head up to look at him, and he's already watching me, his expression soft. I don't pull away. Don't make a joke or put up a wall. I just stay here, in his arms, swaying to the music, letting myself feel this. He smiles, and it's the kind of smile that makes me think maybe, just maybe, I could let myself fall.

"I'm really glad you came tonight," he says.

"Me too."

eighteen

. . .

Jake

WE'RE LYING in her bed, the sheets tangled around us, her body warm and relaxed against mine. It's been like this since Halloween, since that night on the dance floor when I felt something shift between us. I tried to give her space after that, convinced myself I could be patient, wait for her to come to me.

I lasted three days.

Three days before I showed up at her door with more takeout and a flimsy excuse about needing to discuss baby prep. She'd seen right through it, but I know the way to a pregnant woman's heart—it's carbs—and she'd let me in anyway. Now we've fallen into this routine of dinners together, falling into bed, pretending we're still just co-parenting.

But I'm pretty sure I'm not pretending anymore.

The room is quiet the way it only gets after dark, soft shadows across her purple walls, her hair fanned across my chest like she always meant to fall asleep there. My hand traces slow patterns on her hip, and I'm rehearsing something in my head for the fiftieth time, trying to figure out how to ask without spooking her.

"So," I say, keeping my voice casual. "Thanksgiving is next week."

She hums, half-asleep. "Mmm."

"I'm going to Connecticut. To see my mom."

"That's nice."

I take a breath. Just say it. "She really wants to meet you."

Natalie's whole body goes still. Not tense—just awake now. She lifts her head, hair sliding across my chest, and those dark eyes lock onto mine.

"You told your mom about me?"

"Of course I told my mom. She's gonna be a grandmother."

"Right. Yeah." She sits up slightly, the sheet slipping to her waist. "That's sweet, Jake. Really. But I already promised my dad I'd have dinner there."

The disappointment hits harder than it should. "Oh. Okay."

She must hear something in my voice because she reaches out and touches my arm, thumb brushing my skin like she's trying to soften the blow. "Thank you for asking. That was really thoughtful."

"My mom's excited to meet you eventually," I admit. She's been asking about Natalie every time we talk, wanting to know how she's feeling, if she needs anything, when she'll get to meet the mother of her grandchild.

"Maybe over the holidays," she says, but it's noncommittal, a safe placeholder. "There's a lot happening between now and then."

"Right. The holidays."

Silence settles, and I push down the urge to say more. I wanted her to say yes. Wanted to bring her home, show her where I grew up, let her see the house I picture when I think "family." But she's not ready. And pushing her now will only make her pull away.

"So tomorrow," I say, shifting us back to safer ground. "Two o'clock, right? We find out the sex?"

"You don't have to go if you're busy."

"Of course I'm going. It's been on my calendar since the second we scheduled it."

She smiles soft and warm in a way that makes my chest ache. "Super Dad strikes again."

"Ha-ha," I mutter, pulling her closer. "You nervous? About finding out?"

"A little. You?"

"Yeah. Excited-nervous." I pause. "Do you have a preference? Boy or girl?"

She goes quiet, tracing mindless shapes on my chest with her fingertips. "I don't know. I keep trying to picture both and I can't."

"Me neither."

She lifts her head a little. "Did you always want kids?"

"Yeah." I answer without hesitation. "Always. Even when I was a kid myself, I knew I wanted to be a dad someday. My dad worked a lot. I barely saw him when I was young, and I promised myself I'd never be like that. If I ever had kids, they'd never have to wonder where I was or whether they mattered."

She listens quietly, her fingers pausing on my chest.

"What about you?" I ask.

"Honestly? No. Not really." She shifts again. "I never saw myself as a mom. I was focused on my career, on getting a seat in a writers' room, proving myself. Kids felt like something that would derail everything I was working toward."

"And now?"

"I'm terrified," she says softly. "But I want this. The baby. I want to be a good mom."

The vulnerability in her voice does something to me. I can't help myself. I reach up and cup her jaw gently, my thumb brushing her cheek. "You're gonna be amazing, Nat. I know it."

"You don't know that."

"I do." My hand slides to the back of her neck, fingers threading through her hair. "You're already thinking about what's best for her. That's half of it right there."

And the other half is me, I think but don't say. I'm already picturing myself as this baby's dad. Reading before bed, teaching how to ride a bike, showing up to every recital and game and moment that matters. Can't picture a future where I'm not there for every single second of this child's life. The thought terrifies me and steadies me all at once.

She lets out a breath of a laugh. "Her. You keep saying her."

"Just a feeling."

"What if it's a boy?"

"Then I buy him a baseball glove and teach him how to throw a punch."

She snorts. "You're gonna teach our potential son violence?"

"Self-defense. Totally different."

She's smiling now and it makes my heart rate speed up. This. This is what I want. Not just tonight, but every night. Her in my bed, in my life, in my future.

"What if it's a girl and she wants to learn how to box?" she asks.

"Then I'll teach her. Equal opportunity sparring in this household."

"Good to know," she laughs.

The quiet settles again, warm and domestic, and I know I should be careful. Know I'm getting in too deep. But lying here with her, imagining our daughter—or son—learning to walk, starting school, I can't picture anyone else in this role. Can't imagine another man teaching our kid how to ride a bike or show up to their soccer games. The thought of someone else being there for those moments makes me physically ill.

This baby is mine. This future is mine. And somewhere along the way, Natalie became mine too, whether she's ready to admit it or not.

"How many kids did you picture having?" she asks.

"Two or three. Enough that they'd have each other."

"That's a lot of kids."

"What about you? Now that you're doing this—do you think you'd want more?"

"I don't know. Ask me again after I've actually birthed

one and survived it." She pauses. "But...maybe. If the first one doesn't destroy me."

I picture it. Another baby. A house full of kids who look like her. Chaos and noise and love everywhere. Me and Nat, years from now, exhausted and happy and together.

"You're gonna be great at this, Nat." I tilt her chin up so I can see her face. "And I'm gonna be right there with you. Every step. Every moment. I'm not missing any of it."

She searches my eyes for a long moment, and I wonder if she can see what I'm not saying. That I'm not just talking about the baby. That I'm talking about her, about us, about a life I'm already building in my head. Then she kisses me.

It starts soft. Sweet. Then her hand slides to the back of my head and her tongue searches for mine. I roll her onto her back, settling between her thighs, her legs falling open like she's been waiting for this.

The truth is, we're both pretending this is simpler than it is. We're circling the same conversation every time we're together, skirting around it like it's some sleeping animal we're scared to wake. We keep spending nights together, eating dinner together, falling into bed like it's instinct then pretending it's all just part of our "co-parenting plan."

Neither of us is brave enough to say what's actually happening. And I'm terrified that if I'm the one who names it first, she'll panic and shut the door in my face.

So I keep it to myself. That she's becoming part of my routine, part of my thoughts, part of my life in a way that doesn't feel casual at all. I hold all of that back, because pushing her now feels like the fastest way to lose the little bit of closeness she's giving me.

She wraps her legs around my waist, guiding me deeper, her hands sliding over my back like she can't decide if she wants to hold me or anchor herself. Her nails graze my skin, and it sends heat straight down my spine. I move slowly, deliberately, matching her pace, letting her set the rhythm, like this is something we've been doing for years instead of stumbling into it by accident.

I brace my forehead against hers, breathing her in as her body lifts to meet mine, every part of her reaching for me like it's second nature. Like she needs this as much as I do. Like we're both trying to close a distance we keep pretending isn't there.

"Jake," she whispers, and the way she says my name ruins me.

I touch her like I'm telling her everything I can't say. I kiss her like she's something precious. And when she shatters beneath me, eyes locked on mine, I follow her, losing myself completely.

Afterward, we lie tangled together, breathing hard, her head on my chest, my hand in her hair. Eventually, I shift. "I should probably head out."

"Okay," she says, but her hand is still on my stomach, like she doesn't want to remove it.

I kiss her forehead before I pull away and grab my clothes. She watches me get dressed from the bed, the sheet pooled around her waist, my T-shirt somehow already on her body again.

God, she looks good in my clothes.

"Thanks for coming over," she says as I pull on my shoes.

"Thanks for inviting me."

I sit on the edge of the mattress to tie my shoes, and she reaches out, her palm resting between my shoulder blades—warm, grounding, and significant in a way I'm trying not to read too much into.

"Jake?"

"Yeah?"

"I'm glad you're coming with me tomorrow."

I turn toward her. "Me too."

We stare at each other for a beat that stretches and stretches.

"Text me if you need anything before then," I say.

"I will."

"Drive safe," she says.

"Always do."

I go to give her a quick kiss but she lifts onto her toes, fingers framing my face, and deepens it. The kind of kiss you feel in your ribs. When she finally pulls back, we're both breathing harder than we should be.

"Goodnight, Jake."

"Goodnight, Nat."

nineteen

. . .

Natalie

THE NOVEMBER AIR has the nerve to actually feel like November. Cool, overcast, the kind of day LA breaks out maybe twice a year just to remind us it can do weather if it wants to. I'm in leggings and an oversized sweater that's rapidly becoming not-so-oversized. There's a curve now that's small, like a little quiet announcement.

When I spot Jake waiting by the entrance, I stop walking for half a second. Just long enough to feel that weird shift in my chest again. Something really did change last night. I didn't mean for it to. Didn't intend to let it. But there it is, humming under my skin like a secret I haven't decided to keep or destroy.

I wonder if he felt it too.

He turns at just the right moment, like he senses me, and when that smile hits his face, the breath catches in my throat.

"Hey," he says.

"Hey."

His eyes do a quick sweep over me, reading me in that way he's gotten good at. "You look beautiful."

"Thank you." I can feel heat flush across my face. He steps closer, and I realize my whole body is vibrating with this restless energy I can't seem to shake.

Jake must see it, because he reaches out, his hand finding mine. His fingers thread through mine slowly, deliberately, and the warmth of his palm against mine steadies something inside me I didn't know was wobbling.

"Is this okay?" he asks quietly.

I look down at our hands, then back up at him. There's no pressure in his expression. No expectation. Just that steady presence that's been showing up for weeks now, asking for nothing but offering everything.

I nod, giving him a small smile. "Yeah. It's okay."

His thumb brushes over my knuckles, just once, and the gesture is so gentle it creates a cluster of flutters in my stomach. "We're checking on our perfectly healthy baby today. And whatever we find out about the sex, it's gonna be perfect too."

"You sound very confident."

"I'm faking it." His mouth quirks.

Despite everything, I laugh. And just like that, the tension in my shoulders eases. Just having him here settles something in me.

"You ready?" he asks.

"I am now." And it's true.

We walk through check-in, the waiting room, the normal pre-appointment choreography. Fifteen minutes later, I'm lying back in the dim exam room, cold gel on my stomach, Jake beside me.

"So today's the anatomy scan," the tech chirps. "We'll check all the organs, measurements, overall growth. And if you want to know the sex, we can absolutely look for that too."

"We want to know," I say before she even finishes the sentence.

Jake nods. "Definitely."

The wand hits my stomach. I flinch. Jake reaches for my hand without looking away from the screen. His fingers slide around mine like it's the most natural thing in the world.

And suddenly we see the baby.

The tech provides a running commentary as she moves the wand, but I'm barely hearing the words. The baby is stretching, curling, flexing tiny limbs that don't feel so tiny anymore.

"Everything looks great," she says. "Strong heartbeat, good organ development, measuring perfectly."

Jake releases a low exhale, like all the air in his lungs has been waiting for this update. His jaw clenches with emotion but also with something steadier. Relief. Awe.

Then the tech beams at us. "Ready to find out what you're having?"

Jake looks at me. I look at him. Something sparks between us, warm and alive and terrifying.

"Yes," we say together.

The tech moves the wand, angling for cooperation. The seconds stretch. My heart tries to escape through my throat.

"There it is," she announces. "Congratulations. You're having a girl."

A girl.

My lungs forget how to function. I stare at the screen, then at Jake. His eyes lock with mine, and the smile that spreads across his face is pure, unfiltered joy. The kind that pushes color into his cheeks and makes the corners of his eyes crinkle. He looks like someone just handed him the entire world on a silver platter.

"A girl," he says again, like he wants to make absolutely sure he heard the tech right. His voice drops a little, steady but almost reverent, eyes still locked on me. "We're having a daughter."

The words land somewhere in the center of my chest and hit a switch I didn't know existed. Something warm rises up and I have to shift, sitting up a little so I don't accidentally leak emotions all over the ultrasound machine. He moves to help me up and every touch, every gesture sends electricity through me.

We clean up and the tech hands us the printouts. Jake thanks her with a voice that sounds like he's still half breathless. The walk out of the building feels unreal and by the time we reach the parking lot, my heart still hasn't settled. I turn to him and say the first thing my brain can manage. "We're having a daughter."

He doesn't answer. He just steps closer, lifts a hand to my face, and kisses me. A slow, deliberate kiss that I feel deep in my bones. His soft lips covering mine, his tongue gently sweeping inside to find mine. It's tender and sweet and full of something that makes my heart skip.

When he pulls back, his eyes roam my face. "Sorry. I got caught up in the moment."

"It's okay," I say, and I mean it.

He shoves his hands into his pockets like he needs to do something with the excess energy buzzing off him. "You hungry?"

"Starving."

His face lights up again. "I'll grab food. We can celebrate at your place."

There's something so normal and sweet about the way he says that word—celebrate—that warmth slides through me before I can stop it. I nod. "Yeah. I'd like that."

Jake brushes a loose strand of hair behind my ear, gives me a smile that knocks the wind out of me again, and says, "Text me your order. I'll be there as soon as I can."

A half hour later we're on the floor, surrounded by Chinese takeout, my laptop open to a baby-name website as we scroll through endless suggestions.

"What about Emma?" Jake suggests, scrolling through the list like a man on a mission.

"Too popular," I say. "Every preschool has at least three."

"Okay.... Olivia?"

"Same issue."

"You're very picky."

"It's our daughter's name. It needs to have some personality. Something that makes her sound like she might grow up to win an Oscar or overthrow a government."

Jake laughs, leaning back on one hand. "Our daughter. I keep saying it in my head."

"Me too."

I reach for a spring roll. "What about Margot?"

"I like Margot. Strong, elegant."

"Or Sloane?"

He adds both to his notes app. "I'm starting a list."

His dedication to even this somehow makes my heart swoon.

Jake glances at the clock. "I should probably head out."

He says the words, but his body doesn't move. And I'm suddenly, painfully aware of how long it's been since I've wanted someone to stay.

"Yeah," I say. Except my voice betrays how much I don't want him to.

He hears it. I know he does.

"Or…" I hear myself say, heart thundering in my chest, "you could stay."

His brows lift slightly. Not shocked. Not smug. Just hopeful.

"Stay?" he echoes.

I swallow hard. "If you want to."

He studies me for a long breath. Like he's making sure I mean it. Like he's trying not to get ahead of himself even though he already is.

"You sure?" he asks.

"Yeah."

The smile he gives me isn't triumphant. It's not even confident. It's relieved. Almost tender.

"Okay," he says, voice quiet but certain. "I'll stay."

twenty

· · ·

Natalie

THE DRESSING ROOM mirror is unforgiving.

I'm twenty-one weeks now, almost five and a half months, and apparently that's the point at which your body decides subtlety is no longer an option. Last week at the anatomy scan, I could still button my regular jeans if I didn't breathe too deeply. This week? Not a chance.

I'm staring down at my sixth pair of jeans, the button several inches away from success, and I give up. Fully surrender. White flag.

My belly has officially rounded out. There's no hiding it anymore, no strategically oversized sweaters that can disguise the curve. And the weird part? I'm ecstatic about it. Seeing this physical proof that our daughter is growing, thriving, real. But I'm also frustrated because nothing in my closet fits and I refuse to live in leggings for the next four months.

"These don't fit either," I call through the curtain.

Stella's voice floats back. "None of them?"

"None of them."

"What about the stretchy ones?"

"Those are maternity jeans, Stella. I'm not ready for maternity jeans."

"Why not? You're literally pregnant."

I yank the curtain open dramatically, the too-small jeans unbuttoned and clinging to me out of pure spite. "Because maternity jeans feel like…admitting something."

She's leaned back against the wall scrolling her phone, but she lifts her eyes, one brow raised. "Admitting what? That you're growing a whole human? Newsflash, babe, the evidence is literally right there." She gestures at my stomach.

"Admitting my body is changing. That I'm not in control anymore."

Stella softens immediately. The teasing vanishes, replaced by full best-friend gentleness. "Your body is doing the most important job of your life. It's supposed to change."

"I know that. In my brain. My brain is Zen about it."

"And the rest of you?"

I sigh. "Freaking out."

"Then let's get jeans that actually fit instead of torturing yourself. Suffering isn't a personal virtue." She plucks a few pairs off the rack. "Here. These are cute and stretchy, but in a good way."

I take them and disappear again. The first pair slips on without a fight. They look good. Normal. Like maybe I haven't turned into a bloated marshmallow.

"These work," I call.

"Show me!"

I step out. She gives a satisfied nod. "Get them in black, dark wash, light wash, and whatever that fourth color is."

We check out with jeans, sweaters, a dress Stella claims I "need," and then rush to lunch.

The restaurant is all exposed brick, conversations at excessive volumes, and tables the size of small cutting boards. Blair waves us over from the back, Ruby on her knee, babbling away. Jess is showing Sophia something on her phone, causing both to laugh hysterically.

"Hiiii!" Blair calls in her mom-voice.

We're swallowed into hugs. Blair careful, Jess enthusiastic, Sophia giving me double cheek-kisses like the glamorous celebrity she is.

"How was Thanksgiving?" Jess asks as we slide into the booth.

"Low-key," Stella says. "Brandon cooked. I supervised."

"Grant made an entire feast," Sophia says. "For the three of us. Hazel inhaled mashed potatoes like it was a competitive sport."

"How's she doing?" I ask.

"Nine going on nineteen. She wants her ears pierced for Christmas."

"And?"

"Grant said no. I said maybe. She's learning negotiation." Sophia grins.

Blair adjusts Ruby on her lap. "We missed you at your parent's house, Soph. It was actually nice, except when your mother kept asking when we're having another baby."

"Yikes," Jess says.

"Right? I told her to ask me again in two years." Blair looks at me. "What about you, Nat? What did you do?"

"Dinner at my dad's."

Stella gives me a pointed look. "Not with Jake?"

Our server appears, as if she's been summoned by the universe to save me from that question. But once she leaves, the table goes quiet again.

"So?" Jess asks, sipping her iced tea. "Why not Jake?"

I trace circles on my water glass. "I don't know."

Stella snorts. "Lies."

"It's not lies. It's just...complicated."

"Tell us why it's complicated," Blair says gently.

"Thanksgiving in Connecticut with his mom is a relationship thing. That's meeting-the-family territory," I say.

The truth is I've been thinking about him constantly since he left earlier this week. Missing the way he shows up at my door with food I didn't know I was craving. Missing his hand on my stomach to see if the baby is kicking yet. Missing the sound of his laugh and the way he looks at me like I'm something precious.

"You miss him," Sophia observes, reading my face.

"Yeah," I admit. "I do."

I hesitate before saying more, knowing this will open a can of worms. "But writers' room starts Monday. I need my head in the game. This show is everything I've worked for. I can't get distracted."

"Have you told them yet?" Blair asks gently. "About the pregnancy?"

My stomach tightens. "No."

"Nat," Jess says carefully. "You're twenty-one weeks. You're showing."

"I know. I'll tell them. Soon." I shift in my seat. "I just want to prove myself first. Get a few weeks under my belt so they see what I can do before they start seeing me as a liability."

"They're not going to see you as a liability," Sophia says.

"You don't know that. The industry isn't exactly famous for supporting pregnant women." I take a breath. "I've worked too hard to get here. I just need a little more time to show them I deserve to be in that room."

"Being with someone doesn't automatically mean distraction," Sophia says, changing the subject back to Jake.

"For some of us," Jess adds, "it's support."

"I can't ask Jake to play that role for me," I argue. "It's already throwing him into a parenting role he didn't sign up for."

"Actually," Blair says, "I'm pretty sure he would love to play that role. Besides, Jake is one of the best people I know."

"Grant says the same thing," Sophia adds. "One of the few attorneys he actually likes working with."

Jess leans in. "We're not saying jump into a relationship. We're saying stop pretending you don't care about him."

My stomach dips. "I don't—"

Stella cuts me off. "Nat. You've been glowing for weeks, and it's not the prenatal vitamins."

Before I can respond, my phone buzzes.

> **JAKE**
>
> Mom says hi. She's already planning how to spoil our daughter.

A smile pulls at my mouth spontaneously.

Blair sees it. "Oh boy."

"It's just a text."

Jess laughs. "Your face says it's more than the text."

I ignore them and look at my phone as another message comes in.

> **JAKE**
> Missing you. Sorry if that's weird.

My chest tightens, warm and a little achy.

Sophia leans over. "Show us."

I comply—resistance is useless with this group.

Sophia whistles. "That's not baby-related missing you. That's missing *you*."

I shouldn't reply. I know I shouldn't.

But I also know I'm lying to myself about what I feel.

> **NATALIE**
> Not weird. I miss you too.

Stella claps like she's at a sporting event. "She admitted it!"

"Would you stop?" I laugh, covering my face.

We shift to safer topics—Ruby's sleep regression, Hazel's classroom drama, Sophia's potential movie deal—but eventually Blair glances at me with those soft, mom-level intuitive eyes.

"Can I ask something?"

"Do I have a choice?"

"No," she concedes. "What are you so afraid of?"

The question slices right through me. "I was left at the altar," I blurt before I can stop myself.

The table goes silent.

I force myself to keep going, even though my throat feels

like it's closing. "We had the venue booked. The dress. Hundreds of guests. I spent the morning getting ready with my mom and my bridesmaids, and I was so happy. So stupidly, blindly happy." I swallow hard, but it doesn't help.

Jess makes a small, wounded sound.

"His best man told me five minutes before the ceremony was supposed to start. Said he couldn't go through with it. That he was sorry." My voice cracks. "Turns out he'd been cheating on me for months. With someone from his office. He married her six months later."

"Oh sweetheart," Blair whispers.

The memory crashes over me. Standing in that white dress, makeup perfect, hair perfect, feeling like my entire body was made of glass and someone had just taken a hammer to it. The whispers I imagined from the guests, even though my mom rushed everyone out. The flowers that suddenly felt like a funeral arrangement. The terrible, suffocating humiliation of having to tell people, over and over, that there wouldn't be a wedding.

I couldn't eat for weeks. Couldn't sleep. Kept replaying every moment of our relationship, searching for signs I'd missed. Wondering what was wrong with me that he could do that. What I lacked. Why I wasn't enough to keep him.

"It took me a really long time to come back from that," I say quietly, looking down at my hands. "I questioned everything. Was it me? Was I not enough? Was I fundamentally unlovable?" I force myself to look up, meeting their eyes. "And I promised myself I'd never be that vulnerable again. Never let someone have that kind of power over me."

My voice drops to almost a whisper. "Because what if

Jake realizes I'm too much work? Too complicated? What if he decides I'm not worth it and just...leaves? I don't know if I could survive that again."

Jess reaches across the table and squeezes my hand. "That wasn't your failure. That was his."

"Maybe. But there were no signs. I trusted him completely. I just, I'm not interested in going through that kind of pain again."

Sophia's expression softens. "I think Jake is worth the risk."

"How do you know?" My voice is smaller than I'd like.

"Because it's obvious he's all in." Stella says. "I think he's the kind of guy you take the risk on."

"And," Blair adds gently, "you're falling for him. Whether you want to or not."

I don't answer because they're right. I am falling for him. Maybe I've been falling since July fourth. Maybe since that first doctor's appointment when he held my hand. Maybe since he arranged groceries and prenatal vitamins without being asked. The terrifying part is I'm not panicking the way I should be.

With my ex, there were no red flags because everything was performative. Like we were playing the roles we were supposed to play. He said the right things, did the right things, but there was always this distance. This sense that I had to earn his attention, his affection, his presence.

With Jake, it's different. He shows up. Not because he has to, but because he wants to. He listens when I talk about *Spellbound*, asks thoughtful questions, celebrates my wins like they're his wins too.

And the way he looks at me. God, the way he looks at me.

Like I'm not too much. Like my walls and my sarcasm and my fears don't scare him away. Like he sees all of it and wants me anyway.

The thought should terrify me.

But underneath the fear, there's something else. Something that feels dangerously close to hope.

Instead, I turn to Sophia. "So tell us everything about this potential movie."

Everyone glances at each other, fully aware I'm changing the subject. I appreciate the moment they decide to let it go. Sophia shifts the conversation and laughter bubbles around the table again. But under it all, there's a quiet understanding.

They know I heard them. And even though I'm still terrified, some part of me—the soft, foolish part I pretend doesn't exist—hopes they're right about us.

twenty-one

. . .

Jake

I'M STANDING outside Natalie's door with a full-sized Christmas tree balanced on my shoulder, a bag of ornaments cutting into my fingers, and a tiny wrapped box in my pocket that felt sweet at the store but which I now worry might be overkill.

It's been almost a week since I've seen her. She spent Thanksgiving with her dad while I flew to Connecticut. And somehow six days turned into this low-grade ache I carried around everywhere. I missed her. Missed her laugh, her snark, that fucking mint tea that tastes so good on her lips.

Tomorrow is her first day in the writers' room. I wanted to do something that would make her smile and add to her excitement.

I knock with my free hand. As the door swings open, her eyes widen. "Jake. What are you—is that a tree?"

"What tipped you off?" I tease.

"Why did you bring me a tree?"

"Because it's the Sunday after Thanksgiving. Trees go up

this weekend." I shift the tree on my shoulder. "Can I come in? This thing is heavier than it looks."

She moves back, still staring like she's not sure if she should laugh, kiss me, or shove me back onto the porch. I brush a quick kiss on her cheek as I pass.

"I thought maybe..." I start, suddenly awkward. "We could start our own tradition."

Her eyebrows jump. "Our own tradition?"

"Yeah," I say, casually enough that you'd never know my heart sped up. "Like putting up a tree the weekend after Thanksgiving. Making sure our daughter has her first Christmas, even if she's not here yet."

She goes still, and I can't tell if I've stepped over a line or hit something tender she wasn't expecting.

"You brought me a Christmas tree," she says again, slower this time.

"And ornaments," I add, pulling out boxes. "Wasn't sure what you had, so I grabbed basics. We can get more later. Personalized ones for..." I grin. "What are we thinking? Wren? Margot? Sloane?"

She folds her arms. "We haven't decided yet."

"Well, I can keep auditioning names. See what fits." I pull the stand from the box. "Where do you want this?"

She hesitates, like the question is bigger than the tree. Then points. "By the window."

"Perfect."

I kneel, set the stand, tighten the screws. Natalie watches from the couch, arms wrapped around herself, expression drifting between surprised and grateful. Something like she wants this but is scared to want it too openly.

"Thank you," she says quietly. "For all of this."

"Of course." I step back, checking the tree's angle. "It felt important. This is her first Christmas, even if she's still in there." I gesture to Natalie's stomach.

Natalie's eyes follow mine.

"Oh," I say, remembering. "One more thing." I lift a sprig of mistletoe from the ornament box.

She huffs a laugh. "You did not."

"I did." I walk to the doorway between her kitchen and living room, reach up, and hook the mistletoe on the light fixture. It twirls slightly, catching the glow of the lamp.

"There," I say. "Now come over here."

She lifts a brow. "Jake."

"Rules are rules, Nat."

She rolls her eyes but stands, crossing the room. "This is ridiculous."

"Completely ridiculous," I agree.

And then I kiss her. It's supposed to be quick. Playful. Just enough to make her smile before her big week, but the moment our mouths meet, everything tilts. Her hands slide to my chest, my fingers find her jaw, and there's nothing playful about the way she kisses me back. It's warm and slow and threaded with an effort of making up for all the days we haven't been able to kiss each other.

We break apart, both of us catching our breath.

"Hi," I say.

"Hi."

"I missed you."

She swallows. "I missed you too."

Those four words hit something deep.

I pull the small wrapped box from my pocket. "I also...got her something."

"Jake, you didn't have to—"

"I wanted to." I place it in her hands. "Open it."

She peels the paper carefully, and when she lifts the lid, her eyes soften instantly. Inside is a delicate glass ornament etched in silver: *Baby's First Christmas.*

"Oh," she whispers. "It's...beautiful."

She runs her thumb over the script like she's memorizing it.

"You're kind of amazing," she says.

"I try."

She laughs quietly, shaking her head. "Thank you. This is perfect."

"Want to hang it?"

She nods, and we move toward the tree together. The next hour is warm and easy. I string the lights while she argues about spacing. She hangs ornaments with quiet intention, making sure each one is placed exactly where she wants it.

When I plug in the lights, the room glows from the soft gold lights, the baby's ornament hanging front and center catching the light. For a second, it feels like a snapshot of a life we could have. The kind with matching stockings and holiday cards and late-night wrapping-paper disasters. The kind that looks suspiciously like a family.

"Oh," I say lightly, "I read something about talking to the baby. About how she can hear us now."

Natalie's gaze snaps to mine. "You did?"

"Can I...?" I gesture to her stomach.

"You want to talk to her?"

"If that's okay."

Her voice warms. "Yeah. Of course."

I kneel, level with her bump. Up close, it's small but undeniable, the gentle curve that holds everything that changed my life.

"Hey, baby girl," I say softly. "It's me. Your dad." The word settles warmly in my chest every time. "I know you can't see me yet, but I'm here. I'm going to be here for everything."

Natalie's hand drifts down, resting lightly on my shoulder.

"We put up your first tree tonight," I tell her. "Your mom picked where your ornament goes. It's front and center. She's got excellent taste."

Natalie lets out a shaky laugh.

"I can't wait to meet you," I say. "To hear you laugh. To watch you grow up. You're going to have the best mom. She's smart and strong and funny. You're going to learn all of that from her."

"Jake," Natalie whispers, her voice caught somewhere between laughter and tears.

I stand slowly, and she steps into me like she belongs there. I wrap my arms around her. She tucks her face into my chest.

"Thank you," she murmurs. "For the tree. For the ornament. For...everything."

"Always." I press a kiss to her hair. We stay like that for a long moment, her heartbeat steady against my chest.

"Come to bed," she says quietly.

I pull back just enough to see her face. "You sure?"

"I don't want you to leave."

She takes my hand and leads me down the hallway. The bedroom is dim, just the faint glow from the living room spilling through the doorway. She turns to face me, her fingers sliding under my shirt, palms flat against my stomach.

"I really missed you this week," she whispers, her voice low and wanting.

Heat rushes through me. "Nat—"

Her hands move to my belt, and I go still, letting her take the lead. She unbuckles it slowly, eyes locked on mine, and there's something deliberate in the way she moves. Like she's been thinking about this, wanting this. She pushes my jeans down, then my boxers, and when her hand wraps around me, I let out a rough exhale.

"Sit," she says, nodding toward the bed. I do, and she drops to her knees between my legs. The sight of her there, hair falling over her shoulders, lips parted, damn near undoes me before she even starts.

I cup her face, thumb dragging across her bottom lip. "Open for me."

Then her mouth is on me, warm and wet and perfect, and every coherent thought I had dissolves. She takes her time, her tongue working me over in slow, deliberate strokes that make my thighs tense.

I thread my fingers through her hair, needing to touch her. "Fuck, Nat."

She hums around me, and the vibration sends a jolt straight through my spine. I'm already close, tension coiling through my balls, and when she looks up at me, eyes locked on mine while she takes me deeper, I nearly lose it.

"I'm not going to last," I warn, voice strained. "But when I come, I want to be inside you. I missed feeling you wrapped around me."

Her eyes flash up to mine. She pulls back off me and drags the back of her hand across her lips. She stands, stripping off her clothes with quick, efficient movements, and then she's climbing onto the bed, onto me, straddling my hips.

I reach for her, hands sliding up her sides, thumbs brushing the curve of her belly before moving higher. Her breasts are fuller, heavier in my palms, and when I thumb her nipples, she gasps.

"You're so fucking beautiful." She leans down, kisses me hard. She positions herself over me, sinking down slowly, and the tight heat of her makes me groan into her mouth. Her cunt grips me so tight I can barely breathe, every inch of her pulling me deeper.

"Jesus, Jake," she gasps, head falling back. "You feel so good."

I grip her hips, guiding her rhythm, watching the way her body moves above me, the way her hands press against my chest for balance.

"I'm close—Jake," she whispers, and the way she says my name, breathy and desperate, sends me careening toward the edge. I slide one hand between us, finding her clit and the pressure makes her shudder. She cries out and her rhythm falters.

"Come with me," I say roughly. "Let me feel you."

When she lets go, our eyes meet and it feels like everything. I see it all. Me, her, this future we're building. And I know, deeper than I've ever known anything, that this is it. She's it.

She clenches around me as she cries out my name and I follow her over, spilling into her with a groan that tears out of my chest. She collapses onto me, both of us breathing hard, slick with sweat, tangled together in the dim light.

"Don't move," I murmur, kissing her shoulder. "I'll be right back."

I slip into the bathroom, clean myself up, wet a washcloth with warm water. When I come back, she's sprawled on the bed, flushed and gorgeous and mine. I take care of her gently, then toss the cloth aside and climb back in, pulling her against my chest.

She fits perfectly there, her head tucked under my chin, my fingers threading through her hair in slow, soothing strokes. We lie there, hearts slowing, her weight a perfect anchor.

"You nervous about tomorrow?"

"Terrified."

"Just remember, they wanted you. They're lucky to have you."

She lifts her head, eyes soft as she studies me. "Thanks for saying that."

I brush a strand of hair from her face. "You're going to be incredible tomorrow. I can't wait to hear all about it."

She settles back against my chest, and I hold her close as I think about how I don't want to be without her in my arms every night. I don't want mornings where I wake up and she's not there. I want this for as long as she'll let me have it.

twenty-two

...

Natalie

THE TABLE IS COVERED in fresh stacks of neon sticky pads, three untouched packs of dry-erase markers, and a whiteboard so clean you just know it's going to squeak when someone writes on it.

It smells like lavender sanitizer and the faint bitterness of coffee. The room has that unmistakable first-day energy, where every chair is still pushed in and the air feels expectant, like the walls are waiting to inhale their first argument about character arcs.

Rebecca is already at the head of the table with her laptop open, tapping notes into a document like she's been here since dawn. She looks up the second I step inside, her smile warm and sharp at the same time.

I'm hyper-conscious of everything. The way my blazer sits over my stomach. The curve that's harder to hide now, even in carefully chosen layers. I wore black on black today, strategically loose but not obviously maternity. Professional. Put together. Don't look at my midsection.

My heart does a nervous little flip as I cross the threshold, trying to hold myself with confidence while also wondering if everyone can see what I'm trying so hard to conceal. This is it. The room I've dreamed about being in for seven years. The show I created, the characters I built from nothing, finally becoming real.

And I'm terrified they're going to see me as a liability before they see me as a writer.

I want to prove I belong here first. Want them to know I can pitch great ideas, that I can break story, that I'm worth the risk FlixPix took on me. Then maybe, when they already know what I can do, the pregnancy won't feel like a complication.

Just a few weeks. That's all I need. A few weeks to show them I'm serious, that I'm talented, that I earned this seat at this table.

Then I'll tell them.

I shut the door behind me and take the seat she gestures toward, forcing my shoulders back, my chin up.

"You ready?" she asks.

"I think so," I say, though my pulse is doing its best impression of a hummingbird.

"Good. Chaos starts in about ten minutes."

I pour myself a glass of water and start thumbing through the printed script in front of me. Episode One.

Bernard comes in first, with his spiral notebook. He's in his mid-fifties and wears wire-rimmed glasses and a sweater vest over a button-down. He's the kind of guy who's been writing TV since I was a baby. He's worked on three critically acclaimed dramas and has that quiet, observant energy that makes you think twice before pitching something half-baked.

Priya follows, balancing her laptop and an enormous Stanley cup. Early thirties, dark hair in a sleek ponytail, wearing a blazer that somehow looks effortlessly cool instead of corporate. She's written on two FlixPix shows and has this sharp, fast-talking energy that makes every pitch sound like the best idea you've ever heard.

David walks in looking over-caffeinated. He's in his late twenties, a UCLA film school grad, and this is his first staff writer job. You can tell he's trying to absorb everything. He's got that eager, prove-myself energy I recognize because I have it too.

Chris and Lena come in together, whispering about some showrunner meltdown they heard secondhand. Chris is tall, lanky, always in vintage band tees under blazers, known for writing incredible dialogue. Lena is petite, pixie cut, big earrings, and has a dry wit that makes every writers' room story sound like stand-up. They both came from cable dramedies and seem like they've been work-friends forever.

By the time everyone takes a seat, the table feels alive with creative energy.

Rebecca uncaps a marker and faces the board. "All right," she says. "Welcome to the *Spellbound* writers' room. Let's make something great."

I look around the room for some indication as to how we're supposed to respond to that. I guess we stay quiet.

"What are we trying to answer this year?" she asks, turning back to us. "What is the thematic spine? And please do not say 'Can she have it all?' because I will throw my coffee."

"It feels like identity," I say, before I can talk myself out of it. "You know, legacy versus choice. The whole season is basically asking: Are you what you were born into, or do you get to decide who you're going to be?"

Rebecca points at me with her marker. "Yes. That. Exactly that."

Purple ink appears on the board: WHO YOU ARE VS WHO YOU CHOOSE TO BE.

"Okay," she says. "If that is our spine, everything we break today has to hang off it. The sisters, the love interests, the villains, the magic system, all of it."

My shoulders drop a fraction. I'm here. I just said a thing in an actual writers' room and the showrunner didn't immediately regret hiring me. Good start.

We go around, everyone throwing out ideas, and Rebecca writes them all in a messy constellation around the question.

"What I love in your pilot," Priya says to me, "is that the youngest sister is the one who actually wants the magic."

"Right," Chris adds. "And the eldest is the one who's like 'you can take your destiny and shove it.' That contrast is your engine."

I nod, feeling my cheeks warm. "Yeah, I wanted it to feel like a real family argument, just with fire coming out of people's hands."

David chuckles. "As one does."

We sink into it. We throw up character cards on the board, argue over Episode One's final image, dig into whether the grandmother is a benevolent badass or a slightly terrifying wildcard. Somewhere between Rebecca circling "middle sister" and Bernard pitching a season-long mystery around a missing grimoire, my leg stops bouncing.

Around what feels like noon, my stomach growls loud enough that Priya glances over and tries to hide a smile.

"Okay, before we all pass out," Rebecca says, checking the time on her phone, "let's order lunch. There's a sushi place down the street that delivers fast. Everybody good with that?"

The table answers in a chorus of "Yes," "Always," "Bless You."

My brain stalls.

Sushi. Raw fish. Mercury. Parasites. All the pregnant-no-no words parade across my mental screen with little flashing warning lights.

"Actually," I hear myself say, aiming for casual and landing somewhere in the zip code of overly bright, "I'm more of a...non-sushi person."

Rebecca looks up from the menu. "Oh, then we can switch. Plenty of options in this neighborhood."

Panic flares, ridiculous and hot. It's day one; I am not about to derail the lunch order because my uterus is occupied.

"No, it's fine," I say too quickly. "They have bowls and stuff, right? Teriyaki? I'll do something like that."

"You sure?" she asks.

"Totally." I flip open my laptop and pull up the menu like I've done this a million times. "You all get what you want. I'm easy."

That's a lie. In so many ways.

The menu loads. I scroll until I find salvation in the form of "chicken teriyaki rice bowl." There. Safe.

As everyone debates yellowtail versus salmon and whether spicy tuna is overrated, my pulse thuds in my ears.

I'm not even halfway through my first day and I'm already hiding things. It's just sushi. Just one tiny white lie about preferences. But it feels like a preview of the next few weeks.

The afternoon stretches into more whiteboard scribbles and card-shuffling. We start roughing out where the season might land, throwing "possible midseason twist" up on the board and starring it twice. Rebecca keeps us moving without steamrolling anyone, firm and excited and exactly the kind of person you want in charge of your dreams.

By five, my brain feels like someone scraped it out with a spoon, in a good way.

"Okay," she says, dropping the marker and clapping her hands once. "Fantastic work, everybody. You all showed up, you played nice, nobody pitched a talking cat. I'm thrilled. Same time tomorrow."

There is a shuffle of laptops closing and chairs scraping. Everyone starts gathering their things, tossing out goodbyes and see you tomorrows.

"Natalie?" Rebecca says. "You have a minute?"

I have a moment of panic. She knows.

Maybe my blazer shifted wrong when I reached for my water. Maybe I touched my stomach one too many times. Maybe the chicken bowl gave me away.

"Yeah, sure," I say, hoping my voice doesn't give me away.

Rebecca sits back down, but she's more relaxed now, one

ankle resting on the opposite knee. "I just wanted to check in without five people staring at us. How are you feeling after today?"

"Good," I say, honestly. "Tired, but good. It was incredible, actually. Getting to hear everyone bounce off the pilot, start building it out. This is...yeah. It's everything."

Her mouth tips up into a smile. "You did great. You jumped in, you weren't precious about your own pages, your ideas tracked. That's not always a given with first-time creators."

"Thank you." My throat goes a little tight. "And thank you again for taking a chance on the show."

She waves that off. "The show's good. That part was the easy decision."

I want to print that sentence out and frame it.

She hesitates for a beat, then folds her hands on the table. "One more thing. This job gets intense. The closer we get to production, the crazier the hours get. Things blow up, you're rewriting on set, life keeps happening anyway. If there's ever anything you need from me, flexibility-wise, I want you to know you can say it. Conflicts, family stuff, mental health days. I'd rather know and work with it than have someone burn out quietly in a corner."

On the surface, it's thoughtful. Generous. The kind of thing people brag about in interviews when they talk about "good showrunners."

But all I hear is: "Do you have anything I should know about that might make you a problem when we're in production April through August?"

I grip my notebook a little tighter. "I really appreciate that," I manage. "Right now I'm good."

"Good." She smiles, all warm sincerity. "We're lucky to have you. Go home. Turn your brain off for a few hours. You earned it."

Traffic on the way home is its usual mess. I barely notice. My brain loops the same beats: Four months until production. April through August. "If you have any conflicts."

By the time I stumble through my front door, my whole body feels like I've been standing under fluorescent lights for ten straight hours. I toe off my boots, peel off the blazer, and trade my outfit for leggings and one of Jake's T-shirts, the soft gray one that mysteriously never found its way back to his drawer.

It falls over the curve of my stomach and I try not to overthink how much that comforts me.

I pour a huge glass of water, flop onto the couch, and open my laptop. There are already three emails from FlixPix. One is calendar invites for the week. One is notes from Rebecca recapping the day.

The third has the subject line that causes my anxiety to spike again.

From: Rebecca Sullivan
Subject: Production Timeline & Availability.

I click.

Hey team,
Quick reminder that production is scheduled from early April

through August. We'll need all hands on deck during that time. It's long days on set, rewrites, last-minute changes—it's intense, but it's also the best part.

Please confirm you're available for the full production period. If you have any conflicts (vacations, other projects, family stuff), let me know ASAP so we can plan around it. Thanks!

Rebecca

The email is reasonable but it feels like someone just walked into my living room, took one look at my belly, and asked, "So, you going to be a problem?"

What am I supposed to say back?

Hi, this all looks great. Quick thing: I'm going to give birth two weeks before we start twelve-hour days.

Hi, I promise I will totally be available while also figuring out how to keep a tiny human alive and attached to my chest.

Hi, please don't replace me.

My stomach knots.

My phone buzzes against the coffee table, cutting through the spiral. Jake's name lights up the screen.

> **JAKE**
>
> How was day one? Want to celebrate? I can bring dinner.

Just seeing his name does something to my lungs. For a second I picture him here, standing in my kitchen with takeout containers, listening while I word-vomit everything in my head. The way he would say, "We'll figure it out," and wrap his soothing arms around me.

NATALIE
> Day was good but I'm exhausted. I have a lot of work to do tonight. Need to prep for tomorrow.

The second I hit send, guilt unfurls in my chest.

JAKE
> You sure? I can just drop food and go. You need to eat.

NATALIE
> I'm fine. Thanks though.

The dots appear. Disappear. Appear again.

JAKE
> Okay. Let me know if you change your mind.

I put the phone face down. It feels like I just shut the door in his face. Again.

He's trying to show up. I'm the one backing away. But keeping him at arm's length feels like the only way to keep everything else standing. I can't juggle the writers' room, the pregnancy, and the possibility of falling in love with the father of my baby without dropping something.

I close the laptop without replying to Rebecca's email. Adult, professional Natalie will deal with it in the morning. Right now, I just want a five-minute break from being "available for the full production period."

I lean my head back against the couch and press the heels of my hands into my eyes until colors bloom there.

And then I feel it.

A soft flutter low in my abdomen, like someone tracing the inside of my skin with a feather.

I hold still.

It comes again. A tiny tap from the inside, not painful, just insistent. Like a knock. My hands drop to my belly before my brain catches up. I press my palms gently against the stretch of skin where my T-shirt pulls a little tighter.

"Do it again," I whisper, because apparently I negotiate with my uterus now.

For a heartbeat there is nothing, and I wonder if I imagined it. Then there it is. A little thump. Stronger this time. A swirl and push, like something turning in a small space. Air rushes out of me.

"Hi," I say, my voice a wrecked little laugh. "Hi, baby girl."

My eyes sting out of nowhere. I blink too fast, and a tear spills down.

"Your mom's having a very low-key panic attack about her entire life, but I'm so happy you're here."

And in this moment, nothing else matters except her.

twenty-three

...

Jake

IT'S BEEN two weeks since I put up the Christmas tree in her living room, since she let me talk to our daughter through her shirt, since she stood there looking at me like she was letting herself feel something. Two weeks of barely seeing her.

The contract in front of me is a mess of redlines I'm supposed to be cleaning up, but the words won't stick. My phone is sitting on top of the file, screen dark because it hasn't lit up once this morning. Or yesterday. Or the day before that. My thumb keeps hovering over it anyway, like I can will a message into existence.

If we were truly nothing but co-parents, this silence wouldn't hurt. It would be normal. But it hurts like hell, which tells me exactly how far gone I am.

"You look miserable."

I don't even hear Wyatt come in until he's already leaning in my doorway, mug in hand, looking annoyingly rested for someone who has a baby at home.

"I'm fine," I say, even though we both know I'm lying.

"You waiting for a call?" He nods at the phone in my hand as he steps inside and drops into the chair across from me.

"Nat started at FlixPix," I say, setting the phone face down. "I just haven't heard much from her."

"Oh." Wyatt raises a brow.

I shrug. "She says work is crazy. She needs to prep for the next day. She's exhausted. Which is true, I'm sure. But it feels like she's pulling back."

"Do you think she is?"

"I don't know," I say quietly. "I want to be supportive. She told me the writers' room would be intense. She warned me this might happen."

Wyatt watches me for a long moment, and I already know what he's thinking before he says it. "You're serious about her."

I drag a hand down my face. "I miss her. Not seeing her every day makes me feel…" I search for a word that doesn't make me sound like an idiot. "Untethered."

Wyatt's expression shifts, the teasing edge dropping away. He leans forward, his voice quieter. "You need to talk to her, man."

"I know."

If I'm already this tied up in knots after two weeks, I need clarity. Sooner rather than later. If she's pulling away for good, I'd rather know now, before I fall any harder.

"No, I mean really talk to her. Because from where I'm sitting, you're putting everything into this and she's keeping you at arm's length." He hesitates. "I care about Nat. You know I do. But I also care about you. And I don't want to watch you get hurt by someone who doesn't feel the same."

The words land heavier than I expect.

"I'm not saying give up," he continues. "Just make sure you're protecting yourself too. You deserve someone who's all in, Jake. Not someone who only shows up when it's convenient."

My throat tightens. "I know."

"Talk to her. Get some clarity. You can't keep going like this."

Before I can respond, he brightens. "By the way, welcome to the girl-dad community," he says, gesturing to himself like he invented fatherhood. "You're going to love it here."

Despite everything, I laugh. "How's Ruby?"

"Perfect and exhausting. She discovered she can throw things, so Blair and I have accepted our home is a danger zone." He grins proudly. "Worth it though."

I feel the answering warmth in my chest immediately. "That's how I feel every time I look at the ultrasound pictures."

Wyatt leans forward, elbows on his knees. "So how's Natalie doing? Pregnancy-wise?"

"She's good. The baby's good. Everything's on track."

Before he can say more, a knock sounds on the door. Ryan steps inside, holding a file.

"Jake, got a minute? Need to go over the St. James contract."

"Sure," I say, but I feel my shoulders tense.

Ryan glances between the two of us, reads the room instantly, and closes the door behind him. "Everything okay?"

Wyatt answers for me. "Jake's missing his daughter." Then, with a grin, "And her mother."

Ryan's face softens immediately. "How's Natalie settling in at FlixPix?"

"Good," I say. "Busy. Stressed. Focused."

"That sounds like her." He sits beside Wyatt. "When she's overwhelmed, she'll bury herself in work. Shut everything else out until she feels like she's back in control."

That hits a little too close.

"Yeah," I say. "I'm getting that impression."

Ryan hesitates, then leans back like he's calibrating the boundaries between father and boss. "Can I give you some advice?"

"Please."

"Keep showing up for her. She has a tendency to push people away when things feel too close."

I lean forward. "Why?"

Ryan shifts uncomfortably, his jaw tightening. "It's not really my story to share. I've said this before." He pauses, seeming to wrestle with something. "But you should know she was hurt badly in a past relationship. They were supposed to get married, and the way it ended was rough."

The air leaves my lungs.

"Married?" The word comes out strangled. "She was engaged?"

My chest constricts. The room feels smaller suddenly, the walls pressing in. Natalie was going to marry someone. Someone proposed to her, put a ring on her finger, made promises, and I had no idea.

How did I not know this?

Ryan's watching me carefully. "I hoped you knew."

"Hoped?"

"I hoped she'd confided in you. That she was finally opening up to someone." He sighs. "She doesn't talk about it. Not to me, not to her mother. Maybe to Stella, but even then, I doubt she shares much."

My hands curl into fists on my lap. "What happened?"

"I've already said too much." Ryan's voice is firm but not unkind. "You need to talk to her, Jake. Ask her yourself."

"And if she won't tell me?"

"Then give her time." He looks at me directly. "And give her space to get there on her own terms. She'll come around. She just needs to feel safe first."

"And if she doesn't?"

"She will. I've seen the way she looks at you when she doesn't think anyone's watching," he says.

After Ryan leaves, Wyatt whistles low. "That's new news."

"Yeah."

"And you didn't know?"

"We haven't really talked about our past." I stare at my phone again. "I haven't even told her the full story about Lauren. I figured she probably knew from the gossip around town."

"Maybe you should tell her. Open up first. Show her it's safe."

"Maybe."

But even as I say it, I'm not sure it'll make a difference. Because the problem isn't that we don't know each other's pasts. The problem is it feels like she's decided she doesn't want a future. At least not with me.

When Wyatt leaves I grab my phone and decide to make the first move.

> **JAKE**
> Can we talk? Maybe I can come by tonight?

It takes a minute for her to reply.

> **NATALIE**
> I can't tonight. Meeting my writers' group. But I promise we'll spend time together this weekend.

> **JAKE**
> Okay. Let me know when works for you.

> **NATALIE**
> I will. Thanks for understanding.

I turn back to my computer, to the contract I'm supposed to be reviewing, and try not to think about how Natalie was engaged once. How someone else had her heart and broke it so badly she's still protecting the pieces.

And how I'm falling for a woman who's seemingly convinced herself she doesn't need anyone.

Including me.

twenty-four

...

Natalie

JONAH'S APARTMENT door swings open before I can knock twice.

"Natalie!" he says, already reaching for the Tupperware in my hands. "Tell me that's something with sugar."

"Ginger molasses cookies," I say, stepping inside.

The place smells like the holidays. Gingerbread, cinnamon, something vaguely pine-adjacent. White lights loop around the windows, a small fake tree glows in the corner alongside a menorah, and his kitchen counter is covered in enough food to cater a mid-level awards show.

"So you went subtle this year," I deadpan, hanging my bag on a hook by the door.

"Were you expecting something different?" he says, already peeling the lid off my cookies.

Wren and Eric are already here, half arguing, half laughing near the tiny dining table, plates in hand. Iris slips in right behind me, cheeks pink from the chill, holding a metal tin that smells like butter and chocolate. Brody arrives last, balancing a paper bag of even more goodies.

"Traffic was a nightmare," he says. "If I didn't love you people, I would've turned around and gone home to FlixPix and self-pity."

"Aw," Jonah says, clapping him on the shoulder. "He loves us."

"I love the cheese board," Brody corrects, heading straight for the food.

We load up plates and fall into our normal routine of catching up with each other.

"I have an interview to write on a show," Wren says once we're all settled in the living room, holiday music humming low in the background. "Network. Prime time."

"That's huge," I say, genuinely thrilled for her. "What is it?"

She shakes her head. "Can't say. They made me sign a stack of NDAs, but it's an ensemble comedy, workplace, actually funny, so I'm cautiously excited."

"You'll crush it," Jonah says. "You're the queen of secondhand embarrassment humor."

"Thank you?" she says, scrunching her nose.

"And you?" Jonah turns to me. "How's *Spellbound*?"

I lean back against his couch, balancing my plate on my knees. "Good. Really good, actually. We just finished writing the second episode."

There's a little ripple of impressed sounds around the room, which I pretend not to soak in like sunshine. It still hits me in waves. I can't believe I will have a show on TV. I can't believe I'm writing in a real writers' room.

We settle into the couch and floor in a loose circle, plates and drinks balanced on laps, the tree lights blinking gently in the corner. For a second, I let myself enjoy it. This little pocket of people who knew me when *Spellbound* was just an idea.

"I still can't believe it's happening," I say, exhaling. I press my palm lightly against my stomach, grounding myself. "Seven years of trying, and now it's actually real."

There's a beat of silence.

And that's when I realize everyone's eyes have shifted.

Down.

To where my sweater has pulled a little tighter over my stomach because I've unconsciously pressed my hand there.

Wren blinks first. "Um. Nat?"

I look down.

The bump is not hiding. At all.

Fantastic.

"So," I say, my voice weirdly calm. "I'm pregnant."

The room detonates.

"What?" Wren shrieks, launching off the couch so fast her wine nearly sloshes out of the glass.

"You're pregnant?" Brody yelps, eyes bugging.

"Holy shit," Eric says, sitting up straight.

Iris comes in for a hug that threatens to cut off my circulation.

"How far along?" Jonah asks.

"Almost six months," I say.

"Six months?" they all echo, eerily harmonic.

"Have you been hiding under baggy sweaters this whole

time?" Wren demands. "Is that why you 'suddenly discovered' the joys of oversized blazers?"

"Yes," I say.

Jonah recovers first. "Why didn't you tell us?"

The question is gentle, not accusatory. That somehow makes it worse.

"Because I'm terrified," I admit. "I haven't told FlixPix yet. I'm scared it'll ruin everything. That they'll find a way to push me out, even if they don't say it's because of this." I gesture toward my stomach. "I wanted to prove myself first. Show them I can handle the room, the workload, the insanity. I thought if I got a couple of months in, it would be harder to let me go."

The room quiets.

"When are you going to tell them?" Jonah asks.

"After the new year," I say. "I don't think I'll be able to hide it much longer, and by then they'll have seen what I can do."

Eric nods slowly. "I get that. Lead with the work, not the thing they'll use to make you seem 'difficult.'"

"I just didn't want anything to make them question hiring me," I say. "Or make them think I'm not all in because I have this other...massive life thing happening. I've waited my whole career for this shot. I can't lose it."

"You're not going to lose it," Wren says, coming around the coffee table. She's still wide-eyed, but the edge has softened to something almost fierce. "And for the record, we are mildly offended that you didn't tell us you were growing a person in there, but we will shove our hurt feelings down because we love you."

"Deeply hurt," Brody says, hand over his heart. "But also sobbing with joy on the inside."

Jonah looks at me like he's trying to figure out how I've been standing upright with this much weight on my shoulders. "We won't say anything," he says. "Not to anyone. Room's a vault."

Everyone nods.

Iris gives me another squeeze. "Congratulations," she whispers. "Really. This is huge. Both things. The show and the baby."

"Thanks," I say, hugging her back.

We ease back into conversation, but everything feels a little different now. Lighter. As the night winds down, people start gathering their things, slipping leftovers into foil, hugging goodbye near the door while Mariah Carey serenades us in the background.

By the time I get home, my feet ache, my back is threatening mutiny, and my brain is buzzing with story beats and production calendars. I change into one of Jake's T-shirts and a pair of soft shorts, plug my phone in on the nightstand, and collapse onto my bed. The house is quiet, just the faint hum of traffic outside and the soft glow of the Christmas tree coming from the living room.

My phone buzzes.

> **JAKE**
> Hope you had a good night with your writers' group. Sleep well.

I stare at the screen. I miss him. I thought giving us a little space would reset how I'm feeling, but I don't think it's working. In fact, I think I want him more than before. And if I'm being honest, I can't believe he's still here. Still checking in. Still being patient, even though I've given him every reason to back away.

> NATALIE
> Thanks. It was good. They all know now.

> JAKE
> How'd they take it?

I smile, remembering the chaos, the voices, the hug that almost suffocated me.

> NATALIE
> Really well. Supportive.

> JAKE
> Good. You deserve that.

My throat tightens. There's so much more I want to type. I'm sorry I've been distant. I miss you. I'm scared this industry will punish me for wanting both a baby and a career, and I don't know how to let you in without feeling like I'm handing you a grenade with the pin half-pulled.

> NATALIE
> Thank you. I'm headed to bed, but I'll see you this weekend?

The dots appear.

> JAKE
> Definitely. Goodnight, Nat.

I heart the message, set the phone on the nightstand, and

lie there in the dim light, one hand resting over the curve of my stomach. Telling my friends about the baby helped relieve some of my anxiety. It made this feel less like a secret I'm hiding and more like a life I'm building.

But the clock's ticking now. On FlixPix. On the pregnancy. On whatever the hell I'm doing with Jake. I can feel everything shifting under my feet, all at once. And I know that at some point, very soon, not deciding is still going to be a decision.

I just really, really wish I weren't so afraid of wanting the thing that might actually make me happy.

twenty-five

. . .

Jake

I KNOCK on Natalie's door with my arms full of wrapped presents, adjusting the stack so nothing slips before she opens it. Even though she invited me to come over tonight, my heartbeat still kicks up, the kind of steady thrum that always seems to show up right before I see her.

The lock clicks. The door opens. And there she is.

Her face softens the moment she sees me, something small and real shifting through her expression like a quiet welcome.

"Hey," she says.

"Hey." I lift the presents a little. "These are for your tree."

She steps aside, letting me in with that slow, warm ease that tells me she wants me here, even if she's still figuring out what that means.

The Christmas tree glows in the corner, except now I spot a few new ornaments tucked between the branches.

Little additions she made on her own. It makes something in my chest settle.

I kneel near the tree and set the boxes down carefully. One with her name. The other labeled *Isla?* with a question mark.

She steps beside me, her voice quiet. "Isla?"

"I wanted to see what it felt like," I say.

Her face softens as she looks at the name, something tender easing into her expression. She reaches out, her fingers hovering just above the letters like she's afraid to disturb them.

"It's beautiful," she murmurs.

"Yeah?"

She nods slowly, almost as if she's picturing our daughter grown up, introducing herself, carrying this name we're choosing for her right now.

"Yeah," she says, her voice catching just a little. "Isla. Our Isla."

The way she says "our" does something to my chest.

We straighten at the same time, close enough that we almost bump into each other. Neither of us moves away. There's something in the quiet between us that feels gentler than the last couple of weeks. A tiny shift pulling us forward.

"I'm glad you're here," she says softly.

"I'm glad too."

Her eyes flick to mine, full of something restless and tender, and then she clears her throat. "Are you hungry? I was thinking Chinese."

"That sounds good," I say.

She orders without consulting me, because she already

knows what I'll want. When she sets her phone down, she tells me dinner will be here in half an hour, and we drift to the couch, settling into our familiar corners.

Except tonight, the space feels different. Closer. Something in the air is shifting back toward us instead of away.

Natalie traces her fingers along the seam of a pillow, her shoulders lifting in a small breath. "I'm sorry I've been distant."

"You don't have to apologize."

"I think I do." Her eyes stay on the pillow, then lift to me. "You've been kind. And patient. And I haven't been either of those things."

"You've had a lot going on."

"It's not just that." Her hand stops. "It's..."

Her sentence dissolves into a sudden stillness. One hand moves to her stomach, her eyes widening in surprise.

"What happened?" My whole body shifts toward her.

"She's kicking." Her voice is full of awe. "Jake. She's kicking."

Everything inside me tightens. "Can I feel?"

"Yes. Come here."

She reaches for my hand and places it low on her stomach. I hold my breath. Waiting. Then it happens. The smallest tap against my palm. A tiny, determined movement. I don't breathe for a second. Then another kick comes, a little stronger.

"Oh my God," I say quietly.

"I know."

"That's her."

I keep my hand there until the movements slow, and even

when they stop, I don't move right away. It feels like the moment might break if I do.

"Was that the first time you felt her?" I ask quietly.

She hesitates, just a beat. "No. I felt something two weeks ago. I didn't know if it was her or just...I don't know. But yeah. I think it was her."

Two weeks ago. And she carried that alone. Not because she wanted to. Because she trained herself to.

"Why didn't you tell me?"

She looks up at me, startled by the gentleness in my voice. "I'm not sure," she says softly.

I keep my eyes on hers, steady, not accusing. "Nat...why do you do that?"

"Do what?"

"Close yourself off," I say. "Hold me at a distance. Like you're waiting for a reason not to let me in."

She swallows, her fingers curling into the hem of her shirt. "I'm not trying to."

"I know you're not," I say. "That's why I'm asking."

For a long moment, she just sits there, breathing slowly, like she's deciding whether she's brave enough to tell the truth. Then she leans back into the couch, her gaze drifting toward the tree lights reflecting off the windows.

"I was engaged once," she says quietly.

I don't move. Don't speak. Just listen.

"His name was Darren." She says it like the word tastes bitter. "And he wasn't all bad. People always talk about red flags, but sometimes there really aren't any red flags. Sometimes the person shows up on time. Or remembers how you love Reese's mini peanut butter cups. Or fixes the loose cabinet hinge without you asking. And you think: *he loves me. He's good. He's mine.*"

Her eyes soften with something vulnerable. "And then one day you realize you were wrong. Completely wrong. And you wonder how anyone could miss something that big. You start doubting not just the person...but yourself. Your judgment. Your ability to tell when someone is true."

She looks at me then, and the rawness in her eyes hits me in the chest. "That's why I get scared. I trusted someone I shouldn't have. And I didn't see it coming."

"It wasn't your fault," I say softly.

She shakes her head. "It feels like it was."

"Nat," I say, leaning closer, my knee brushing hers, "people who want to hurt you are good at lying. They don't give you flashing warning signs. They make you feel safe. They make sure you don't see the escape hatch until they're already halfway out."

Her breath catches, and she looks at me with something like recognition.

I settle a little deeper into the cushions, letting the truth in me rise to the surface. "I understand that feeling more than you think."

She tilts her head, waiting.

"I never thought Lauren would betray me," I say. "Not once. Not even when she left our honeymoon early. Not when she skipped out on my friends. Not when she always had somewhere else to be. I kept telling myself everything was fine. That I was the one overreacting."

Natalie eyes are focused on me, listening to every word.

"I thought I knew who she was," I say. "I thought I was a good judge of character. And I was completely wrong."

Her face softens. "What did she do?"

I inhale, then let it out slowly. "She went through my files and emails. She sold private information about my clients to tabloids."

Her eyes widen, the shock immediate and honest. "Jake..."

"I didn't see it coming," I say. "Not even a little. And afterward, I had the same questions you did. Am I blind? Did I miss every sign? Am I the kind of man who can't tell when someone's lying to him?"

She nods with understanding. They're the exact questions she's been living with too.

"But here's the thing," I continue. "She took enough from me. She doesn't get to take everything. And definitely not the part that lets me believe good things can still happen."

Natalie's breath catches, just a little.

"I learned from it," I say. "Not in a way that made me shut down. In a way that made me pay attention. It taught me to look for someone who actually shows up. Someone who's here because they want to be."

I take her hand, slow and careful. "Lauren wasn't the whole world. She was one person who made terrible choices. She doesn't get the right to define the rest of my life." I pause, then add quietly, "And Darren doesn't get the right to define yours either."

I say his name like it's nothing. Like he's nothing. Because he is. Her eyes shine, but she doesn't pull her hand away.

"You're not broken," I say. "You're cautious. There's a difference."

She sucks in a slow breath, her fingers tightening around mine.

"And I'm not naive," I add. "I'm hopeful. Big difference there too."

Her lips part, like she wants to respond but isn't sure how yet. And that's fine. I'm not asking her for anything immediate. I just want her to know the door is open and I'm not walking away from it.

We sit there like that for a long moment, our hands linked, the tree lights flickering softly through the room.

When she finally speaks, her voice is barely above a whisper. "I don't want to push you away."

"Then don't," I say.

She stares at me, breath held tight, and I see the exact second something inside her shifts. Not completely. Not all at once. But enough to open a door that's been locked for a long time.

And that's when she leans closer, her voice barely above a whisper. "Will you stay tonight?"

"Yeah," I say softly. "I'll stay."

She doesn't move right away. Just looks at me with those dark eyes that have been guarding so much for so long. Then she stands, offering me her hand.

I take it.

She leads me to her bedroom, and when we reach the bed, she turns to face me. Her hand lifts to my face, palm warm against my jaw. I lean into the touch, and she kisses me.

Soft at first. Tentative. Then deeper.

Her hands slide up my chest, fingers curling into my shirt. I cover her hands with mine, slowing her down, and she looks up at me. I brush her hair back from her face, my thumb tracing her cheekbone, taking my time.

She reaches for the hem of my shirt and I let her pull it over my head. Her hands flatten against my chest, fingers splaying wide like she's memorizing the feel of me. I do the same with her sweater, easing it up and off, my knuckles grazing her sides.

When I reach for the clasp of her bra, she doesn't help. Doesn't rush. Just watches my face while I undress her, piece by piece, like I'm unwrapping something precious.

Her breathing changes when I lay her back on the bed. Usually she's the one pulling me down, rolling us over, taking control. Not tonight. Tonight she stays where I put her, her eyes locked on mine as I settle over her.

I bracket her face with my hands and kiss her slowly. Thoroughly. Like I have all the time in the world and nowhere else I'd rather be. I feel the exact moment her body relaxes underneath mine. I slide my hand down her side, over the curve of her hip, feeling the slight swell of her stomach under my palm. Our daughter. Right there between us.

She arches into my touch, her breath catching, and I take my time. Kissing her throat. Her collarbone. The curve of her breast. Learning her all over again, but slower this time. Paying attention to every small sound she makes, every place on her body that makes her gasp.

When I finally move inside her, her hands grip my shoulders and she breathes my name against my neck. I go slow. Steady. Watching her face in the dim light, seeing every flutter of her eyelashes, every part of her opening up to me in a way she hasn't before.

Her nails dig into my back and I kiss her, swallowing the soft sounds she's making. She wraps her legs around my waist, pulling me deeper, and I feel the shift in her breathing that tells me she's close.

"Jake," she whispers.

I press my forehead to hers, keeping that same steady rhythm until she breaks apart beneath me, her whole body tightening around mine. I follow her over, burying my face in her neck, and for a long moment neither of us moves.

Afterward, we lie tangled together, her head on my chest, my hand tracing slow circles on her bare shoulder. The room is silent except for our breathing.

She's quiet for a long moment, then her hand finds mine, threading our fingers together over her stomach where our daughter is growing. She doesn't say anything. She doesn't have to. For the first time in weeks, I feel like we're finally on the same page.

twenty-six

. . .

Natalie

I WAKE UP SLOWLY, blinking into the pale light spilling through my bedroom curtains, and the weight of Jake's hand resting over my hip. He's pressed up behind me, warm and solid, his breath moving in a lazy rhythm against the back of my neck. His fingers are curved protectively over the curve of my stomach.

I stay still and let myself enjoy the way his body relaxes around mine. He's been here more nights than not lately, the evidence accumulating. A toothbrush in the bathroom. His hoodie on the back of my chair. A second pair of shoes by the door.

A month ago, seeing his things scattered through my house would have sent me spiraling. Would have felt like too much too fast, like I was losing control of my own space, my own life.

Now? It settles something in me.

Maybe it's the baby. Maybe having her inside me, growing and real and impossible to ignore, makes it easier to let him in too. Like she's the excuse I needed to stop fighting what I actually want. Or maybe it's just him. The way he doesn't push. The way he shows up and stays without making it feel like a demand.

"Are you awake?" His voice is low and rough with sleep, right against my hair.

"Kind of," I murmur. "What time is it?"

He shifts just enough to reach for his phone on the nightstand, his arm tightening around me so I don't move when he does. "A little after eight."

"Too early for Christmas Eve," I say, closing my eyes again.

He laughs softly. "I thought you were the one who liked this holiday."

"I like this holiday when it starts at ten."

He's quiet for a moment, then I feel him move. The bed shifts as he sits up, and I open my eyes to find him reaching for something on the nightstand.

"What are you doing?"

"Hang on." He turns back to me, a small, gift-wrapped box in his hand. "I was going to wait until tonight, but this feels like the right moment."

My nerves take over. "Jake, you didn't have to—"

"I know I didn't have to." He settles back against the headboard, pulling me up with him. "I wanted to. Open it."

I take the box, the wrapping paper soft under my fingers. It's small, maybe the size of my palm, wrapped in silver paper with a white ribbon. I pull it loose and tear through the paper carefully, revealing a simple white jewelry box. When I open it, my breath catches.

It's a necklace. Delicate gold chain with a small pendant —a crescent moon with a tiny star nestled inside the curve.

"Jake," I whisper.

"The moon is you," he says quietly. "The star is Isla. I saw it and thought.... I don't know. It felt right."

My eyes sting. I blink hard, trying to keep it together, but my throat is tight. "It's beautiful."

"Can I put it on you?"

I nod, not trusting my voice, and turn so my back is to him. He lifts the necklace from the box, his fingers brushing the nape of my neck as he fastens the clasp. The pendant settles just below my collarbone, cool against my skin.

I turn back to face him, my hand automatically going to the pendant. "Thank you. Really. This is—" I swallow. I lean forward and kiss him, slow and deep, trying to say everything I can't quite put into words yet.

When I pull back, he cups my face, his thumb brushing my cheek. "Merry Christmas, Nat."

"Merry Christmas."

His thumb brushes absently against my stomach, sending a jolt of desire through me. We've been good since the night she kicked for him. Not perfect, not suddenly cured of all our baggage, but there's been an ease to us lately.

He presses a kiss to my shoulder. "I have to go get my mom from the airport," he says quietly. "Her flight lands around noon."

"Wait. I have something for you too."

His eyebrows lift. "You do?"

"Don't look so surprised." I climb out of bed, grabbing his shirt from the floor and pulling it on as I cross to my closet. I reach up to the top shelf, behind a stack of notebooks, and pull down a small, gift-wrapped package of my own. I climb back onto the bed, sitting cross-legged in front of him. "Here."

He takes it carefully, like he's afraid it might break. "Nat, you didn't have to."

"Neither did you." His eyes linger on me, moving around my face like he's trying to unravel a hidden meaning.

He grins and tears through the paper. Inside is a leather-bound journal, with thick, creamy pages and a strap that wraps around to keep it closed. His initials are embossed in gold on the bottom right corner.

"Nat," he says quietly, running his fingers over the leather.

"I know you keep everything on your phone and your laptop," I say, suddenly nervous. "But I thought maybe you'd want something for the important stuff. For Isla. You could write to her, or about her, or just whatever you want."

He opens it, and I watch his face as he sees what I wrote on the first page.

For Jake. May you fill these pages with all the moments I know you'll never want to forget.
— N

His eyes lift to mine, and they're bright.

"This is perfect," he says, his voice rough. "Thank you."

He sets the journal carefully on the nightstand, then

pulls me into his arms, holding me tight against his chest. I feel his heartbeat under my cheek, steady and strong.

"I love it," he murmurs into my hair. "I love that you thought about this. About me."

I love you.

The thought fills my head before I can manage it or control how I want to feel in this moment. The words sit right there, pressing against the back of my teeth, wanting out.

But I'm not ready. Not yet.

So I pull back slightly, clearing my throat, forcing myself back to practical territory. "Is your mom excited to visit?" I ask.

"Yes," he says. "And she's really excited to meet you," he adds, his voice softer.

I bite back a smile. Meeting someone's mother is...big.

"My mom is excited to meet you too," I say. "And your mom. She's making enough food to feed half of Los Angeles."

The baby decides that's the moment to give one solid kick against the inside of my ribs. I wince and press a hand there.

"You okay?" he asks, instantly alert.

"She's clearly pro–grandmother summit," I say, exhaling. "Or just protesting how long we stayed in bed."

He slips his hand over mine, palm warm against the stretch of skin. "She's making her opinion known."

"Wonder where she gets that from," I mutter.

He leans in and kisses me, slow and steady, like he has time, like he's not about to run to the airport, like we're not both suddenly standing at the edge of a very big step.

When we pull back, he rests his forehead against mine. "See you at your mom's house later?"

"Yeah."

"And Natalie?"

"Hm?"

"Thank you," he says. "For inviting us."

I swallow. "Don't make it weird. It's just dinner."

He gives me a look that says we both know it's not just dinner, then kisses my forehead and finally rolls out of bed.

By the time I get to my mom's house, the sun is already starting to dip lower, the sky turning that pale, washed-out blue that makes Christmas lights look brighter against the houses. The air is mild, the kind of cool that feels good after a warm day, not the bone-deep cold people up north complain about in December.

It smells like roasted garlic and something sweet when she opens the door. She pulls me into a hug before I even step over the threshold, careful but firm, her hands automatically bracketing my stomach the way they always do now, like she's checking on both of us at once.

She pulls back to look at me, eyes scanning my face like she's trying to read whatever I brought in with me. "How are you feeling?"

"Uncomfortably full of human," I say. "Otherwise okay."

She smiles, then glances over my shoulder, clearly expecting someone behind me. "Is he coming?"

"Yes," I say. "They'll be here around six, I think."

Her eyebrows lift, just a little. "I can't wait," she says, a little excitement in her voice.

We move into the kitchen, where every surface is covered with bowls, platters, cutting boards, and half-chopped herbs.

She's already in full Christmas Eve mode. A pot bubbles gently on the stove.

She pulls a pan from the oven, the heat washing over us. "So, it's going well with Jake?" she ask, not looking at me.

"It is."

I inhale slowly, letting that settle in. My instincts have betrayed me before. I've missed things that were right in front of me. And yet, there's nothing jangling in the back of my mind with Jake. No quiet wrongness I'm trying to ignore. Just the steady, unfamiliar feeling of being seen and chosen and not rushed.

The doorbell rings, slicing through the moment. My mom wipes her hands on a towel.

"Please don't say anything embarrassing," I mutter as I slide off the stool.

"No promises," she says, and heads for the front door.

Jake stands on the porch in a navy button-down and dark jeans, that glimmer in his eyes that says he's missed me. Standing next to him is a woman with kind eyes and his same dark hair threaded with silver, cut in a neat, practical bob.

"Hi," I say, suddenly very aware of how pink my cheeks feel.

"Hi," Jake says, his gaze softening the moment it lands on me. He reaches for my hand, giving it a quick squeeze before letting go.

I turn to the woman beside him. "Hi. You must be Jake's mom. I'm Natalie."

"Linda," she says. Her smile is warm and immediate, and she goes straight in for the hug. "It's so nice to finally meet you. I feel like I already know you."

My mom appears at my side, and I shift so they're all in front of me. "Mom, this is Jake, and his mother, Linda," I say. "And this is my mom, Elena."

"It's wonderful to meet you," my mom says, stepping forward, giving Jake a big hug, and then taking Linda's hand in both of hers.

"Thank you for having us," Linda replies. "And for feeding us."

My mom laughs. "Come in. There's plenty of food. Always."

Once we make it to the living room, Linda's gaze drops to my stomach with an impatient fondness. "May I?"

"Of course," I say, a little surprised at how okay I am with that.

She rests a gentle hand there, a light touch, nothing invasive. "Hello in there," she says softly. "I'm your grandmother."

The words hit me somewhere deep, in a place that's still getting used to the reality of all of this. I glance at Jake, and the look on his face tells me he feels it too. My mom's eyes shine as she watches us, something satisfied in her expression, like a piece of a puzzle has just clicked into place.

Dinner is loud in the best possible way.

My mom keeps bringing food to the table like we're secretly expecting six more people. Linda insists on helping serve despite my mom's protests, which leads to both of them laughing over who gets to carry what. By the time we sit down, the table is covered with roasted chicken, potatoes, green beans with slivered almonds, everything delicious, and in quantities appropriate for about twice as many people.

Jake sits next to me, close enough that our knees keep finding each other under the table. Our moms sit across from us, already in a deep conversation about holiday traditions.

The conversation moves, flowing around the table. They ask about my work, my mom tells old stories about me as a kid. Linda talks about their hometown and Jake and what he was like growing up, little details that make him more real in a way I didn't know I needed. There are moments where I forget to be nervous. Moments where it feels like this has been happening for years.

At one point, I feel his fingers brush mine under the table. "You okay?" he murmurs.

"Yeah," I say, surprised to find that I mean it. "More than okay, actually."

His hand lingers for a second before he pulls back, but the warmth stays. When it's finally time for them to go, night has fallen and the air has cooled down. The moms trade numbers and promises to talk again, which I believe entirely.

"Thank you," Jake says quietly once they're at the door, his voice meant just for me.

"It went well, yeah?" I say.

"It did," he agrees. There's something steady in his eyes.

He steps closer, just enough, and cups my face in his hands, his fingers cool against my skin. He kisses me softly. When he pulls back, he rests his forehead against mine for a second.

"Merry Christmas Eve," he says.

"Merry Christmas Eve."

He gives me one last look, then turns to go, helping his mom into the car before climbing into the driver's seat. I stand there until the taillights disappear at the end of the street, the sound of the car folding back into the quiet of the neighborhood.

My mom opens the door behind me a crack. "You coming in?"

"In a minute," I say.

I rest my hands over my stomach and feel the faintest movement beneath my palms, like someone turning over to get comfortable.

"Okay," I whisper, more to myself than anyone else. "We can do this."

I just stand there for a beat longer, letting the day settle. And I feel happy.

twenty-seven

...

Jake

I WAKE up to Natalie wrapped around me like a vine.

Her head is on my chest, one leg thrown over mine, her hand resting on my stomach. She's completely dead to the world, breathing deep and even, her dark hair spilling across my shoulder.

This has become our routine for the last few weeks. We haven't talked about what this means or what we're doing. We're just...doing it.

I press a kiss to the top of her head, careful not to wake her, and she shifts slightly, burrowing closer. The morning light filters through her curtains, soft and golden. It's New Year's Eve. The last day of a year that changed everything.

Carefully, I extract myself from her grip, replacing my body with a pillow that she immediately hugs. I pull on my jeans and head to her kitchen.

Eggs, toast, fresh fruit. I plate everything and carry it back to the bedroom, setting the tray on her nightstand.

"Nat," I say softly, sitting on the edge of the bed. "Wake up."

She makes a grumbling sound and burrows deeper into the pillow.

"I made breakfast."

Both eyes open now. She sits up slowly, her hair a mess. She's wearing another one of my T-shirts, and the sight of her in my clothes makes me want to rip them off her. Honestly, at this point half her wardrobe is my shirts, and I don't hate it.

She takes the plate I offer, and we eat together in her bed, the morning stretching out lazy and comfortable around us.

"So," I say, setting my empty plate aside. "Tonight is the Hays & Cole New Year's Eve party. I was wondering if you'd want to go with me."

She pauses mid-bite, her fork hovering in the air. "To your office party?"

"Technically it's your dad's office party. But yeah." I reach over, tucking a strand of hair behind her ear. "I want to take you out. Ring in the new year together. It's going to be a big year for us."

She sets her fork down, her fingers playing with the edge of the blanket. "Jake—"

"Plus, it's just the firm. Most people there already know about the baby, or they won't care. You don't have to hide."

She's quiet, her eyes fixed on her plate. I can see the wheels turning, the hesitation written all over her face.

"You don't have to if you don't want to," I add gently. "No pressure."

"Okay," she says finally, her voice soft.

Relief floods through me. "Yeah?"

"Yeah. Let's go."

The smile that breaks across my face is probably ridiculous, but I don't care. I pull her closer, kissing her forehead.

Later that evening, I'm in Natalie's living room, adjusting my tie and trying not to pace. She's been in her bedroom for the past hour getting ready, and I'm equal parts excited and nervous.

This is our first real date. Our first time going out as... whatever we are. Maybe not quite a couple yet. But something.

"Okay," she calls from the bedroom. "I'm ready."

I turn around, and my breath catches.

She's wearing a dress I've never seen before. Deep emerald green, velvet, with long sleeves and a neckline that shows just enough. It hugs her curves, accentuating every line—her shoulders, her breasts, the swell of her hips.

And her belly.

The dress doesn't hide it. Doesn't try to. It showcases it, the fabric draped perfectly over the curve where our daughter is growing.

She's stunning.

"Is it too much?" she asks, a hint of uncertainty in her voice. "I wasn't sure about the dress, but Blair said—"

"You're beautiful," I interrupt. "Nat, you're absolutely beautiful."

A blush creeps up her neck. "Thank you."

Her hair is down in soft waves, dark against the green of the dress. She's wearing makeup—not a lot, just enough to make her eyes look even more dramatic. And she smells incredible.

But it's the belly that I can't stop looking at. The visible proof that she's carrying our daughter. That in a few months, our entire world is going to change.

"You're staring," she says softly.

"I know. I just..." I place my hand gently on her stomach, feeling the firm curve through the velvet. "You're growing our baby. You're the mother of my child. And you're so goddamn beautiful it actually hurts to look at you sometimes."

Her eyes are shining now. "Jake."

"I mean it."

She rises on her toes and kisses me, soft and sweet, and I have to force myself not to suggest we skip the party entirely.

"We should go," she murmurs against my lips. "Before I change my mind about this dress."

"The dress is perfect. You're perfect."

She laughs, grabbing her clutch from the couch. "You're biased."

"Completely."

The party is at a hotel ballroom in downtown LA, all twinkle lights and champagne flutes and people dressed to impress. The party is legendary. Ryan goes all out, and everyone from the firm shows up.

When we walk in together, I rest my hand on the small of Natalie's back, and I don't miss the way several people's eyes track to her belly before quickly looking away.

We find a table and I get her sparkling cider while I grab a beer. The DJ is playing something upbeat, and couples are already on the dance floor.

"Want to dance?" I ask.

"I do."

I lead her onto the floor just as the song hits its peak. We move together, her laughing as I spin her carefully, and for a few minutes it's just fun. Light. Easy.

Then the song ends, and the DJ's voice comes over the speakers. "All right everyone, let's slow it down a bit."

The opening notes of something slower, more romantic, fill the room. Couples around us shift, pulling each other closer.

I offer Natalie my hand. "One more?"

She smiles and takes my hand. I pull her in close, one hand settling on her waist, the other cradling her hand against my chest. She fits perfectly against me, her free hand resting on my shoulder. We sway together, barely moving, and I'm hyper-aware of every point of contact. The warmth of her palm through my shirt. The curve of her waist under my hand. The way her belly presses gently against my stomach, a constant reminder of what we're building together.

Her fingers trace small circles on my shoulder, absent and intimate, and it sends heat straight through me. I tighten my hold on her waist, pulling her closer, and she doesn't resist. Her head tilts up, her eyes meeting mine, and there's something vulnerable in her expression that makes my chest ache.

"This is nice," she says.

Her hand slides from my shoulder to my chest, her palm resting over my heart. I wonder if she can feel how hard it's beating.

"Jake," she says quietly, and there's something in her voice that makes me hold my breath.

"Yeah?"

She opens her mouth, then closes it. Whatever she was

going to say, she's not ready. I press a kiss to her forehead instead. Her eyes close for a second, and when she opens them again, they're bright.

"Thank you," she whispers. "For being patient with me."

"Always," I say, and I mean it.

We keep swaying, our bodies moving together like we've done this a thousand times. Her fingers trace the buttons of my shirt, a gentle, unconscious gesture that's driving me insane. I slide my hand lower on her back, right above the curve of her hip, and she shivers.

"Cold?" I murmur.

"No." Her voice is barely audible. "Definitely not cold."

The heat in her eyes when she looks up at me nearly undoes me. I want to kiss her. Want to take her home and show her exactly what she does to me. Want to tell her I'm in love with her and I can't keep pretending this is casual.

I'm snapped back to reality by a glimpse of Ryan and his wife across the room.

"Hey," I say to Natalie. "I see your dad."

"Oh good. Where?"

We make our way over, and Ryan's face lights up when he sees us.

"There you two are!" He pulls Natalie into a hug, careful of her belly, then shakes my hand. "You both look very nice."

"Thanks, Dad."

Rachel leans in to hug us both. "Natalie, that dress is stunning. You're glowing."

"Thank you."

"How are you feeling?" she asks Nat. "I remember when I was that far along. Everything hurt."

"I'm good. Feeling a little swollen, but good."

"Save me a dance later?" Ryan asks Natalie.

"Of course."

We chat for a few more minutes before Ryan gets pulled away by someone from accounting. Rachel gives Natalie's hand a squeeze before excusing herself to find some friends, and Natalie and I are about to head back to the dance floor when she turns and nearly collides with someone.

"Oh! I'm so sorry—" Natalie stops short. "Rebecca."

I watch as the blood drains from Natalie's face and she looks as if she's seen a ghost. I turn to see a woman in her forties in a sleek black dress, standing with a man I vaguely recognize as one of the senior associates.

The women's eyes widen slightly when she sees Natalie. Specifically, when she sees Natalie's very pregnant belly in that form-fitting dress.

For a moment, neither of them speaks. The air between them feels charged.

"Natalie," Rebecca finally says. "I didn't expect to see you here."

"I'm here with Jake. He works at the firm." Natalie gestures to me. "Jake, this is Rebecca Sullivan, my showrunner."

Oh fuck.

I shake her hand. "Nice to meet you."

"You too." Rebecca glances at her date. "This is Mark. He's a partner here."

"Nice to meet you both," Natalie says, her voice steady but tight.

There's another beat of silence. Rebecca's eyes flick to

Natalie's stomach again, but she doesn't say anything. Doesn't ask.

I feel Natalie go rigid beside me, her whole body tensing like she's bracing for impact.

Everything in me wants to step in. To pull Natalie behind me, to tell Rebecca that whatever she's thinking, she can keep it to herself. To shield her from the judgment I can see forming in the other woman's eyes.

But I can't. This is Natalie's career. Her show. Her relationship with her showrunner. All I can do is stand here and watch her crumble, and it's killing me.

"I know this probably looks—I was going to tell you after the new year, I just wanted to—" Natalie starts.

"Let's talk when we're back at work," Rebecca interrupts smoothly. Her expression is neutral, unreadable. "Enjoy your evening."

And just like that, she walks away, Mark following.

My hand finds the small of Natalie's back instinctively, trying to ground her, but she's already spiraling. I hate this. Hate that I can't fix it. Hate that all I can do is be here and hope that's enough.

"Nat—"

"I need to leave." Her voice is barely above a whisper.

"Okay. Let's get our coats."

We make our way toward the exit, but the countdown to midnight is starting. The ballroom erupts in noise—people shouting numbers, glasses clinking, the anticipation building.

"Ten! Nine! Eight!"

I grab our coats from the coat check.

"Seven! Six! Five!"

Natalie's already at the door, but I catch her hand, pulling her gently to a stop.

"Four! Three!"

"Jake—"

"Two!"

I cup her face, forcing her to look at me.

"One! Happy New Year!"

And I kiss her. Right there in the hotel lobby, with the celebration erupting behind us, I kiss her like she's mine. Like this year mattered. Like the next one will too.

When I pull back, her eyes are wide, surprised.

"I'll take you home," I say quietly. "But I want you to know that I'm grateful you came into my life this year. And I'm excited about being with you in the next one."

Her eyes shine with tears she won't let fall. She just nods.

The drive back to her place is quiet. She stares out the window, and I don't try to coax any conversation out of her.

When I pull up to her bungalow and put the car in park, she finally speaks.

"Will you stay with me tonight?"

"Yes," I say immediately. Relief floods through me. "Of course I will."

twenty-eight

. . .

Natalie

I HAVEN'T SLEPT MORE than three hours a night since New Year's Eve. Every time I close my eyes, I see Rebecca's face. That unreadable expression. When she looked at my belly and said, "Let's talk when we're back at work."

Which is today. The nausea hits before I'm even out of bed, sharper than usual, my stomach churning with what I wish was only morning sickness but I know is pure dread. My phone lights up on the nightstand.

> JAKE
>
> Morning. You looked so peaceful, so I didn't want to wake you when I left. I left you some breakfast. Good luck today - call me when you can.

He's stayed with me all week offering reassurances and saying Rebecca won't fire me, that she's too smart for that, that my talent speaks for itself. But I'm not sure he gets it. It's not his fault, it's just that men never have to walk into rooms wondering if their career will implode the second someone notices their body.

I type back with shaking hands.

> NATALIE
> I will.

I force myself into the shower, letting the hot water beat against my shoulders, trying to wash away the exhaustion that's settled into my bones. The baby's been kicking constantly, like she knows I'm stressed. Like she's reminding me she's here, that this is real, that there's no going back now.

I press my hand to my stomach, feeling a flutter of movement beneath my palm. "We've got this," I whisper, though I'm not sure which one of us I'm trying to convince.

Getting dressed takes longer than it should. Every outfit feels wrong. Too tight across my belly, too obviously maternity, too much evidence of what I've been hiding. I finally settle on black leggings and an oversized sweater, the same uniform I've been wearing for weeks.

I'm sitting in my car outside the FlixPix offices, gripping my steering wheel and trying to remember how to breathe. I force myself out of the car and into the building. The elevator ride to the third floor feels like it takes a year. When I step out, the assistant at the desk gives me a sympathetic look.

"She's waiting for you in her office."

Great.

I walk down the hallway on shaky legs, past the writers' room where I've spent the last month proving myself, past the offices of other producers and executives, and straight to Rebecca's door at the end.

I stop outside, pressing my hand to my stomach. The baby kicks, a solid thump against my palm, and something in my chest loosens just a fraction. I knock.

"Come in."

Rebecca's sitting behind her desk, looking polished and professional as always. She gestures to the chair across from her.

"Close the door and sit down."

I sit, my heart hammering so hard I'm sure she can hear it. She studies me for a long moment, and I can't read her expression at all.

"How far along are you?" she asks finally.

"Six months. I'm due at the end of March."

Rebecca nods slowly. "Why didn't you tell me sooner?"

I take a breath. "I wanted to prove I could do the work first. That I deserved to be here. I didn't want you to think I was a liability or that I'd be distracted or—"

"That's not your call to make," Rebecca interrupts.

The words hit like a slap.

"I'm sorry, I just—"

"Do you know what makes a good writers' room work?" She leans forward. "Trust. Teamwork. Communication. You keeping this from me undermines all three."

Tears are already burning behind my eyes, but I force them back. "I know. I'm sorry."

"You should have told me. Not because I needed to plan around you, but because you deserved support, or possibly accommodations." She pauses. "Instead, you've been hiding in oversized sweaters and lying about why you won't eat sushi."

"I wasn't lying, I just—"

"Natalie." Rebecca's voice softens slightly. "I get it. I do. This industry is brutal to women. Especially women who want families. But you made a choice that affected more than just you."

I nod, unable to speak past the lump in my throat.

Rebecca sits back in her chair, and something shifts in her expression. Less anger, more weariness.

"I didn't have kids," she says quietly. "I chose this career instead. Every time I thought about starting a family, there was another show, another project, another opportunity I couldn't pass up. And now I'm forty-three and it's too late."

I wasn't expecting that. "Rebecca—"

She lifts her hand, indicating she's not finished talking. "I'm telling you this because you need to understand something. You can have both. You're allowed to have both. But only if you let people help you. Let me help you."

The tears spill over now, and I swipe at them angrily. Relief is crashing through me in waves, mixing with gratitude and something that feels like—*fuck me*—I think it feels like hope. Rebecca isn't firing me. She's supporting me. She's giving me exactly what I need, and I didn't even know how to ask for it.

My hand finds my stomach again, protective and instinctive. The baby shifts beneath my palm, and I think about what Rebecca just said. That she chose her career over having kids. That it's too late for her now. And here I am convinced I have to choose too.

But maybe I don't. Maybe she's right. Maybe I really can have both.

I wipe my face again. "I'm sorry. Hormones."

"Don't apologize for crying in my office. I've cried in here plenty." She opens her laptop. "Now let's figure out how we make this work."

"Make it work?"

"You think I'm firing you? Natalie, you're one of the best writers I've had in a room in years. I'm not letting you go because you're having a baby." She pulls up what looks like a production calendar. "Here's what I'm thinking. We push production."

"Push it?"

"Originally we were slated to start in April. But if we push to July, you can take maternity leave from April through June. Will that be enough? Can you come back in July?"

I stare at her. "You'd do that?"

"The network's flexible on timing. And honestly, another few months of prep won't hurt." She makes a note on her screen. "The writers' room will continue through March. We'll have all the scripts locked before you go on leave. Then when you come back in July, you'll be on set for production."

"I don't...I don't know what to say."

"Say you'll communicate with me from now on. If you're tired, if you need a break, if you're struggling—tell me. I can't help you if I don't know what you need."

"I will. I promise."

"Good." Rebecca closes her laptop and gives me a very direct look. "This job is hard. Pregnancy is hard. Doing both at once? Even harder. But I believe you can do it. I just need you to trust me enough to let me support you."

The tears are coming faster now, and I can't stop them. "Thank you. Really. Thank you."

"You're welcome. Now go get yourself together and meet me in the writers' room in twenty minutes. We have episodes to write."

I stand, wiping my face. "Rebecca?"

"Yeah?"

"I really am sorry. For not telling you sooner."

She nods. "I know. And for what it's worth, I'm excited for you. You're going to be a great mom."

When the meeting ends, I practically run to the bathroom, lock myself in a stall, and let myself fall apart. Relief crashes over me in waves. I'm not fired. They're supporting me. I get maternity leave.

When I can finally breathe again, I pull out my phone. My fingers hover over Jake's name for just a second before I press call. The realization hits me square in the chest that he's the first person I want to talk to.

He answers on the first ring. "How'd it go?"

His voice is low and warm and steady, and something in my chest cracks open. I close my eyes, picturing him at his desk, probably gripping his phone too tight, waiting to hear if I'm okay.

"I'm not fired."

"I told you." There's relief in his voice, thick and real. "What did she say?"

"They're pushing production to July. I'll have maternity leave from April through June."

"Nat, that's amazing."

The baby kicks hard, right beneath my ribs, like she's

celebrating too. I press my palm there, feeling her move, and a watery laugh escapes me.

"I was so scared, Jake. I thought she was going to tell me I wasn't committed enough or that I'd lied to her or—"

"But she didn't. You're okay. You did it."

I grab a few pieces of toilet paper, dabbing at my eyes even though more tears just keep coming. Happy tears this time. Relieved tears.

"She said I can have both," I whisper. "Career and baby. That I'm allowed to have both."

"You are. You deserve both."

I close my eyes, leaning against the stall door. The relief I feel is overwhelming. Somewhere deep down I didn't believe I could have it all. But Rebecca believes it. And Jake believes it.

Maybe I can start believing it too.

The baby kicks again, stronger this time, and I laugh through my tears. "She's kicking so much. Like she knows everything's going to be okay."

"She knows her mom's a badass."

"Okay," I say, as my throat tightens. "I need to get back to the writers' room."

"Okay. I'll see you tonight?"

"Yeah. Definitely."

"I'm really proud of you, Nat."

The words settle warm in my chest. "Thank you. For everything."

After we hang up, I clean myself up in the mirror. My eyes are red and my makeup is smudged, but I don't care. I fix what I can and head to the writers' room.

When I walk in, everyone looks up. The energy in the room shifts slightly, and I realize they must have heard I was meeting with Rebecca this morning.

"Hey," Bernard says carefully. "You good?"

"Yeah. I'm good."

Rebecca walks in behind me, coffee in hand. "Okay, people. Let's get to work. We have an episode to write."

And just like that, we're back to normal. Breaking stories, pitching jokes, building the world of *Spellbound*.

Around lunchtime, we break for the catered spread that's been set up in the corner. I'm loading my plate with more food than I've eaten in weeks when Priya appears beside me.

"So," she says quietly, "I take it the meeting went well?"

I glance at her. "How did you—"

"Rebecca called me in on Friday. Wanted to talk through production timeline adjustments." She grabs a sandwich. "Said we might be pushing our start date to accommodate a team member's maternity leave. Didn't take a genius to figure out who."

Heat floods my face. "Oh."

"If you want my take?" Priya leans closer, her voice warm. "I think it's badass that you're doing this while pregnant. Like, actual superhero levels of badass."

I smile despite myself. "Thank you."

On the drive home, I let myself feel it. All of it. The relief, the gratitude, the overwhelming sense that maybe, just maybe, things are going to be okay.

twenty-nine

. . .

Jake

I'M WAITING in the FlixPix parking lot when Natalie emerges from the building. She's walking slower these days, one hand at her lower back, the other cradling her belly. Seven months pregnant and still showing up every day, still breaking stories, still proving she can do it all.

She spots my car and smiles, and something warm settles under my ribs.

God, I love her. I'm completely gone for this woman.

This is our routine now. I pick her up when I can, drive her home, stay for dinner. We've been practically living at her place since right before Christmas. Her cozy bungalow is nice, and I know she's been slowly converting the guest room into a nursery, but with the baby coming, I keep thinking about space. About what comes next. And there's something I've been wanting to show her for weeks now.

She climbs into the passenger seat with a groan. "My feet are killing me."

"Long day?"

"We're on episode four. Everyone's getting punchy." She adjusts the seatbelt under her bump. "Bernard pitched a joke about menstrual blood being the key to unlocking the curse and Rebecca just stared at him for a full minute."

"Did she use it?"

"Shockingly, yes. With tweaks." She leans her head back. "How was your day?"

"Good. Closed the St. James deal. Ryan's pleased."

"That's great."

I pull out of the lot, but instead of heading toward her place, I take the highway north.

It takes her a few minutes to notice. "Where are we going?"

"My place."

She sits up a little straighter. "Your place?"

"Yeah. I want to show you something."

She quiets, and I can feel her watching me. She hasn't been to my house since that night months ago, the night that got us here.

"I've only been to your place once," she says. "I'm not sure I remember much besides your bedroom."

I grin. "Well, you'll get the full tour this time."

"Should I be nervous?"

"Why would you be nervous?"

"This feels very deliberate."

"It is deliberate," I say. "Just not in a scary way."

"Now I'm definitely nervous."

I reach over, take her hand. "Trust me."

She threads her fingers through mine. "Okay."

When I pull into the driveway and turn off the engine, she stares up at the house, taking it in slowly, quietly.

"Come on," I say softly. "I'll show you inside."

I help her out of the car, and we walk up the front path. Inside, the entry opens into a wide, light-filled space—hardwood floors, high ceilings, and the living room flows into the dining area and kitchen.

"Wow," she says under her breath. "This is so much bigger than my place."

"Three bedrooms, two and a half baths. Bought it earlier this year. After the divorce."

She wanders into the living room, fingers brushing the back of the couch. "I love the fireplace."

"It's gas. Easy to use. Nice on cold mornings."

She moves to the windows overlooking the backyard. "I remember this backyard. Beautiful."

"There's plenty of space for a swing set or sandbox or whatever she needs."

She turns toward me, something unreadable flickering in her expression.

"Come upstairs," I say quietly. "There's something I want to show you."

I lead her up the staircase. The guest room is on the left. My room at the end of the hall. But it's the room on the right I open.

The nursery.

Soft lavender walls. The crib that matches the one at her house. A changing table. A bookshelf filled with baby books and toys and more space for whatever she ends up loving.

Natalie's hand lifts to her mouth.

"Jake," she whispers.

"I know we haven't talked about custody or any of the logistics." I keep my voice low. "But I want her to have a space here. A room that's hers. So when she's with me, she's not just visiting."

The words feel wrong even as I say them. When she's with me. Like we'll be handing her back and forth, splitting time, dividing our daughter's life into shifts.

It's not what I want. What I want is Natalie here every night. The baby down the hall. All of us under one roof, building something real together.

She steps inside like she's afraid she'll disturb the air. She touches the crib rail, gentle and careful.

"This is perfect," she says quietly.

"You think so?"

"Yeah. It's exactly what I pictured."

I lean against the doorframe, watching her hand drift over her belly. Everything about her in this moment makes something tighten in my chest.

"Nat," I say. "Can I say something?"

She looks up immediately. "Of course."

"I know you love your place. And Blair's been a great landlord. But I've been thinking..." I exhale, trying to find the right words. "You're renting month to month."

"Yeah."

"And after the baby comes, after maternity leave, you're going to need support. Someone who can help with the day-to-day."

She's watching me without blinking.

"I have space," I say, crossing to stand in front of her.

"Real space. A house that can be a home for all of us. I'm not asking for an answer now. I'm just putting it out there. If you ever want to live here. With me."

Her eyes go wide, soft, almost startled. "Jake..."

"I'm not rushing you," I say quickly. "I just want you to know the option exists."

She looks around the room and then back at me.

"Can I think about it?"

"Of course. Take however long you need."

She touches the crib again before turning toward me.

"Thank you," she says. "For this. For thinking about her. For...everything."

"Always."

We grab takeout on the way back to her place and spread it across the coffee table the way we do most nights. She curls into the corner of the couch with her laptop, working on notes for tomorrow's session. I settle into the armchair with my laptop, reviewing a contract.

It's domestic in a way I never had with Lauren. Lauren lived everywhere but home. Natalie lives here, in the moment, in the work, in the connection. Even when she doesn't say it out loud.

Around nine, I notice her laptop has gone still. Her eyes are closed, her head tipped back against the cushion. I set my computer aside and cross to her silently. She's out, one hand curved protectively over her belly. I close her laptop, set it gently on the table, then slide an arm behind her back and another under her knees.

She stirs. "Jake?"

"I've got you. Just taking you to bed."

She burrows into my chest. "You smell good."

I smile, carry her down the hall. I get the covers back one-handed and lay her down gently. She's already in her pajamas, so I leave her as she is. I pull the blanket up, kiss her forehead.

"Stay," she murmurs.

"I'm staying."

I change quickly, then climb into bed beside her. She immediately rolls into me, fitting her body to mine like it's instinct. Her belly presses against my side, warm and real and full of our daughter. The baby kicks against my side.

"What do you think?" I whisper, brushing my thumb over the curve. "Think your mom's ready for more?"

Another kick.

I take it as a yes.

thirty

. . .

Natalie

THE STUDIO for *On the Red Carpet* is smaller than I expected. Just a soundproof room with two microphones, some recording equipment, and Jess sitting across from me with her notes and a warm smile.

"You ready?" she asks, adjusting her headphones.

"As I'll ever be."

"Don't be nervous. This is going to be great. You're a natural storyteller."

"I write stories. I don't usually tell them about myself."

"Same skill set." She glances at her producer through the glass window. He gives her a thumbs up. "Okay, we're recording in three, two, one..."

The red light blinks on. "Welcome back to *On the Red Carpet*, the podcast where we pull back the curtain on Hollywood's biggest stories. I'm Jess Lexington, and today I have a very special guest. My friend, the incredibly talented screenwriter Natalie Cruz, creator of the upcoming FlixPix series *Spellbound* is here. Natalie, welcome."

"Thanks for having me, Jess."

"So let's dive right in. *Spellbound* has been generating a lot of buzz. Can you tell our listeners what the show is about?"

I take a breath, settling into the familiar territory of talking about my work, and explain the premise.

"It sounds incredible. How would you say it's different than other supernatural shows airing right now?"

"At the heart of the show are hints of generational trauma, a little of what it means to be a woman with power in a world that wants to control you, and how family can be both your greatest strength and your deepest wound."

"Well, you've managed to hit all of the heavy, political, and controversial themes in one go. What made you want to tell this particular story?"

"I've always been drawn to stories about women who are told they're too much—too powerful, too emotional, too ambitious. Magic felt like the perfect metaphor for exploring that."

Jess nods, making notes. "What's it been like going from solo writer to writers' room?"

"Honestly? Terrifying and exhilarating. I'm not the showrunner—that's Rebecca Sullivan, who's incredible—but being a producer and having creative input on every episode has been a dream. Our writers' room is phenomenal. Everyone brings such unique perspectives."

"Speaking of the writers' room, production was originally scheduled to start in March but got pushed to July. Can you talk about why?"

Here it comes. This is why I'm interviewing with Jess today. She wanted to acknowledge some of the biases I feared about being pregnant and writing on this show. She feels like anything we can do to help reduce the stigma is imperative.

"Yeah. So, as you can probably see—" I gesture to my very pregnant belly "—I'm having a baby. Due at the end of March. We pushed production so I could take maternity leave."

"That's a pretty significant accommodation. How did FlixPix and Rebecca react when you told them?"

I choose my words carefully. "Rebecca was incredibly supportive. She and the network worked with me to create a timeline that works for everyone."

"But you didn't tell them right away, did you?"

I should have known Jess wouldn't let me off that easy. "No, I didn't. I was about twelve weeks along when I signed my contract, and I didn't tell anyone until after the new year."

"Why not?"

"I was scared. This industry has a history of sidelining women who get pregnant. I wanted to prove I could do the work first, that I deserved to be there, before giving them a reason to doubt me."

"That's a lot of pressure to put on yourself."

"It is. But it's also the reality for a lot of women in this business. We're constantly asked to choose between our careers and our personal lives in ways men never are."

Jess leans forward slightly. "When you did tell Rebecca, how did that conversation go?"

"It was hard. She was understandably frustrated that I'd kept it from her for so long. She said it undermined trust and communication, which are essential in a writers' room. And she was right."

"But she also supported you."

"She did. More than I could have hoped for. She told me something that really stuck with me—that I'm allowed to have both. A career and a family. That I don't have to choose."

"That's remarkably supportive," Jess says.

"It was. Rebecca's been an incredible mentor and advocate. I'm really lucky to work with her."

"Do you think your experience—hiding your pregnancy, being afraid of the consequences—do you think that's common in Hollywood?"

"Absolutely. I've talked to other women writers, actresses, directors who've all felt the same pressure. There's this unspoken expectation that you have to be one hundred percent available, one hundred percent of the time, or you're not serious about your career. And pregnancy is seen as a liability."

"What would you say to women who are facing that same fear?"

"I'd say find people who support you. Build a team that values you as a whole person, not just as a content generator. And don't be afraid to advocate for yourself, even when it's scary. Because you deserve to have it all if you want it." I pause. "I'd also say, if you are a woman, it's imperative we support each other."

"That's beautiful advice. And in the words of the late, great Madeline Albright, 'there's a special place in hell for women who don't help other women.'" Jess laughs. "Okay, let's talk about the show itself. *Spellbound* premieres in the fall. What can viewers expect?"

We spend the next twenty minutes diving into the show—the casting process, the tone, what makes it different from other supernatural dramas. By the time Jess wraps up the interview, I'm feeling good. Proud, even.

"That was perfect," she says as the producer signals we're done recording. "You're a natural."

"That wasn't as terrifying as I thought it would be."

"See? I told you." She takes off her headphones. "Want to grab coffee or tea? We can go off the record."

"Sure."

We head to the coffee shop next door and settle into a corner table.

"So," Jess says, stirring her latte. "How are things with Jake?"

I should have seen this coming. "Things are good."

"Just good?"

"Really good. Great, actually."

"Blair says you two are basically living together."

"We're not living together. He just stays over a lot."

"Every night, from what I hear."

I laugh. "Okay, most nights. But it's not official or anything."

"Are you going to move in together? After the baby's born?"

The question catches me off guard. "I don't know. We haven't really talked about it."

"But you've thought about it."

"Of course I've thought about it. But I'm trying not to get

ahead of myself. Things are going well right now, and I don't want to rush into something just because it's convenient."

Jess studies me over her coffee. "What are you afraid of?"

"Who says I'm afraid?"

"Nat. Come on."

I sigh, running my finger along the edge of my cup. Everyone has always told me what a force Jess is, I'm starting to understand what they mean.

"I just want to prioritize the baby right now. Figure out how to be a mom before I worry about being a girlfriend or whatever Jake and I are."

"You can be both."

"I know that intellectually. But emotionally? I'm not there yet, and I like where we are. I need to focus on her. Make sure I'm doing this right before I add anything else to the equation."

"And Jake's okay with that?"

"He seems to be. He's been incredibly patient."

"He's in love with you, you know."

The words land like a physical blow. My heart stutters, then kicks into overdrive. Heat floods my face, crawls down my neck.

"He hasn't said that."

But even as I say it, I know it's true. I've known for weeks, maybe longer. The way he looks at me. The way he shows up every single day without asking for anything in return. The nursery he built. The groceries he sends. The way he holds me at night like I'm something precious.

"He doesn't have to. It's obvious to everyone who sees you two together."

"Jess—"

"I'm not trying to pressure you. I'm just saying, when a guy shows up the way Jake shows up for you? That's love. And maybe it's worth letting yourself feel it back."

I want to. God, I want to so badly it scares me. I want to let myself fall completely, to trust that he'll catch me. But what if I'm wrong? What if this is just him being a good guy, doing the right thing because I'm carrying his baby? What if I let myself believe this is real and it all falls apart?

"I'm not ready."

The words taste like a lie. Or maybe like fear dressed up as truth.

Jess reaches across the table and squeezes my hand. "I'm not trying to tell you what to do. I just want you to be happy. And from where I'm sitting, it looks like Jake makes you happy."

"He does."

"Ok then, tell me about baby names. Have you guys decided yet?"

We spend the next hour on lighter topics like name options, nursery colors, and the terrifying reality of labor and delivery. By the time we part ways, I'm feeling lighter.

But Jess's words stick with me.

He's in love with you.

And somewhere deep down, underneath all the fear and doubt and self-protection, I know the truth.

I'm in love with him too.

thirty-one

. . .

Jake

I'M STILL shocked Natalie agreed to come to my house. We haven't been back since I showed her the nursery, and honestly, I wasn't sure she'd say yes when I asked her to dinner tonight.

I take the salmon out of the oven and set the pan on the stovetop to rest. It looks good. Crisp edges, center still soft. I check one piece with the back of my fork to make sure it flakes but doesn't fall apart. Perfect.

The table's already set. I probably went overboard on the flowers, but if that's the worst thing I do tonight, we're fine. I check my phone on the counter, look at the text that came in about twenty minutes ago.

> **NATALIE**
> Just leaving the office. Be there in 20.

> **JAKE**
> Drive safe.

She should be here any minute. I adjust the oven to low

so the salmon stays warm, toss the salad one more time, double-check the dessert in the fridge. We've basically been living together since just before Christmas. She never said no when I floated the idea of her and the baby moving in. She just said she needed time. And in the weeks since, we've slipped into a life that already feels like the answer.

Tonight is about saying it out loud.

I open the drawer by the stairs, touch the small velvet box resting there, then close it again. My heart kicks a little harder, but my hands are steady.

Headlights sweep across the front windows. I wipe my palms on a towel, take one slow breath, and walk to the door. When I open it, she's there on the porch in leggings and one of her oversized blazer jackets, hand automatically resting at the top of her stomach like it's second nature. Her hair is down, the ends curling from the day, her bag slipping off her shoulder.

"Hey," I say, and this time my voice comes out even. I step forward to grab her bag.

"Hey yourself," she says, a small smile tugging at her mouth. "Something smells good."

Her gaze slips past me into the house and I watch as her eyes dart across the space looking at the candles, the flowers, and the decorated table.

She hesitates in the doorway. "What's all this?"

"Dinner," I say. "Come in."

She steps over the threshold and, for a second, her shoulders tense, like her body clocks something before her brain catches up.

"It's Valentine's Day," I say quietly.

"I didn't know we did Valentine's Day."

"We can start."

Something shifts in her expression and her shoulders relax. "Okay," she says finally. "The flowers are beautiful."

"Let me grab your drink, then we'll sit."

I get the sparkling cider and pour it into flutes.

"You look nice," I say, setting her glass down.

She glances up at me, surprised. "My work clothes?"

"You look good in everything."

Color warms her cheeks. "You clean up nicely too."

I serve the salad, salmon, the rice, and the roasted vegetables. She watches me for a second, then looks down at her plate.

"Did you work today?" she asks, looking at the spread like maybe I didn't cook all of this.

"I did," I say. I take the seat across from her.

Her eyes flick to mine, then away. She picks up her fork, takes a careful bite. "This is really good," she says. "I'm impressed."

She tells me about her day, and I share mine. It feels easy. Familiar. The thing I want every night for the rest of my life.

When we're finished, I clear the plates and serve her favorite bakery cake I picked up on the way home from the office.

She raises an eyebrow when she sees it. "Okay, now I'm suspicious," she says. "What did you do?"

"Nothing," I say. "Yet."

She narrows her eyes at the "yet," but she takes a bite and closes her eyes for a second, clearly appreciating the sugar hit.

We finish, and for a moment I just watch her. The way

her hand moves absently over her belly while she listens. The way she looks around my house like she's starting to get familiar with it.

"Come sit with me," I say, nodding toward the living room. "I want to talk to you."

There it is. The shift. Her shoulders straighten. Her hand stills. She hears what I didn't say.

"Okay," she says carefully.

We move to the couch. She settles into the corner, angled slightly toward me, her feet tucked under her, one hand at her side, the other resting over the baby. I sit close, but not crowding her.

For a second, I just take her in. The woman I'm in love with sitting in my living room, carrying our daughter.

"I've been thinking a lot," I begin.

Her mouth tips knowingly. "That sounds serious."

"It is," I admit. "But I'd like you to hear me out."

"Okay."

"When we first talked about this—about keeping things simple, being co-parents, not making it more complicated than it had to be—I agreed. Mostly, I didn't want to push you into anything. I didn't want you to feel trapped with me just because of the baby."

She swallows, eyes on my face.

"But since before Christmas, we've been living something completely different," I continue. "I pick you up from work. We eat dinner together. We fall asleep together. We wake up together. We talk about our days. We've planned her room. Her name. Her future. That's not casual, Nat. That's building a life together."

Her eyes shine a little, but she doesn't look away.

"You didn't say no when I asked you to think about moving in," I say quietly. "You said you needed time, but babe, we're running out of time, and I'd like to make it official, to make it real."

I stand, my heartbeat steady now instead of jumping, and cross to the drawer by the stairs where I left the ring box. When I turn back, she's watching me, completely still.

"Jake," she says, and my name sounds more like a warning.

I drop to one knee in front of her. Her hand flies to her mouth.

"Let me say it," I ask. "Just once. All the way through."

She's frozen, so I take advantage of the silence.

"I'm in love with you," I say. The words land between us, heavy and clear. "Not because this got complicated or because there's a baby on the way. I love you. I see the person I want to come home to. The person I want to fight with and make up with and fall asleep next to every single night. When I'm with you, I'm steadier. Better. Calmer in a way I didn't know I could be. You're the first person I've ever been with where nothing feels performative or fragile. It just feels right. It feels like home. You make my life feel...whole."

A tear slips down her cheek. She doesn't move to wipe it away.

"I love our life," I say. "The one we're already living. And I want to build on it. I want you and the baby here. With me. Not as my roommate. Not as my co-parent who happens to share my bed. As my partner. As my wife."

I open the box. The ring catches the light. It's simple,

elegant, something I could picture on her hand from the first moment I saw it.

"Natalie," I say, my voice steady, "will you marry me?"

For a moment, everything in the room goes very quiet. Even the clock on the wall seems to pause.

Her eyes are locked on the ring, then on me. I watch the shift I know too well. Her shoulders tighten, her eyes look vacant, and her lips shift into a forced grin.

"Jake," she whispers, and my name sounds like it hurts.

Something cold settles in my gut, but I keep my voice steady.

"You don't have to answer this second," I say gently. "But I needed you to know where I am. I needed you to know this isn't an accident I'm just managing. This is what I want. You. Her. Us. Permanently."

Her throat works around words that take a moment to form.

"I thought we agreed," she says finally, her voice rough, "that we were just co-parenting. That we weren't doing this."

The words hit harder than they should. We've been living together in everything but name for months. I've been inside her, held her while she slept, felt our daughter kick against my hand. And she's calling it co-parenting.

I swallow hard, force myself to stay calm. "What we said," I correct quietly, "and what we've been living aren't the same thing."

Her eyes flash, something like panic or anger or pure fear surfacing for the first time. "You knew from the beginning," she says. "I told you I don't do relationships. Not like this."

My jaw tightens. I flex my fingers, releasing the tension before it can show in my voice.

"You say that," I answer, still calm, "but you've been in one with me for months."

"That's not fair."

"Is it not true?"

She looks away. She's shaking now, small tremors she's trying to control.

Every instinct tells me to stand, to pull her close, to make her see what we have. But I stay on one knee, the ring box still open, my heart pounding against my ribs like it's trying to break free.

"I'm not trying to trap you," I say, and my voice comes out lower now, rougher. "I'm not asking you to play house because it's tidy before the baby comes. I'm asking because I love you and I want you."

"I can't do this," she says.

Something cracks in my chest. The pain is sharp and immediate, but I keep my expression neutral. "Can't say yes right now?" I ask. "Or can't even think about it?"

"It's all too much," she says, shaking her head. "Work. The show. The baby. Everyone having opinions about how I should do everything. I feel like I'm barely keeping my head above water and you're asking me to stand at the altar again and—I have to go."

The mention of the altar makes my stomach drop.

"I'm not him," I say softly, and it takes everything I have to keep the frustration out of my voice. "I'm not going to disappear. I'm not going to leave you standing there alone."

She's breathing fast now. I can see her pulling away one piece at a time.

"I need space," she says suddenly.

The words land like a punch to the gut. My hand tightens around the ring box, the velvet crushing under my grip.

"Space?" I repeat.

"I need to think," she says. "I need to figure out how to be a mom without also trying to be someone's fiancée. I barely recognize myself right now. I can't make a decision like this when I don't even know who I am in this version of my life."

I stand slowly, closing the ring box with a quiet snap. The sound has a feeling of finality to it.

"Nat—"

She pushes to her feet, slower than she used to, one hand braced on the arm of the couch, the other over her stomach. "I think we might need to take a step back," she adds, and that's the one that really cuts. "Just for a while. So I'm not making choices because there's a clock ticking."

My throat feels tight. I swallow hard, force myself to nod.

"For how long?" I ask, and my voice comes out quieter than I intended.

"I don't know." Her eyes gloss again.

The not knowing is worse than a clean no. It leaves everything suspended, uncertain, like I'm supposed to just wait while she decides if I'm worth the risk.

"I'm sorry," she whispers. "I really am."

She reaches for her bag, fingers fumbling with the strap.

My chest aches. Every muscle in my body wants to move, to stop her, to make her stay and talk this through. But I stand there, holding the ring box, watching her pull away from everything we've built.

"I never wanted to make you feel cornered," I say, and I have to work to keep my voice level. "That wasn't the point of tonight."

"I know," she says, and for the first time since I opened the ring box, she steps closer, resting a hand on my arm. The touch is brief but real. "You were trying to give me something solid. I'm just not there yet."

She hesitates at the door, fingers tightening around the handle. For a second, I think she might turn back, say something different. She doesn't. The door closes behind her with a soft click.

For a long time I stay where I am, the house suddenly too quiet. The table still set. The flowers still perfect. The candles burned down to stubs. I set the ring box on the mantel and press the heels of my hands against my eyes.

The frustration burns hot in my chest, mixing with the hurt, with the fear that maybe she'll never be ready. That no matter how much I show up, how patient I am, how much I love her, it won't matter. Because she's still running from something I can't fight. If love and showing up aren't enough to make her feel safe, what is?

thirty-two

. . .

Natalie

MY MOM'S house smells like coffee and cinnamon rolls.

It's been eight days since Jake proposed. Eight days since I walked out of his house and left him standing there with a ring box in his hand and devastation written across his face.

Eight days of silence.

No texts. No calls. No showing up at my door with groceries or takeout or that stupidly perfect smile that always made my defenses crack just a little.

Nothing.

I haven't slept more than a few hours at a time since that night. My bed feels too big, too empty, too cold without him taking up half the space and pulling me against his chest in the middle of the night. I keep reaching for him in my sleep, my hand finding only empty sheets and the sharp reminder that I did this. I chose this.

And I'm miserable.

I sit at her kitchen table, the same one at which I ate breakfast growing up, and watch her move around the kitchen with the ease of someone who's done this a thousand times. I came here because I didn't know where else to go. Because my house felt suffocating and I needed someone to tell me I'm not ruining my life.

"You want another one?" she asks, gesturing to the cinnamon roll on my plate.

"I shouldn't. I've already had two."

"You're eating for two."

"That's a myth, Mom. I'm supposed to eat like three hundred extra calories a day, not double everything."

She sits down across from me with her coffee, giving me that look mothers perfect over decades of practice. "You look tired."

"I haven't been sleeping."

"Why not?"

I press my hand to my belly, feeling the baby shift beneath my palm. "She moves a lot at night. Keeps me up."

It's not entirely a lie. The baby does move at night. But that's not why I can't sleep.

I can't sleep because every time I close my eyes, I see Jake's face. The way he looked at me when I said I needed space. The hurt he tried to hide. The ring box closing with that quiet snap that sounded like an ending.

"That's not what I mean," she says gently.

I take a sip of my decaf tea, avoiding her eyes. "Work's been intense. We finished breaking all season one episodes last week. It's the mad rush before our deadline."

"That's exciting."

"It's surreal to see it all come together. Like, these were

just ideas in my head a year ago, and now we're about to have eight full scripts ready to shoot."

"I'm so proud of you, sweetie."

"Thanks, Mom."

"And how's the baby? Everything good?"

"Everything's great. She's measuring right on track. And she's very active." As if on cue, I shift in my chair, the baby pressing against my ribs. "Dr. Nelson says everything looks perfect for a late March delivery."

Mom nods, taking a sip of her coffee. "And how's Jake?"

It takes me a minute to answer. "Fine."

She gives me that look again. The one that says she knows I'm lying. "Fine?" she repeats.

"Yeah. Fine."

"Natalie."

I set down my mug. "Can we not do this right now?"

"Do what?"

"The thing where you ask me questions you already know the answers to."

"I don't know the answers. That's why I'm asking." But her expression has shifted from casual to concerned. "What happened?"

I close my eyes. I haven't told anyone about Valentine's Day. Not even my friends. I've been carrying it around for a week, this heavy thing sitting on my chest, making it hard to breathe.

"He told me he loved me," I say finally.

Mom goes very still. "And?"

"And asked me to marry him."

I see the shock hit her face and watch as she tries to put on her professionally neutral face.

"When was this?"

"Last week. Valentine's Day. He cooked this whole dinner, had flowers and candles." My throat tightens. "He got down on one knee and told me he loved me. That he wanted us to be a family. That I made his life feel whole."

The memory makes my chest ache. Because he meant it. Every word. I could see it in his eyes, hear it in his voice. Jake loves me. Really, truly loves me. And instead of letting myself feel the joy of that, the wonder of being loved by someone like him, I ran.

"What did you say?"

"I told him I needed space."

"Space," Mom repeats, her voice neutral.

"I panicked, okay? He just sprang it on me, and I wasn't ready, and I needed time to think."

But that's not entirely true either. Of course he thought I was ready. Because I've been acting like I was ready. I just couldn't say it out loud when it mattered.

"Have you talked to him since?"

"No."

"Has he tried to contact you?"

"No."

And God, that hurts more than I expected. Part of me thought he'd push. That he'd show up at my door, refuse to let me shut him out, fight for us the way he's been fighting since the beginning.

But he didn't. He gave me exactly what I asked for.

Space.

And that's what's killing me. The silence. The absence of him. It's been a week of nothing, and it feels worse than being left at the altar. Because this time, I'm the one who left. I'm the one who hurt someone who didn't deserve it. Someone good and kind and patient. Someone who has been showing up for me every single day since the moment he found out I was pregnant. Someone I'm in love with.

Mom is quiet for a long moment, just watching me. Then she asks, "Do you love him?"

"It doesn't matter."

"That's not what I asked."

I stare down at my coffee. My hands are shaking slightly, and I press them flat against the table to steady them. "I don't know. Maybe. Probably. Yes. I think I've loved him for a while now. And that's what scares me the most."

"So you left him instead."

"I didn't leave him. We'll still co-parent. We just won't... we're not doing the relationship thing."

"You're already doing the relationship thing, Natalie. You've been doing it for months. You just won't call it that."

I don't have an answer for that.

Mom leans forward, her elbows on the table. "Can I tell you something?"

"Do I have a choice?"

"No," she replies, but she's smiling slightly. "What Darren did to you was terrible. The hurt and humiliation you felt were very real. I watched you go through that, and it broke my heart."

"Mom—"

"But you survived it. More than survived—you thrived.

You found your own place, built a career, sold your show. You never let that pain stop you from going after what you wanted." She pauses. "So why are you letting it stop you now?"

"Because this is different."

"How?"

"Because I have a baby to think about. It's not just me anymore. If I let myself love Jake and it doesn't work out, it affects her too."

Mom sits back in her chair, considering. "Having a baby is the biggest risk you'll ever take. There are no guarantees. You could do everything right and still face challenges you never imagined. But you didn't let that stop you from wanting her, did you?"

"That's not the same thing."

"Isn't it? You're about to love someone more than you've ever loved anyone in your life. This baby is going to have the power to hurt you in ways Darren never could. And you're choosing it anyway."

I open my mouth to argue, but nothing comes out.

"Life doesn't come with guarantees. You could go to the store to buy ingredients for a cake and get home and realize all the eggs are bad. You could get in your car to drive somewhere important and get a flat tire on the way. Bad things can happen at any time. But you don't let those thoughts stop you from grocery shopping or driving, do you?"

"Maybe." I say. And she gives me the look all moms have perfected when they think their child is being ridiculous. I try to explain. "But love—"

"Love is the same. Yes, it might not work out. Yes, you might get hurt. But refusing to try because you're afraid?

That's just another kind of pain. A slower, quieter kind. The kind that eats away at you until you wake up one day and realize you built a whole life around fear."

I feel tears burning behind my eyes. "What if I'm not brave enough?"

"You're brave enough to have a baby by yourself. You're brave enough to build a career in one of the hardest industries in the world. You're brave enough to face down a writers' room full of strangers and prove you belong there." Mom reaches across the table and takes my hand. "You're brave enough for this too. You're just choosing not to be."

"I don't know how to do it differently."

"Yes, you do. You just have to decide that the possibility of happiness is worth the risk of pain."

We sit in silence for a moment. The baby kicks hard, and I press my hand to my belly.

I swipe at the tears on my face. "I don't know what to do."

"You don't have to know right now. But you do have to think about what you actually want, not just what you're afraid of." She stands, coming around the table to pull me into a hug. "And whatever you decide, I've got your back."

I let myself sink into her embrace, breathing in the familiar scent of her perfume and laundry detergent. "What if I ruin it?" I whisper.

"What if you don't?"

When I finally pull away, Mom brushes the hair back from my face like she used to do when I was little. "You want to stay for lunch? I was going to make enchiladas."

"Yeah. I'd like that."

We spend the rest of the afternoon cooking together,

talking about safer things, pretending I'm not having a complete romantic crisis, but Mom's words stay with me, echoing in the back of my mind.

You just have to decide that the possibility of happiness is worth the risk of pain.

And maybe, for the first time, I'm willing to risk it.

When I leave that evening, Mom walks me to my car. "Think about what I said," she tells me.

"I will."

"And Natalie? Don't wait too long. Good men who love you the way Jake does? They don't come around often."

I nod, not trusting myself to speak.

On the drive home, I keep replaying the conversation. Mom's voice mixing with my own doubts, my fears, the small, quiet hope I've been trying to ignore. The baby kicks, strong and insistent, and I press my hand to my belly.

"What do you think?" I ask her. "Am I being an idiot?"

She kicks again, and I take it as a yes.

thirty-three

. . .

Jake

"YOU'RE NOT EATING."

My mom sets a plate of scrambled eggs in front of me. I've been sitting at her kitchen table for twenty minutes, staring out the window at the frozen backyard. The oak tree I used to climb as a kid is bare, branches black against the February sky.

I flew out here eight days ago. Called Wyatt after Natalie left, told him what happened. That I'd proposed. That she'd walked out. That I needed to get away before I did something stupid like show up at her door and start begging.

"Go see your mom," Wyatt had said. "Take a few days. Clear your head."

So I booked a flight for the next morning. Didn't tell Natalie I was leaving. What would I even say? She asked for space. I'm giving her space.

Even if it's killing me.

"I'm not hungry."

"You haven't been hungry since you got here." She sits down across from me, her own coffee untouched. "Jake."

I force myself to look at her. At sixty-three, Linda Reyes is still sharp, still sees through every defense I've ever tried to build. She's wearing her favorite jeans and one of my dad's old flannel shirts that she's had for thirty years and refuses to throw away.

"I don't know what you want me to say, Mom."

"I want you to tell me what happened. The real version, not whatever you said on the phone when you told me you were coming to visit."

I pick up my fork, push the eggs around. They're perfect, the way she's always made them—fluffy, with just a little cheese. My childhood breakfast. But they taste like nothing. "I told Natalie I loved her."

Mom is quiet. Waiting.

"Valentine's Day. I cooked dinner, finished the nursery. I had this whole plan." The words feel heavy in my mouth. "I proposed to her. Had a ring. I asked her to move in with me. Told her I wanted us to be a real family."

"What did she say?"

"She said she needed space." I set the fork down. "It's been a week. Haven't heard from her since."

"Have you tried calling?"

"She asked for space. I'm giving her space."

"Jake—"

"What am I supposed to do?" My voice comes out sharper than I intend. "Chase after her? Beg? I put myself out there. I told her everything. And she walked out."

Mom is quiet for a long moment, her hands wrapped

around her mug. Outside, a cardinal lands on the bird feeder, a shock of red against the gray morning.

"You know what I remember most about your father?" she says finally.

The shift catches me off guard. "What?"

"How patient he was. When we first started dating, I was terrified. I'd been hurt before, badly, and I kept waiting for him to prove he was just like the others." She looks at me. "He didn't push. He just showed up. Every day. Until I finally believed him."

"Natalie's not going to believe me, Mom. She's convinced everyone leaves. And now I pushed too hard and she ran."

"Did you push too hard? Or did you just finally tell her the truth?"

I don't have an answer for that.

"She's having my daughter in less than a month," I say quietly. "And I'm in love with her. Not just because of the baby. Because of her." My throat tightens.

"But I can't make her love me back. I can't make her trust me. And I'm terrified that I'm going to spend the rest of my life co-parenting with a woman I'm in love with, watching her eventually find someone else. Some guy who she'll let in because enough time has passed and she's not scared anymore. And my daughter will have a stepfather who gets to be there for all of it while I'm just the every-other-weekend dad who—"

I have to stop. The words are choking me.

My chest feels tight, like there's a weight pressing down on my ribs. I stand abruptly, the chair scraping against the floor. The kitchen walls feel like they're closing in.

I pace to the window, back to the table, my hands clenching and unclenching at my sides. Everything inside me is chaos. Thoughts crashing into each other, none of them making sense, all of them leading back to the same place.

Natalie walking out. The door closing. The silence.

I press the heel of my hand against my chest, trying to ease the pressure there. It doesn't help.

Mom reaches across the table, but I'm already moving, needing space, needing air. "You're not going to be the every-other-weekend dad. You're already not that. You're building a nursery, showing up for appointments, learning how to love your baby's mother."

"But what if it's not enough? What if I do everything right and she still won't let me in?"

"Then you love your daughter and you keep showing up for Natalie anyway. Not because you expect something back, but because that's what love is. It's showing up even when it's hard."

"I don't know if I can do that. Watch her live her life without me in it. Not the way I want it to be."

"You're stronger than you think."

"I don't feel strong. I feel like I'm barely holding it together."

The words come out rough, scraped raw. I can't breathe. I need to get out of this house.

Mom stands, concern clear on her face. "Then fall apart. You're allowed to fall apart. Just don't give up on her yet."

The kitchen suddenly feels too small, too warm. "I need to go for a run."

"Jake, it's twenty-eight degrees out there."

"I need to clear my head."

I need open sky. Fresh air. Something other than these four walls and the spiral of my own thoughts.

"At least eat something first—"

"I'm fine, Mom."

I'm already moving toward the stairs, toward my old bedroom where my running gear is. I can feel her watching me, can sense all the things she wants to say but doesn't.

The cold hits my lungs like knives.

I head toward the beach path, the route I've run since high school. Surfside in February is dead—summer homes shuttered, the beach empty except for a few brave souls walking dogs. The wind off the Long Island Sound is bitter, slicing through my running jacket.

My feet find the rhythm. Left, right, left, right. Breathe in, breathe out.

I think about the nursery at my house. The crib I assembled, the mobile I hung, the bookshelf I filled. All of it waiting for a baby who'll visit but never really live there. Not the way I imagined.

I think about Natalie's face when she saw it. The tears in her eyes. The way she said "You did this for our little girl" like she couldn't believe someone would.

I think about waking up without her these past few days. The bed too big, the house too quiet, the mornings too empty.

I think about the next eighteen years. Coordinating schedules, splitting holidays, being polite and careful with each other. About dropping my daughter off and watching Natalie close the door. About birthday parties where we're both there, but not together. About some future version of this where she brings a date to our daughter's soccer game and I have to shake his hand and pretend I'm fine.

About my daughter calling someone else Dad.

The thought makes my chest tight, makes it hard to breathe, and I'm running faster now, trying to outrun the images in my head.

The path curves inland, away from the water. There's a section here that cuts through some trees, mostly pines, the ground uneven where roots have pushed up through the pavement over the years.

I'm not paying attention. Not to where I'm putting my feet, not to the patches of ice from last night's freeze, not to anything except the spiral of thoughts I can't escape.

What if this is it? What if I did everything right and it still wasn't enough? What if she never—

My foot hits something.

The world tilts sideways.

I'm falling and there's nothing to grab, nothing to stop it. My body hits the frozen ground hard—shoulder first, then my wrist as I try to brace myself against the blow.

The crack is audible.

Then my head.

The impact sends white light exploding through my vision. Pain, sharp and immediate, radiating from the back of my skull.

A low groan escapes me before I even realize it's coming. My chest heaves, breaths choppy and uneven, shallow. Nausea coils tight in my gut, threatening to turn me inside out.

The sky above me is gray. The trees are spinning, or I'm spinning, I can't tell which.

I try to move and the world lurches violently. Everything tilts. My fingers twitch, flexing weakly like they're testing whether they still work. My hand moves toward my pocket but finds nothing. Did I bring my phone? Can't remember.

This is bad.

Everything feels wrong.

The edges of my vision darken, closing in like a tunnel. My eyelids flutter, each blink slow and heavy, taking effort I don't have. Cold seeps through my clothes, the icy ground penetrating fabric and skin. When did I get so cold? Why am I so damp?

My teeth grit against the pain pulsing through my skull. Each breath is a struggle. My whole body trembles, shock and fear tangled in every nerve.

Someone's shouting. Far away. Getting closer. Louder now.

"—okay? Sir? Can you hear me?"

I try to respond but my throat won't cooperate. My chest tightens. The trembling gets worse.

Then nothing.

thirty-four

. . .

Natalie

THE KNOCK on my door startles me.

I'm still in my pajamas on the couch, working on notes Rebecca asked for on a potential second season of *Spellbound*. Just preliminary thoughts, character arcs we could explore, nothing formal.

Except I can't focus. My pen hovers over the notebook, the same sentence half-finished for the past twenty minutes. My mind keeps drifting back to Jake and what I'm going to say when I finally call him. To the speech I've been rehearsing in my head.

I'm sorry. I was scared. I love you. Please give me another chance.

The words are right there, pressing against my ribs, demanding to be spoken. I just need to be brave enough to pick up the phone. To admit I was wrong. To tell him what I should have said a week ago when he was on one knee in front of me with his heart completely exposed.

Today. I'll call him today.

My heart skips at the thought, nerves and anticipation tangling together in my chest. I set the pen down, my fingers trembling slightly.

The baby's been kicking all morning, restless. I press my hand to the spot where her foot keeps jabbing my ribs.

"I know, I know," I mutter. "You're running out of room."

The knock comes again. More insistent.

I wrap the blanket around me in an effort to disguise the fact that I've not gotten ready for the day yet and heave myself off the couch. Everything takes twice as long when you hit nine months.

Blair and Wyatt are standing on my doorstep.

"Hey," I say, surprised. "What are you guys doing here?"

Blair's face is pale. Wyatt's jaw is tight, his hands shoved in his pockets.

"Can we come in?" Blair asks.

"Yeah, of course." I step aside, and something cold starts to creep up my spine. "Is everything okay? Is it the house? Do you need to do repairs, or...are you selling it?"

The panic hits me all at once. I can't move right now. I'm almost nine months pregnant, I don't have time to find a new place and pack and—

"It's not the house," Wyatt says.

They're both just standing in my living room now, and neither of them is moving to sit down. Blair's hands are twisted together. Wyatt won't meet my eyes.

"Okay, you're scaring me. What's going on?"

"Can we sit?" Blair asks gently.

"Sure. Yeah. Sit."

We all settle—me back on the couch, them in the chairs

across from me. The silence stretches out for what feels like forever.

"Have you talked to Jake recently?" Wyatt asks finally.

The question catches me off guard. I try to keep my face neutral. "We've both been busy. Why?"

"Natalie." Wyatt leans forward, elbows on his knees. "I know about Valentine's Day."

The words hit like ice water.

"Oh," I manage.

His eyes are warm, understanding, and hold no blame or judgment.

Blair moves from her chair to the couch, sitting next to me. Her hand finds mine, and that's when I know. That's when the real panic starts clawing up my throat. My heart kicks into overdrive, slamming against my ribs. Something's wrong. Something's very wrong.

"Why are you asking if I've talked to Jake?" My voice sounds strange, too high. "What happened? Is he okay?"

Wyatt's face is grave. "There was an accident."

The room tilts.

"What kind of accident?"

"He went home to Connecticut. To see his mom. Went out for a run yesterday morning and slipped on ice. Hit his head." Wyatt pauses, and I can see him choosing his words carefully. "He has swelling in his brain. They've put him in a medically induced coma to keep the pressure down while it heals."

The words don't make sense. My brain refuses to process them. Accident. Coma. My mind is screaming. My chest constricts, a crushing weight pressing down until I can't breathe. My hands start shaking. The room feels too small, the air too thin.

I'm standing before I realize I'm moving. "I need to go. I need to get to Connecticut. Where is he? What hospital?"

"Nat—" Blair's up too, her hands on my shoulders.

"I need to see him. I need—" I'm looking around for my phone, my keys, my bag. My thoughts are jumbled, none of them making sense, all of them screaming the same thing: Jake. I need to get to Jake. "I can book a flight. Or I can drive. How long does it take to drive to Connecticut? I can—"

"You can't fly," Wyatt says quietly.

"I don't care—"

"The airlines won't let you on the plane. Not this far along. It's policy."

"Then I'll drive. I'll leave right now. I just need to pack a bag and—"

My breathing is shallow, too fast, my heart racing. My jaw clenches so tight it hurts. This can't be happening. This can't be real. Jake can't be—

No. I won't think it. Won't let the thought form.

"Natalie, stop." Blair's voice is firm. She turns me to face her, her hands still on my shoulders. "You can't drive across the country right now. You're about to have a baby."

"He needs me." My voice cracks, and I realize I'm crying. When did I start crying? The tears are hot, relentless, blurring my vision. My whole body trembles. "He can't—he has to wake up. He has to be here for the birth. He has to meet his daughter."

He has to know I love him. That I want him. That I made a terrible mistake and I need the chance to fix it.

"His mom's with him," Wyatt says. "And I'm flying out this afternoon. They're doing everything right, Nat. He's at a good hospital. He's getting excellent care."

"I should be there." The tears are coming faster now, hot and desperate. My chest heaves with sobs I can't control. The weight pressing down is unbearable, crushing everything inside me. "I should be the one sitting with him."

"You need to stay here and take care of yourself and the baby," Blair says gently. "That's what Jake would want."

"Jake would want me there." My legs feel weak, unsteady. Blair guides me back down to the couch, sitting close beside me. "I made a mistake. I told him I needed space, but I don't. I don't need space. I need him."

"I know," Blair says softly.

"No, you don't understand." I turn to look at her, and everything I've been holding back for the past week comes pouring out. "He told me he loved me. He wanted to marry me, for us to be a family. And I panicked. I told him I needed space, and I left. I walked out on him."

Wyatt's face is pained. He already knows this, but hearing me say it out loud makes it real in a different way.

"The last thing he heard from me was that I couldn't do this. That I needed to be alone." My voice breaks completely. "And now he's lying in a hospital bed unconscious, and I can't even tell him I was wrong. That I love him. That I want everything he was offering me, and I was just too scared to say it."

Blair pulls me into her arms, and I dissolve. I'm sobbing into her shoulder, my whole body shaking with it. The baby's moving frantically now, responding to my distress, and that just makes me cry harder.

"He has to wake up," I manage between sobs. "He has to be okay. I love him so much, Blair. I love him and I never told him and now—"

"He's going to wake up," Blair says firmly, pulling back to look at me. "And you're going to tell him everything. I promise you, Nat. You're going to get that chance."

"What if I don't? What if he doesn't—"

"He will." Wyatt's voice is certain, and when I look at him, his eyes are red too. "Jake's stubborn as hell. He's not going anywhere. Not when he has a daughter to meet. Not when he has you to come back to."

I want to believe him. God, I want to believe him so badly. But the fear is overwhelming, crushing my chest, making it hard to breathe.

Wyatt stands, checking his phone. "I need to head to the airport. My flight leaves in two hours. But I'll call you as soon as I see him, okay? As soon as I have any news."

"Tell him—" My voice catches. "Please tell him I'm sorry. Tell him I love him."

"You can tell him yourself when he wakes up." Wyatt comes over and squeezes my shoulder. "Hang in there, Nat. He's going to be okay."

After he leaves, Blair stays. She makes me tea and sits beside me on the couch while I stare at my phone, waiting for news that doesn't come. The minutes crawl by, each one heavier than the last. She tries to get me to eat something, but the thought of food makes me nauseous.

My phone buzzes and I grab it immediately, but it's just

my mom asking how I'm feeling. I can't even begin to answer that question right now, so I set the phone back down without responding.

The baby kicks again, a sharp jab under my ribs, and I press my hand to the spot. She's been moving constantly since Wyatt and Blair showed up, like she knows something's wrong. Like she's asking where her father is.

"He's going to be okay," I whisper to her, to myself, to anyone who might be listening. "He has to be okay. Because I love him."

thirty-five

. . .

Jake

THE LIGHT IS TOO BRIGHT.

That's the first thing I notice. White and sharp, stabbing through my eyelids even before I open them. Then sound—steady beeping, the hum of machines, voices somewhere nearby.

My head feels like it's been split open.

I force my eyes open, and the hospital room comes into focus slowly. White ceiling tiles. An IV line running into my left arm. My right wrist is in a cast. I lift my good hand slowly, fingers finding the thick bandage wrapped around my head. The pressure there is tender, aching.

"Jake?"

Everything hurts so I turn my head slowly, and see my mom leaning over me. Her face is pale, eyes red like she's been crying.

"Mom," I croak. Or try to. The sound that comes out is barely audible, more breath than word. My throat is sandpaper, my mouth so dry my tongue feels stuck.

"Oh thank God." She's grabbing my hand, squeezing it too tight. "You're awake. You're finally awake."

"Water," I manage, the word rasping out.

Mom's already reaching for the pitcher on the bedside table, pouring water into a plastic cup with a straw. She brings it to my lips carefully, supporting my head with her other hand.

"Small sips," she warns.

The water is cool, soothing, the best thing I've ever tasted. I take two careful sips before she pulls it away.

"How long—" My voice is still rough, quiet, but at least the words are forming now.

"Three days." Another voice. I shift my gaze and see Wyatt standing on the other side of the bed. He looks like shit —unshaven, wearing rumpled clothes, dark circles under his eyes. "You've been out for three days, man."

Three days. I try to process that, but can't quite wrap my head around it.

"What happened?"

"You went for a run," Mom says, her voice shaking. "Slipped on ice. Hit your head pretty badly. You had swelling in your brain, so they put you in a medically induced coma to let it go down."

The memories come back in fragments. The path. The cold. Thinking about Natalie. About the proposal. Then falling.

"Is Natalie okay?" The words come out urgent, panicked. "The baby—did I miss anything? Is she—"

"They're fine," Wyatt says quickly. "They're both fine. Nat's okay, the baby's okay. You didn't miss anything."

The relief is so intense I have to close my eyes for a second.

"Does she know? About the accident?"

"Yeah. I told her the minute I found out. I've been keeping her updated." Wyatt pauses. "She's been texting almost every hour to check on you."

"I should call her," I say. "Let her know I'm okay."

"Yeah, you should." Wyatt glances at my mom. "Except there's a small problem."

"What?"

"Your phone." Mom gestures helplessly. "The paramedics couldn't find it at the scene. We think maybe the ambulance ran over it. Or it fell in the water. Either way, it's gone."

"Great." I close my eyes again. Everything hurts, and now I can't even call Natalie to tell her I'm alive.

"Here." Something presses into my good hand. I open my eyes to see Wyatt holding out his phone. "Use mine. I think she'd really want to hear from you."

"She asked for space."

"Jake." Wyatt's voice is firm. "Call her. Trust me on this."

Mom's already moving toward the door. "We'll give you some privacy."

They step out into the hallway, and I'm alone with Wyatt's phone in my hand.

I pull up the video call app and see Natalie's number in his recent contacts, evidence of all the updates he's been giving her. I hit call before I can overthink it.

It rings once. Twice.

Then her face fills the screen.

She's in her living room, I think. But I barely register the background because all I can see is her. Hair pulled back in a messy bun and puffy eyes with no makeup. Her eyes go wide when she sees me.

"Jake," she breathes.

And then she's crying.

"Hey." The word comes out slower than I intend, quieter. My head throbs with each syllable. "Don't cry. I'm okay."

My eyes wince against the pain, and I have to pause, gather strength before continuing.

"I'm fine," I add, though even I can hear how unconvincing it sounds. My voice is barely above a whisper, still scratchy from days of disuse.

"You're awake." Tears are streaming down her face. "Oh my God, you're awake."

"Yeah." I close my eyes for a second, the light from the phone screen making my head pound harder. "I'm awake. And I'm okay, I promise." Another pause to breathe through the pain. "Please don't cry, Nat."

"I can't—I can't stop. I was so scared. I thought—" She can't finish the sentence. "Jake, I love you."

The words hit me like a freight train. "What?"

"I love you. I'm so in love with you and I was so stupid on Valentine's Day. I panicked and I ran and I've been miserable ever since and then Wyatt told me about the accident and I couldn't get to you and I thought I might never get to tell you—" She's talking fast, the words tumbling over each other. "I love you. I want to marry you. I want to move in with you. I want everything you were asking for. I want us to be a family, a real family, and I'm so sorry it took me this long to say it but I love you so much—"

"Nat, breathe."

She takes a shaky breath, wiping at her tears with the back of her hand.

"I love you too," I say, and my voice cracks. "God, I love you so much. I'll be there as soon as I can."

"I need you to listen to the doctors," she says, her voice fierce despite the tears. "I need you to stay as long as they tell you to. Do not play superhero. Do not risk your recovery."

"Nat—"

"I mean it, Jake. I want you back here whole and healthy, not because you pushed yourself too hard to get to me." She wipes her eyes. "Promise me you'll do what they say. Promise me you'll take care of yourself."

"I promise," I say quietly. "But I'm coming home as soon as they clear me. Not a day longer than necessary."

"That's all I'm asking." She smiles through her tears. "Just get better. We'll be here waiting when you're ready."

"Okay."

Mom and Wyatt are already back in the room, having heard the whole conversation. Mom's eyes are wet, and even Wyatt looks a little choked up.

"The doctors said at least another day, maybe two," Mom says gently. "They want to monitor you, make sure the swelling doesn't come back."

I look back at the phone, at Natalie's face on the screen. She's still crying, but she's smiling now too.

"I'll get there as soon as I can," I tell her. "One or two more days and then I'm on the first flight home."

"Okay." She wipes her eyes again. "Okay. I'll be waiting."

"Nat?"

"Yeah?"

"I love you. In case that wasn't clear."

"It's clear. I love you too." She laughs through her tears. "You should rest," she says finally. "Let them take care of you."

After a few more updates, I end the call and hand the phone to Wyatt, as my mom grabs my hand and gives it a squeeze.

"Two days," I say. "That's it. After that, I'm out of here whether they like it or not."

Mom gives me that look that says she's not going to let me do anything stupid, but she's also not going to argue right now. "Two days," she agrees. "And then we get you home to your girls."

My girls. Natalie and our daughter.

I lie back against the pillows, ignoring the pain in my head and my wrist, and let myself feel it. The happiness, the relief, the overwhelming certainty that everything's going to be okay.

thirty-six

...

Natalie

"**THIS BOX IS** full of books about why relationships are doomed to fail."

I look up from the dresser drawer I'm organizing to see Stella holding up a cardboard box, peering inside with barely contained delight. She's already smiling like she's about to read back to me every poor decision I've ever made.

"That's research," I say.

"For what? Your thesis on dying alone?"

"For characters. For writing. Not everything is about me."

"This one's called *The Myth of Happily Ever After*." She pulls it out triumphantly, waving it in the air like she's caught me in a lie. "You literally highlighted passages, Nat."

Blair walks in carrying a lamp, Ruby strapped to her chest and making contented little noises. "Please tell me you didn't bring the anti-love library to Jake's house."

"It's not an anti-love library—"

"There's one here called *Self-Partnered: A Guide to*

Thriving Solo," Stella interrupts, digging deeper. "With your name written inside the cover."

"I was going through a phase."

"You were sure going through something," Blair murmurs, amusement in her voice.

Sophia appears in the doorway with an armful of clothes still on hangers. "Where do you want these? And also, I found your vision board from last year. It has a picture of a cabin in the woods and the words 'no men allowed' written across it."

"Oh my God, can we please focus on unpacking instead of roasting me?"

"We can multitask," Stella says cheerfully, setting the box down. "This can go in the garage, right? Or should we donate it? Or set it on fire?"

"Garage," I mutter.

Jess emerges from unpacking my things in the bathroom. "I'm just saying, for someone who swore she'd never live with a man, you're moving into his house awfully fast."

"I'm nine months pregnant with his child. It's not that fast."

I sit on the edge of Jake's bed, well, our bed, and press a hand gently against my belly. Everything inside me feels stretched and full and settling into something new all at once.

"Are you guys going to help me, or just keep giving me a hard time?"

Blair smiles at me, soft and warm, bouncing Ruby lightly. "For the record, we're really happy for you. We're just enjoying the moment. You've been very insistent about your anti-love stance over the years."

"I never thought I'd see the day," Jess adds. "Natalie Cruz, moving in with a man, having a baby, admitting she was wrong about love."

"I didn't say I was wrong about love in general—"

"You literally had a box full of books about how love is a lie," Stella repeats.

"Okay, fine. I was wrong. Happy?"

"Ecstatic," she says.

A laugh slips out of me before I can help it. I feel good.

Sophia starts hanging my clothes in the closet next to Jake's. "I still can't believe he had cleared out half the closet for you. It makes my heart melt."

Jess pokes her head out of the bathroom, eyebrows high. "He cleared the space in the bathroom like he thought you would say yes. Nat, this man's serious."

"I know." And I do. The certainty sits warm and steady under my ribs, even with everything that's happened.

We work for another hour, filling drawers and hanging clothes and stacking my books on the shelf Jake cleared for me in his office. And as we move around the house, it starts to look like our home. My yoga mat in the corner by the nightstand. My favorite mug inside his cabinet. The ultrasound photos on the fridge. Small things that make it feel like I'm settled here.

When we heard Jake had to stay longer than expected in the hospital, I used it as an opportunity to enlist my friends to help me move into his house. The doctors refused to clear him to fly, but Wyatt stepped in without hesitation and is driving him all the way home now.

When I told him I wanted to move in, that I didn't want

to spend another night in separate places, he responded with a single word: "Yes." Then gave me the key code to his house. So here I am, surprising him by having everything moved in before he gets home. My books on his shelves. My clothes in his closet. My life woven into his. And I hope when he walks through that door, he still wants this.

"This is surreal," I say at last, standing in the kitchen and looking around at the house that looks more like ours every time I blink.

"Good surreal?" Blair asks.

"Really good." I rest a hand on my belly. "It's just wild to think that last year I barely talked to Jake and now we're here and—"

"In love," Sophia finishes with a little smile.

"Yeah. In love."

Blair's phone buzzes. She checks it, then looks up with an excited grin. "Wyatt says they're twenty minutes out."

My heart lifts and tightens at the same time. "He's almost here?"

I waddle into the bathroom to check my reflection. I have zero makeup on, and my hair is up in a messy bun. But my eyes are bright and I've never looked happier.

"He's not going to care what you look like," Blair calls from the living room. "The man crossed state lines with a concussion to get back to you."

I step back out, and all four of them are watching me like I'm about to walk down the aisle.

"What?"

"Nothing," Stella says with a soft grin. "We're just happy for you."

"You already said that."

"It bears repeating," she says, stepping forward to touch my arm gently. "You deserve this, Nat. You really do."

My throat goes tight. "Thanks. And thank you for helping me move. I know this is chaotic and last-minute, but I didn't want to spend another night apart from him."

We hear the rumble of an engine pulling into the driveway. And I'm moving before I realize it. I fly out the front door and down the steps. The air is warm, a soft Los Angeles evening settling around me as I reach the driveway and see Wyatt climb out of their rental car.

The passenger door opens and Jake steps out slowly. He looks tired, pale. There's a bandage near his hairline. The moment his eyes find mine, something inside me breaks open in a rush of relief so strong it feels physical. I move toward him as fast as my belly will let me, and he meets me halfway, his good arm wrapping around me, pulling me into him until I'm pressed against the safest place I've ever known.

"You're here," I breathe against his chest, my fingers curling into the fabric of his T-shirt.

"I'm here," he says quietly, voice rough and real and full of every mile he drove to get to me. "I'm home."

I pull back just enough to look at his face, and before I can stop myself, I kiss him. It's not soft or careful. It's weeks of missing him, of being scared, of needing to feel him whole and real beneath my hands. He kisses me back just as fiercely, his hand coming up to cup my jaw, and for a moment the world narrows to just us.

When we break apart, I keep my hand on his chest, anchoring myself. My other hand comes up to gently touch the edge of the bandage. "How's your head? Are you okay? Do you need to sit down?"

"I'm fine," he says, but I can see the exhaustion around his eyes.

"You're not fine. You just drove across the country with a concussion." I slide my hand down to his chest, feeling his heartbeat steady beneath my palm. "Let me take care of you now. Please."

His eyes soften. "Nat—"

"I mean it. You've been taking care of me for months. It's my turn." I keep my hand over his heart. "I want to be your safe place too. The person you come home to. The one who makes sure you rest and heal and know you're loved."

Something shifts in his expression, vulnerability mixing with relief. "You already are," he says quietly.

"Good. Then let me prove it." I thread my fingers through his. "Come inside. I have a surprise for you."

thirty-seven

. . .

Jake

SHE TAKES my good hand and leads me toward the house. That's when I notice all the cars in the driveway. Blair's SUV. Sophia's Range Rover. Two others I don't immediately recognize.

"Are we having a party?" I ask.

"Not exactly."

We walk through the front door, and I stop dead.

My living room is full of boxes. Natalie's boxes. Her books are stacked on my coffee table. Dishes are stacked on my counters waiting to be put in their place inside my cabinets.

"Surprise," she says quietly beside me.

I turn to look at her. "You already moved in?"

"I hope that's ok? I called everyone and—"

I kiss her, cutting off the words. Deeper this time, my hand sliding into her hair, trying to pour everything I feel into it.

When we break apart, she's breathless.

"I'll take that as a yes?" she says.

"That's a hell yes."

Blair appears from the kitchen, Ruby still strapped to her chest. "Welcome home, Jake. Sorry for the mess."

"Mess is good. Mess means she's staying."

Stella, Sophia, and Jess emerge from various rooms, all of them grinning.

"We tried to organize everything," Jess says. "But Natalie has a lot of books."

"And opinions about where things should go," Sophia adds.

"I heard that," Natalie calls.

I'm still holding her hand, still processing that she's here, that all her stuff is here, that we're really doing this. My chest feels too full, like my heart might actually burst.

"Thank you," I say to all of them. "For helping her. For being here."

"Of course," Blair says. "That's what—"

Natalie gasps.

It's a sharp, sudden sound that cuts through the room. Her hand tightens on mine, her other hand going to her belly.

"Nat? You okay?"

She looks down. I follow her gaze.

There's water pooling at her feet, and for a second, nobody moves. We all just stare.

Then chaos erupts.

"Oh my God!" Stella shrieks.

"Her water broke!" Blair's already moving, shifting into crisis mode.

"We need to get her to the hospital!" Jess is looking

around wildly, as if an ambulance might materialize spontaneously.

"I can't carry her," I say, panic rising. "My arm—"

"I've got her." Wyatt's already there, his hand on Natalie's elbow. "Come on, Nat. Let's get you into the car."

"My go bag," Natalie says, her voice tight. "I need my go bag. Stella, can you grab it? I think it's in the bedroom. Or maybe it's still at my old place? I don't remember if I brought it over—"

"I'll find it!" Stella's already running toward the bedroom.

Wyatt and I help Natalie toward the door. She's walking carefully, one hand pressed to her belly, breathing through what I'm realizing is a contraction.

"You're okay," I tell her. "We're going to get you there. You're okay."

"I know. I just—oh God, Jake, we just got you home and now—"

"And now we're going to meet our daughter." I squeeze her hand with my good one. "It's perfect timing."

"It's terrible timing," she gasps, but she's smiling.

Wyatt gets the car door open and helps ease Natalie into the back seat. I climb in beside her, my cast making everything awkward, but I manage to get my good arm around her.

Stella comes sprinting out of the house with a duffel bag. "Got it! It was in the closet!"

She tosses it to Wyatt, who puts it in the trunk.

"We'll meet you there!" Blair calls, already heading for her own car.

Wyatt slides into the driver's seat. "Everybody buckled?"

"Yes," I say. "Go."

He pulls out of the driveway, and I realize we literally just got home. I was in this car five minutes ago. And now we're racing to the hospital.

Natalie leans into me, her breathing controlled but tense. "This isn't how I imagined today going."

"No?"

"I thought we'd have time. To talk. To settle in. Maybe eat dinner."

"We can still do all that. After."

She laughs, then winces. "Another contraction."

"Time them." Wyatt says. "How far apart?"

I check my watch. "I don't know. Five minutes? Six?"

"We've got time," Wyatt calls from the front. "Hospital's ten minutes away."

Those ten minutes feel like an hour. Natalie has one more contraction, and she grips my hand tighter. I talk her through it, keeping my voice steady even though inside I'm terrified and excited and completely overwhelmed. By the time we pull up to the emergency entrance, Blair and the others are right behind us.

A nurse appears with a wheelchair, and we get Natalie settled. I'm right beside her as they wheel her in, my good hand holding hers.

"Name?" the nurse asks.

"Natalie Cruz."

"Due date?"

"March 28th. I'm only thirty-six weeks."

The nurse's expression sharpens. "Okay, let's get you upstairs. Dad, you coming?"

"Yes," I say immediately. "I'm coming."

The labor and delivery room is all white walls and medical equipment and excessively bright lights. Natalie slips into a hospital gown, and as she slides into the bed, nurses get her hooked up to monitors. After a few minutes, the baby's heartbeat fills the room, steady and strong.

"You're at four centimeters. Still got a ways to go, but you're doing great," the on-call attending physician tells us after a quick examination.

"How long?" Natalie asks. "And can you call Dr. Nelson?"

"Hard to say. Could be a few hours. Could be longer. First babies like to take their time. And Dr. Nelson is on her way."

When the doctor leaves, the silence only amplifies the beeping monitors and the soundtrack of the baby's heartbeat. Natalie's quiet in the bed looking simultaneously terrified and determined, so I pull a chair close and take her hand.

"Hey," I say softly.

"Hey."

"Our daughter really wanted to meet me, huh?"

She laughs, a little breathless. "She probably feels how I'm feeling. Like she couldn't wait another second."

"I couldn't either." I lean forward, careful of my cast, and kiss her forehead. "I'm sorry I wasn't here. I'm sorry I scared you."

"I'm sorry I pushed you away. I'm sorry I wasted so much time being scared when I should have just been with you."

"We're together now. That's all that matters."

"I love you." She says it clearly, firmly, like she needs me to hear every syllable. "I love you and I want this life with you. All of it. The house and the baby. I want everything."

"I want everything too." I kiss her properly this time, soft and slow, trying to show her what words can't quite capture. When we pull apart, her eyes are shining. "I'm all in, Nat. Whatever comes next, we're doing it together."

"Together," she agrees.

Then her face twists, her hand gripping mine so tight I think she might break my good wrist too.

"Contraction," she gasps.

I check the monitor, watch the number climb. "Breathe. In through your nose, out through your mouth. You've got this."

She breathes through it, her eyes locked on mine, and when it passes, she slumps back against the pillows.

"That one was worse."

"You're doing amazing."

"I haven't done anything yet."

"You grew a human and are about to push her out. That's something."

The hours blur together. Contractions getting closer, stronger. Natalie squeezing my hand until I lose feeling in my fingers. Me talking her through each one, getting her ice chips, adjusting pillows, doing everything I can with one working arm.

Blair and the others come in and out to encourage and distract her. Wyatt gives me a fist bump and tells me I've got this. Stella takes approximately eight thousand photos that I'm sure Natalie will hate later.

And then, finally, Dr. Nelson comes in.

"All right, Natalie. Sounds like you're ready. So unless you'd like an audience, I'd say everyone out except dad, and let's get this baby out."

Everything shifts into high gear. Nurses repositioning her, setting up equipment, giving instructions. I watch as Natalie gives everything she has and then…a cry. Sharp and indignant and perfect.

"She's here!" the doctor announces.

I'm crying. I don't remember when I started, but tears are streaming down my face as they lift this tiny, screaming creature and place her on Natalie's chest.

Our daughter. She's perfect.

Natalie's sobbing, her hands cradling the baby, and I'm leaning over both of them, my forehead pressed to Natalie's temple, staring at the miracle we made.

"Hi," Natalie whispers to her. "Hi, baby girl. We've been waiting for you."

The baby's cry softens to a whimper, then settles as she feels her mother's skin, her heartbeat. Her hair is dark and wet, her eyes squeezed shut.

"She's beautiful," I manage. "She's so beautiful."

A nurse lifts her back up before we get too comfortable and she's calling me over to cut the cord.

"Do you want to hold her, Dad?" a nurse asks.

"Yes." My voice cracks. "Yes, please."

They help me, showing me how to support her head with my good hand, how to cradle her against my chest despite the cast. She's so small, so light, and yet she feels like the weight of the entire world.

"Hi," I whisper to her. "I'm your dad. I've been waiting to meet you."

She opens her eyes—just a little, just enough for me to see they are a dark blue—and my heart explodes.

"Say hello to your little girl," the nurse says, smiling.

I look up at Natalie. She's watching us with tears streaming down her face, her hand reaching out to touch the baby's tiny foot.

"Hello," I say to our daughter. "Welcome to the world."

thirty-eight
. . .
Natalie

ISLA IS asleep in Blair's arms, completely unbothered by the chaos of eight adults and two other children crowded into Jake's living room.

Our living room, I remind myself. I'm still getting used to that.

It's been three days since Isla was born, small but healthy, her lungs strong despite arriving a month early.

We spent two nights in the hospital while the nurses monitored her temperature and feeding. She struggled a bit with breastfeeding at first, needing help latching, and they wanted to make sure she was gaining weight before sending us home. But yesterday afternoon, they cleared us both, and Jake drove us home to our house.

This is our first full day home with her. Our first time having everyone we love in the same room to meet our daughter. My mom is sitting next to Blair, her eyes never leaving Isla's face. She's been here since the moment we texted that we were home. My dad is standing near the windows with

Rachel, both of them smiling at the baby with that grandparent glow.

Jake's mom beaming from the screen of the laptop propped on the coffee table, her face bright even through the video call. "She's absolutely precious," Linda says for probably the tenth time. "I can't wait to hold her in person."

"We'll fly you out soon," Jake promises.

"No rush," Linda says. "You two focus on adjusting. I'll be there when you're ready."

"She's so tiny," Blair whispers. "I forget how small they are when they're brand new."

"Seven pounds eleven ounces is not that small," I say from my spot on the couch. Everything still hurts—sitting, standing, existing—but I'm too happy to care. "The nurses said she was a great size for thirty-six weeks."

"And twenty-one inches long," Jake adds from beside me. His good hand is resting on my knee, his cast propped on a pillow. "She's going to be tall."

"Just like her dad," Wyatt says, appearing from the kitchen with a beer. "Congrats again, man. She's beautiful."

"She really is," Sophia agrees. She's sitting on the floor next to Hazel, who's been surprisingly gentle and curious about the baby. "That dark hair is gorgeous. And those eyes—do you think they'll stay blue?"

"We're hoping," I say, though honestly I don't care what color her eyes end up being. She's perfect exactly as she is.

Stella emerges from Jake's kitchen. It's turning into what I'm learning is her favorite spot. She's carrying a plate of cookies she's just made for us. "Okay, I have a very important question. How did you decide on Isla?"

Jake and I exchange a glance.

"Jake suggested it, and I loved it immediately. It felt right."

My mom smiles. "It's a beautiful name. Strong and feminine at once."

My dad nods. "Isla Elizabeth Reyes. It suits her."

"It's perfect," Jess says. She and Lucas are wedged together in the armchair, his arm around her shoulders.

Brandon appears from the hallway where he'd been taking a phone call. "Sorry, work thing. Did I miss anything?"

"Just Natalie explaining the name," Stella says, moving to make room for him on the couch.

"Isla's a great name. Strong and delicate." He grins at me. "Also, Stella and I left something in the nursery for you guys. Don't freak out."

"Why would I freak out?"

"Because it's big."

"How big?"

"You'll see."

Before I can ask more questions, Grant stands from where he's been sitting with Sophia and Hazel. "We should probably head out. It's getting close to Hazel's bedtime, and I'm sure you guys want some quiet time with the baby."

"You don't have to leave," Jake starts, but I can hear the exhaustion in his voice. We've been running on adrenaline and about three hours of sleep for the past two days.

"We do," Blair says gently, standing and carefully transferring Isla back to me. The baby stirs but doesn't wake, her tiny fist curling near her face. "You two need rest. And bonding time. And all the things new parents need without an audience."

The exodus happens quickly after that. Hugs all around, promises to check in tomorrow, reminders that they're just a phone call away if we need anything. Stella points dramatically toward the nursery when she leaves, mouthing "you're welcome" at me.

And then it's quiet.

Just me, Jake, and Isla.

I look down at the baby, still amazed that she's real. That she's ours. "Should we put her in the nursery? Let her sleep in her actual crib?"

"We can try."

We make our way upstairs slowly—me still moving carefully after delivery, Jake still ginger with his injuries. The nursery door is closed, and when Jake pushes it open, I see what Stella and Brandon left.

A rocking chair. Not just any rocking chair—a beautiful, cushioned glider in soft gray fabric with an ottoman to match. There's a card taped to the armrest.

"For the late-night feedings and the early morning cuddles. Love, Stella & Brandon"

"Oh," I breathe. "That's perfect."

"It really is."

Jake helps me settle into the chair while he gets the room ready. He adjusts the mobile, makes sure the sound machine is set up, checks that the monitor is on. Even with one arm in a cast, he's completely in his element.

He comes back and carefully takes Isla from me, carrying her to the crib. He lays her down with such tenderness it makes my throat tight, adjusting her sleep sack, making sure she's positioned safely on her back.

We both stand there for a moment, watching her sleep. Her chest rises and falls in that rapid newborn rhythm. Her tiny fingers twitch. She makes a small sound—not quite a cry, just a sleep noise—and settles again.

"I can't believe she's ours," I whisper.

"I know." Jake's good arm comes around my waist, pulling me against his side. "We made her."

"We made a whole person."

"A perfect person."

We stay like that, watching her breathe, until my legs start to protest from standing for too long. Jake guides me to the new rocking chair, and I sink into it gratefully.

He sits on the ottoman, facing me. "How are you feeling?" he asks.

"Sore. Exhausted. Deliriously happy."

"That's a good combination."

"How's your head? Your wrist?"

"Getting better. The headaches are less frequent. The wrist is just annoying." He reaches over and takes my hand. "Nat, I need to tell you something."

My heart skips. "Okay."

"I'm going to marry you."

I blink, confusion crossing my face. "I know. I already said I would marry you."

"I want to make it official. As soon as you're ready. As soon as we can get things together."

The words settle over me, warm and certain and right.

My chest tightens, emotion swelling so fast it steals my

breath. After everything we've been through, every wall I built, every time I pushed him away, we're here. Together. With our daughter sleeping ten feet away.

My heart races, pounding so hard I'm sure he can hear it.

"Let's do it here. Just us, our friends and family, the people we love." The words tumble out, my voice shaky with happiness.

"Are you sure?"

"Absolutely. I had the fanfare, this time I'll just take the man."

A laugh escapes me, watery and breathless, and I squeeze his hand maybe a little too hard. My whole body feels alive with this, with the certainty of us.

I think about how far we've come. From that one night in July to this moment right here. From me running scared to me choosing him, choosing us, choosing this life we're building together. I'm finally letting myself believe in something I thought was impossible. He leans forward, cupping my face with his good hand, and kisses me. It's soft and sweet and tastes like promise.

From the crib, Isla makes a small sound. We both turn to look at her—our daughter, sleeping peacefully in the room her father built, surrounded by love. And I realize I feel something I never thought I'd feel. Hope. Not the false god I convinced myself it was, but something real and solid and worth believing in. Hope for tomorrow. Hope for our future. Hope for all the messy, beautiful, imperfect moments ahead.

epilogue

. . .

Jake - Six Years Later

THE BACKYARD IS madness in the best possible way.

I'm standing at the grill, flipping burgers and trying to keep track of all the children running around the pool. My pool. In my backyard. With my wife inside getting more drinks and my daughters somewhere in the pack of kids screaming with laughter.

Forty years old. Never imagined it would look like this.

"Dad! Watch me!" Isla's voice cuts through the noise. She's standing at the edge of the pool in her purple swimsuit, goggles already on. Six years old and fearless.

"I'm watching!" I call back.

She jumps in with a spectacular cannonball that soaks Hazel, who's sitting on the edge with her feet in the water, scrolling through her phone. At sixteen, Hazel's too cool to swim with the little kids, but she's good-natured about getting splashed.

"Nice one, Isla!" she calls, brushing water off her face.

Wyatt appears beside me, beer in hand. "You need a refill?"

"Not yet. How's Ruby doing in the deep end?"

"Like a fish. She and Isla are trying to teach the younger ones how to dive." He takes a sip of his beer. "June's convinced she can do it, but she's only five, so Blair's hovering."

I spot Blair in the pool, keeping a careful eye on her middle daughter while also managing Ivy, who's three and determined to swim without her floaties. She's managing three kids as efficiently and competently as she runs a talent agency.

"Where's Brandon?" I ask.

"Kitchen, helping Nat with the drinks. Or trying to. You know how Natalie gets about her kitchen."

I do know. Over the years the kitchen has become her domain. Not that I'm complaining, the woman can cook.

Stella emerges from the house carrying a tray of lemonade, Brandon right behind her with a tray of adult beverages. Their son Beckett is attached to Brandon's leg, riding along.

"Drinks!" Stella announces. "And before anyone asks, yes, the lemonade is fresh-squeezed, and yes, Nat made me do it the hard way."

Natalie follows them out, laughing. "I didn't make you do anything. I just suggested that fresh is better than powder."

"Suggested very firmly," Stella says, grinning.

Natalie catches my eye across the yard and smiles. Six years of marriage and that smile still does things to my chest. She's wearing a sundress and her hair is up in a messy bun, and she looks exactly like home.

"Mommy!" Sloan's voice rises above the pool noise. Our three-year-old is paddling toward the shallow end in her mermaid floaties. "Look! I'm swimming!"

"I see you, baby! You're doing so good!"

Sophia and Grant finally make it out back. Sophia's carrying a bakery box that I'm hoping contains the chocolate cake she promised, while Grant has Violet perched on his shoulders. At five, Violet is tiny and fierce, just like her mom.

"Sorry for the delay," Sophia says, kissing my cheek. "Someone decided she needed a wardrobe change right quick."

"I wanted the sparkly one!" Violet announces.

"And you look beautiful," I tell her.

Grant sets her down and she immediately runs to join the other kids in the pool. He shakes my hand. "Happy birthday, man. Forty. How's it feel?"

"Like I'm responsible for too many people."

"Welcome to the club."

Jess and Lucas arrive moments later with their boys, Finn and Theo. Finn makes a beeline for the pool while Theo, being three, needs more convincing.

"Come on, buddy," Lucas says, crouching down. "You love the pool."

"Want Daddy to come," Theo says, grabbing Lucas's hand.

"Okay. Let's do it together."

I watch Lucas walk his son to the shallow end, patient and gentle, and think about how far we've all come. Lucas went from being the guy who never wanted kids to being completely wrapped around his sons' fingers.

Jess joins Natalie and Sophia on the patio, and within seconds they're deep in conversation. Probably about work. Jess's podcast is bigger than ever, Sophia's production company just green lit three new projects, and Natalie's in post-production on season five of *Spellbound.*

"Food's ready!" I call out.

The kids descend like locusts. Isla leads the charge, wrapping herself in a towel and getting in line. Ruby's right behind her, with June and Violet close behind. Sloane needs help, so Natalie scoops her up, toweling her off while she chatters about her swimming.

We fill plates, find spots around the yard. The adults cluster on the patio while the kids spread out on the grass, a mess of wet bathing suits and ketchup-covered faces.

Wyatt raises his beer. "A toast. To Jake. Forty years old and still somehow younger-looking than me."

"That's because you have three daughters," I point out. "They age you."

"Fair point." He grins. "But seriously. To Jake. Best friend, coworker, fellow exhausted dad. Happy birthday."

"To Jake!" everyone echoes.

I look around at all of them. My friends. My family. The people who showed up when Natalie went into labor early, who helped us move in together, who've been there for every birthday and holiday and every milestone since.

Natalie appears beside me, sliding her arm around my waist. "Good birthday?"

"The best."

"Wait until you see what I got you."

"Is it another tie?"

"It's not another tie." She leans up and kisses my cheek. "But you'll have to wait until later. When the kids are asleep."

"Now I'm intrigued."

Isla runs up, still dripping. "Daddy, can we do the cake now?"

"Let people finish eating first, pip."

"But I'm done eating."

"You had half a hot dog."

"I'm full!"

Natalie laughs. "Why don't you go play with Ruby for a few more minutes? Then we'll do cake."

Isla considers this, then nods and runs off.

"She's so much like you," I tell Natalie.

"Stubborn and impatient?"

"Determined and strong-willed."

"Nice save."

The cake comes out eventually, a chocolate masterpiece with "Over the Hill" written in frosting because Stella thought it was funny. The kids gather around to sing, their voices loud and off-key and perfect. Isla helps me blow out the candles while Sloane tries to stick her finger in the frosting.

As the sun starts to set, the younger kids begin to fade. Theo is asleep on Lucas's shoulder. Ivy's curled up in Blair's lap. Beckett is lying on a towel, staring at the sky.

"I think that's our cue," Jess says, gathering their things.

The departures are gradual. Hugs and promises to do this again soon. Kids being carried to cars, still in their bathing suits. Wyatt and Blair live close by now, so they walk home,

Ruby holding her dad's hand while Blair manages the younger two.

Finally, it's just us.

"Best birthday party ever," Isla declares, yawning.

"Agreed," I say.

We get the girls bathed and into bed. Isla wants a story, so I read her favorite while Sloane falls asleep to the sound of my voice. When I'm done, I tuck them in and kiss their foreheads.

"Love you, Daddy," Isla says.

"Love you too, pip."

Downstairs, Natalie's cleaning up the kitchen. I wrap my arms around her from behind, resting my chin on her shoulder.

"Leave it," I say. "We can deal with it tomorrow."

"It'll take five minutes."

"I don't care. Come sit with me."

She turns in my arms, looking up at me. "You sure you're okay with forty?"

"Are you kidding? I've got you, two amazing daughters, a job I love, amazing friends." I kiss her softly. "This is everything I ever wanted."

"Even when the kids are throwing tantrums?"

"Especially then."

She laughs and pulls me toward the couch. We sink into it together, her head on my shoulder, my arm around her waist.

"Remember when we found out we were pregnant?" she asks.

"How could I forget? You looked like you were going to pass out."

"I was terrified."

"So was I."

"And look at us now."

"Yeah. Look at us now."

"Ready for your gift?" Natalie asks, sitting up.

"Now?"

"Now." She stands and holds out her hand. "Come on."

I let her pull me off the couch and lead me through the house. When she opens the back door, I'm confused.

"We're going outside?"

"You'll see."

The backyard is quiet now, the pool lights glowing soft blue in the dark. She walks me to the edge of the pool, then turns to face me.

"Close your eyes."

"Natalie, what are you doing?"

"Just trust me."

I close my eyes. I hear the rustle of fabric, the soft sound of her sundress hitting the deck. Then her bra. Her underwear.

"Okay," she says. "You can look."

I open my eyes. She's completely naked, standing at the edge of the pool with that mischievous smile I fell in love with seven years ago.

"Your gift is a reminder," she says, "that we're not too old for a little fun."

Then she dives in. I'm already stripping off my shirt before she surfaces. My shorts and boxers follow, and I dive in after her. The water is warm and when I come up, she's waiting for me, treading water in the deep end, her hair slicked back and shining in the pool lights. I swim to her, pulling her close. Her legs wrap around my waist.

"Best gift ever," I tell her.

Tomorrow, we'll clean up the mess. We'll go back to work, to school drop-offs and soccer practice and the million small things that make up a life. But tonight, it's just us. Just this moment. Just the life we built from a one-night stand and a little hope.

While *The Backlot Series* ends here, this world isn't disappearing entirely.

Your path to what's next runs through a familiar name. Jess Lexington's brother, Austin, is trading the glitz of the big city for Stillwell, Texas, a small town where baseball brings everyone together and the real drama unfolds off the field.

Turn the page for a sneak peek of *Bases Loaded*.
Book one in the Stillwell Sliders series
coming Summer 2026.

*The following chapter is unedited and
may change in the final format.*

one
. . .
Harper

THE SUITCASE WON'T CLOSE.

I lean my full weight on it, trying to compress eight years of marriage into two pieces of luggage, but the zipper keeps catching on something. Probably the sweater I haven't worn in three years but kept telling myself I'd wear eventually. I won't need it in Texas anyway.

I yank it out and toss it on the bed. Try the zipper again. This time it cooperates.

Two suitcases. That's all I'm taking. It's mostly clothes, a few books, the framed photo of Stillwell's town square my dad gave me, and a set of chipped mugs I found at a Brooklyn flea market. If I wasn't so numb right now, it might actually shock me that this is all I have to show for almost a decade with a man I was supposed to spend the rest of my life with.

Everything else in this apartment, the Italian leather couch, the abstract art I pretended to understand, the price tags that made my stomach tighten, none of it was ever really mine. And the baseball bat lamp he loved? He can have it. I'm done with baseball.

My phone buzzes on the nightstand for the fifteenth time in an hour. I don't look at it. I already know what it says. Reporters asking for comment. My husband's agent pitching some united-front bullshit, like I'm meant to smile for the cameras while his client raw-dogs the team physical therapist.

I zip the second suitcase and haul both to the bedroom door. I pause and look back. The bed is still absurdly big. His closet is still a monument to him. I've packed up my entire side, and nothing looks different.

I remember being twenty-four and stupidly happy. He was playing in the majors. We were living in New York. Everything I'd bent or postponed or quietly set aside felt worth it, like I'd bet on the right future and won. Spoiler alert: apparently winning doesn't stop your husband from sleeping with the team physical therapist.

And that's the problem with packing. It gives you too much time to think. I need to keep moving, keep making small decisions about what stays and what goes, because the second I stop, I'm going to have to feel the full weight of this morning.

My phone buzzes again. This time it's a FaceTime call. Lisa's contact photo lights up the screen showing off her and Craig at the Ribeye Tavern's grand opening, holding champagne flutes, and grinning like they'd just won the lottery.

"You look like shit," Lisa says the second the video loads. She's in her kitchen, hair piled up, wearing an old Texas A&M hoodie that's definitely Craig's.

"Thanks. Love you too."

"Sorry. I just—" She stops, her face doing that thing where she's trying not to look too worried. "How are you really?"

"Never better," I say. "Thinking about taking up yoga. Maybe getting a cat."

"Harper."

"I'm packing. I'm fine."

"You're using your scary calm voice."

I prop the phone on the counter in the kitchen and zip my duffel bag. "I don't have a scary calm voice."

"So you're really coming home?" she asks.

"I don't think I have any other choice."

"Good. Okay. You can stay with me and Craig. We've got the guest room set up." She pauses. "Or Grams' guest house is open if you don't want to stay with us. I'm not sure there's a fridge or if the stove works, but there's a bed."

I'd already been planning to hide out at the guest house. It's small, private, and far enough from the main house that Grams wouldn't hover. Perfect for avoiding questions and pitying looks.

"I'll probably stay at Grams," I say. "But thank you."

"When's your flight?"

"Tonight."

Lisa's eyes go wide. "Tonight? Harper, it's already—"

"I know what time it is."

"Who's picking you up at the airport?"

"I already booked a car service," I lie. I haven't booked anything yet, but I will, and the last thing I need is my little sister driving late at night to rescue me like I'm some kind of disaster she needs to manage. "I'll text you when I land."

She looks like she wants to argue, but something in my face must convince her to let it go. "Okay. But please text me. And if you change your mind about staying with us—"

"I know. Thanks."

She goes quiet for a minute and I know it's coming. "I'm really sorry, Harper."

I don't want her to be sorry. I don't want anyone to be sorry. I want to rewind to age twenty-one and tell my younger self not to follow my newly drafted boyfriend. I want to tell that girl to take the sports photography mentorship and trust the part of her that had a future. Because if she does, she doesn't end up married to a cheating piece of shit, booking late-night flights back to her hometown like she's the one who did something wrong.

But I can't say any of that, so instead I just nod. "Yeah. Me too."

After we hang up, I walk to the window and look out at Central Park stretching to the north, all those trees and paths and people who have no idea that the wife of their favorite shortstop just found out he's been cheating on her with someone who can apparently get pregnant without even trying.

I hope the baby has teeth that come in crooked and need braces and cost him a fortune.

No. That's not fair. It's not the kid's fault.

I hope Kyle ages badly. I hope his hairline recedes and he gets a soft belly the second he stops playing. I hope his knees give out and he loses all that muscle definition he's so proud of. I hope he has to buy reading glasses at CVS and gets lower back pain every time it rains.

My phone buzz interrupts my voodoo wishes. This time it's a text from a number I don't recognize, and the preview makes my stomach drop.

> **UNKNOWN**
>
> Hi Harper, this is Rachel Kim from the Post. We're running a story about—

I delete it without reading the rest.

Then I call my publicist Emily, because if I'm about to become a tabloid headline, I should probably know what I'm dealing with.

She answers on the first ring. "Thank God. I've been trying to reach you all day."

"The Post is running something tomorrow, aren't they?"

"Yeah. An affair with his physical therapist. Pregnancy still technically unconfirmed, but—"

"It's confirmed," I say flatly. "Found out at mediation this morning when his lawyer asked for more time to review assets because of 'impending family expenses.'"

There's a pause. "Jesus, Harper."

"Yeah. His lawyer couldn't even look at me. Mine had to ask three times what that meant before Kyle's attorney finally said it out loud." I laugh, sharp enough to cut glass. "Turns out the physical therapist is about two months along. Funny how that timeline works out, isn't it?"

I hadn't known. That's the part I keep snagging on. I sat in the room wearing my good blazer because I wanted to look like I was handling his infidelity, and I had no idea. I thought I was there to divide up furniture and close a bank account. I thought the worst thing that was going to happen that morning had already happened.

And then his lawyer said *impending family expenses* and the air just left the room. I looked at Kyle. He was looking at his phone.

That image won't leave me. When his attorney said it out loud, Kyle couldn't look at me. He acted like I was the embarrassing part, the problem to be managed while his real life waited somewhere else. And that's the truth, isn't it. He has this whole other life I was never part of. There will always be permanent evidence of every night I didn't ask the right questions, every road trip I didn't think twice about, every time I believed him because it was easier than not believing him.

"Where is he now?"

"Road trip. Eight games on the West Coast. Didn't even stick around after we signed." He was probably already at the airport before I made it to the elevator.

Emily's quiet for a second. "Do you want to release a statement?"

"No. I just want to get the hell out of New York."

"Okay," she says slowly. "And when you say out of New York..."

"I'm going back home to Texas."

"Are you coming back?"

The question catches me off guard, but the answer is easy. "No reason to. We signed the papers this morning. It's done."

There's a pause. "Wait, the divorce is already final?"

"Judge signed off right there. No kids, no shared property worth fighting over, and apparently Kyle was eager to move things along." The bitterness in my own voice surprises me. "Guess he's got a timeline to worry about now."

"Good," Emily says, the approval clear in her voice. "Listen, I know we've only worked together a short time, but if you ever need anything—"

Something loosens in my chest. "Thanks, Em."

After we hang up, I grab my camera bag from the coat closet. Dust clings to the strap. The bag sags into my grip exactly the way it always did, worn soft in all the right places.

I unzip and find my old Nikon nestled in the foam padding like I never left it. I pick it up and my thumb finds the shutter button without thinking, and my heart aches for the girl who used to love taking photos. I had an eye for timing and for finding the story inside the motion. After the wedding, the bag went in the closet, and the part of me that reached for it just went quiet. I press the shutter button once. The click sounds the same as it always did.

I zip it closed and add it to my pile. My phone buzzes one more time, and this time the name on the screen makes me smile for the first time in three days.

Larkie Jean Queen. My best friend for as long as I can remember.

I swipe to answer and put her on speaker. "Well, hello, Miss America."

"Ah, I was just runner up." Larkie Jean's voice is pure Texas honey, the kind of drawl that sounds like it should be selling sweet tea on a front porch somewhere.

"Lisa said you're coming home. Please tell me it's true and not just wishful thinking on her part."

"It's true."

"Hallelujah. When do you land?"

"Late."

"Want me to pick you up?"

I lean against the wall and close my eyes for a second. The honest answer is yes. I want Larkie Jean to pick me up and talk the whole drive home the way she does, filling every inch of silence so I don't have to. But if I let her do that, I'm going to cry in the car. And if I cry in the car, I'm going to fall apart a little, and I don't have the energy to put myself back together tonight.

"I'm good. I've got a car."

"Harper."

"Larkie Jean," I plead. "I love you. I genuinely cannot wait to see you. But it's been the kind of day where if someone's too nice to me right now, I'm going to lose it completely, and I'd really like to make it home first."

There's a pause, and I can hear her deciding whether to push.

"Okay," she says finally. "But you call me tomorrow. First thing."

"First thing," I promise.

She lets out a long breath, the kind that means she has more to say and is choosing not to say it. "Where are you staying?"

"Grams' guest house for now."

"Does anyone else know you're coming?"

"Lisa. You. That's it."

"What about your dad?"

"I'll go see him tomorrow. I just—" I stop, trying to find

the right words. "I don't want to deal with people yet. The questions, the sympathy, all of it."

"Say no more. Your secret's safe with me." Her voice softens. "I'm glad you're coming home, Harper."

"Yeah, me too," I say, and for the first time in three days, I almost mean it.

I stand in the middle of the living room and look around one last time. Not sad. Angry, betrayed, humiliated — but not sad.

The door clicks behind me as I step on to the elevator. I drag the suitcases behind me as I step outside to meet my driver. I slide into the back seat of the Uber and watch the building disappear.

At JFK, I check my bags and clear security. At ten-fifteen, I board the plane and find my seat by the window. And when the wheels lift off and New York falls away beneath me, I don't look back.

I'm already gone.

Not ready to say goodbye to Natalie and Jake? Scan the QR code to join my newsletter family and unlock an exclusive bonus scene that wasn't in the book! You'll also be the first to hear about upcoming releases, behind-the-scenes peeks, and special offers. No spam, just bookish joy delivered straight to your inbox!

The Backlot Series
Second Act
Center Stage
On the Record
Behind the Scenes
Off Script

Thank you!
I hope you fell in love with Natalie and Jake's journey in *Off Script*! If their story captured your heart, I'd be so grateful if

you'd consider leaving a review. Reviews are like literary fairy dust for indie authors—they help other readers discover our books and help open doors we sometimes can't open ourselves without social proof. Thank you for being part of this adventure! 🤍

acknowledgments

If you've read more than one of my books, you already know this part of the story.

My family and my people are my center of gravity. Mom, Kristy, Jamie, Cami, Holly, and my daughter Brooklynn—you are my circle of sanity. Your constant encouragement, cheerleading, reality checks, and belief in me mean more than I can ever put into words.

To Staci, my cover designer from day one—thank you for giving every book in this series a visual home and for somehow making each cover feel fresh while still belonging together. Your talent and consistency have been a gift.

To Nicole, my editor from books two through five—finding you when I did changed everything. Thank you for helping me sharpen these stories, push the emotional beats further, and grow as a writer. I'm so grateful you've been part of this series and hope you'll be with me for many books to come.

To Ellie and Love Notes PR: I genuinely don't know how I would have done this series without you. From ARC signups to cover reveals to release days, you've been the bridge to readers, bookish friends, and a community I'm so grateful to be part of. Thank you for your patience, support, and kindness!

To The Plot Twist Book Bar in Denton, TX—thank you for showing up for me again and again. Supporting indie authors the way you do is an incredible gift, and I'll always be grateful for the space you've made for my stories.

And to my bookish friends: I adore you. Thank you for the love, the sharing, the recommendations, and for letting me learn from all the cool, smart, wildly creative things you're doing. Watching you work is half the fun of this life.

Finally, to the readers—thank you for taking a chance on these books, these women, and this world. Closing out *The Backlot Series* is bittersweet, but knowing these stories found their way to you makes it worth every late night and every moment of doubt.

about the author

Kimberly Page is a contemporary romance author who loves writing about strong heroines and the irresistible heroes who fall for them. After a career spent crafting stories for major players in the entertainment industry, she decided to create stories of her own.

When she's not writing, you can find Kimberly planning for beach time, at a theme park with her daughter, or getting lost in a good sports romance book. Follow her on TikTok and Instagram for news and updates.

www.authorkimberlypage.com

www.ingramcontent.com/pod-product-compliance
Ingram Content Group UK Ltd.
Pitfield, Milton Keynes, MK11 3LW, UK
UKHW042002230426
12048UKWH00009B/499